ALEXANDER WILSON was a writer, spy and secret service officer. He served in the First World War before moving to India to teach as a Professor of English Literature and eventually became Principal of Islamia College at the University of Punjab in Lahore. He began writing spy novels whilst in India and he enjoyed great success in the 1930s with reviews in the *Telegraph*, *Observer* and the *Times Literary Supplement* amongst others. Wilson also worked as an intelligence agent and his characters are based on his own fascinating and largely unknown career in the Secret Intelligence Service. He passed away in 1963.

a&b

Wallace at Bay

ALEXANDER WILSON

Allison & Busby Limited
12 Fitzroy Mews
London W1T 6DW
allisonandbusby.com

First published in 1938.
This edition published by Allison & Busby in 2016.

A CIP catalogue record for this book is available from
the British Library.

10 9 8 7 6 5 4 3 2 1

ISBN 978-0-7490-1835-1

Typeset in 10.5/15.5 pt Adobe Garamond Pro by
Allison & Busby Ltd.

The paper used for this Allison & Busby publication
has been produced from trees that have been legally sourced
from well-managed and credibly certified forests.

Printed and bound by
CPI Group (UK) Ltd, Croydon, CR0 4YY

CONTENTS

CHAPTER ONE

An Affair in the Strand

Gale Preston, the well-known film and stage actor, threw the manuscript upon a table close to where he was standing, and looked thoughtfully at his friend, the producer, who sprawled comfortably in an easy chair.

'It's a good show,' he decided, 'strong, clever, and with plenty of action. I am not altogether certain, though, that I fancy myself in the part of Stanley Ferrers.'

'Why not?' queried the other. 'I think it is the best part you have had for years.'

'Perhaps, but it is not in my line, is it? I have never played a temperamental, neurotic role either on the stage or in a film. I am not saying that the part itself is not good; I am simply doubting my ability to play it.'

'Bosh!' snorted the other. 'You'd make a success of anything you played.'

Preston smiled.

'Thanks for the few kind words, Tony,' he returned. 'Coming from a producer they are indeed a compliment.'

'Look here,' observed the man in the chair, stretching himself even more comfortably, though not so very elegantly, 'you know I wouldn't say anything I didn't mean. I certainly would not suggest your playing a character for which I knew you were unsuited. I'm not an idiot, though perhaps some people think I am. What's the snag?'

'At the moment I can't imagine how a fellow of the temperament of Ferrers would react to a charge of murder.'

'Hasn't the author shown you?'

'Up to a point, yes. Ferrers is innocent, but he is also highly strung, and people of that type are difficult to gauge. He is portrayed as being so overcome by the shock that he becomes hysterical in his denunciations, making it appear that he is guilty, or, at least, knows a good deal more about the murder than he actually does. To my mind, his behaviour is exaggerated, and I hate exaggeration. What do you think?'

The producer reflected for a few moments.

'The same thing occurred to me,' he admitted at length, 'and it was my intention to tone the hysteria down a good bit.' Suddenly he sat bolt upright, and laughed softly. 'I've an idea,' he announced; 'why not go out for a walk and study the men you meet? When you come across one who looks of a similar type to Stanley Ferrers, clap your hand on his shoulder, and tell him you arrest him for murder. Watch carefully how he behaves, what he says, and the expression that appears on his face. Afterwards you can apologise, take him in somewhere and give him a drink.'

Gale Preston laughed.

'By Jove!' he exclaimed. 'It is certainly a notion. I'll do it.'

Thus, by a casual, irresponsible decision, did an actor in search of inspiration upset the well-laid plans of the British Secret Service, and render trebly difficult a task that was already bristling with complications. By a chance in a million, he selected the one man who, at that time, was most seriously engaging the attention of the authorities; a man whom they had traced after endless disappointments and setbacks.

Eager to try the experiment suggested by his friend, Gale Preston started off, after lunching at Romano's, in search of a man whose face and demeanour would suggest that he was similar in temperament to the character, Stanley Ferrers, in his new play. He walked the length of the Strand to Trafalgar Square; then slowly retraced his steps, keenly studying the countenances of men he met and passed. Several appeared likely subjects for his rather unpardonable experiment, but they were always with companions, or something else about them stayed him. At length he reached Waterloo Place, and was waiting for the traffic to pass to enable him to cross towards the Gaiety, when he caught sight of a man standing on the island in the middle of the road. He, also, was waiting for the long stream of vehicles to go by, and Preston had ample time to study him. He was about medium height, and thin almost to the point of emaciation. Clothed in a long coat of some dark material, a voluminous bow tie adorning his high collar, and a black felt hat drawn low over his forehead, there was a suggestion of the foreigner about him. It was his hands, however, that had first attracted Preston's attention. Long and white, with fingers almost like talons, they were never still. His mouth was half open, and the underlip appeared to be trembling, though it was difficult to be certain of that, but it was his eyes that decided the actor. Despite the hat shading them, he observed how they constantly moved from side to side, as though their owner were in a high state of nerves, while they contained a burning intensity that, he decided, denoted a passionate, highly-strung disposition. Perhaps if he had been a better judge of human nature he would have hesitated. As it was, he became convinced that if he searched the whole of London he would not find a better subject.

The traffic subsided temporarily, the man crossed towards him. Preston allowed him to pass, and fell in behind him. He had no wish to try his experiment amidst a crowd of people. The results might be embarrassing. When opposite the Tivoli Theatre, however, he suddenly found himself comparatively alone with the man. There appeared no one else within yards. Acting promptly, he stepped forward; placed his hand firmly on the other's shoulder.

'I have a warrant for your arrest,' he began, 'on the charge of—'

He got no further. Abruptly, and with extraordinary violence, he was flung across the pavement, only preventing himself from falling by a great effort. He had a vision of the dark-coated stranger darting swiftly into the road between the numerous vehicles passing by, heard shouts and the grinding of brakes. For a moment he felt dazed; then a hand gripped his arm. He was swung unceremoniously round to face a huge, broad-shouldered man with clean-shaven face, clear-cut features, determined chin, and keen grey eyes.

'Having a little game?' demanded the newcomer in an attractive voice that somehow suggested a great sense of humour.

'Who are you, sir,' asked Preston indignantly, 'and why are you holding on to my arm?'

'If you will play at being a spinning top in the Strand,' came the sarcastic retort, 'you surely can't object to a little steadying influence.'

'I – I was most grossly assaulted by a man who—'

'Yes; we know all about that. But you interfered with him first, and I'm afraid you will have to do a little explaining. Seem to know your face,' he added, frowning thoughtfully.

'I am Gale Preston,' replied the actor with dignity.

'Gale Preston! Gale Preston!' The big man rubbed his chin reflectively with his disengaged hand. 'You appear to think I ought to know it. Sorry and all that, but—Oh, I get you. You're the film *Johnny*, aren't you?'

'I am a well-known star,' came the reply with more dignity than before.

'You were almost a fallen star just now,' commented the other.

'May I ask you to be good enough to release my arm?'

'Presently, sonny, presently. Don't be in such a hurry. We'll cross the road, if you will permit me to escort you.'

The actor protested vehemently, but he might as well have ordered the sun to cease shining. Willy-nilly he was led to the other side, his captor guiding him unerringly between the taxicabs, omnibuses and all the other motors passing in both directions in never-ending streams. They arrived opposite the Adelphi Arches.

'He went down there,' observed the big man, 'and, thanks to you, has probably got clear away.'

'Of whom are you speaking?' asked the irate actor.

'Of whom would I be speaking, but your boyfriend – the fellow you gripped on the shoulder with such bonhomie?'

'He was no friend of mine. He was not even an acquaintance.'

His companion gazed down at him, a frank look of disbelief on his face.

'Do you usually grip hold of perfect strangers with such brotherly cordiality?' he asked.

'I—' Preston got no further. It occurred to him that his explanation would sound absolutely ridiculous. Who would believe it? But why should he have to give an explanation to anybody but the man he had chosen for his experiment? Indignation surged up within him with greater force than ever. 'I don't know who you are, sir, and I don't care,' he declared forcibly, 'but I should like to know by what right you are detaining me in this unwarrantable manner, and why? If you do not release me at once I shall be forced to call a policeman.'

At that the other laughed outright.

'Call away,' he encouraged. 'I've no wish to interfere with your amusements.' He took out a gold cigarette case, which he opened and proffered to the actor. 'Have one?' he invited.

'No,' was the blunt reply.

'You won't? Well, I suppose you have no objection to my smoking? No luck?' he called to a man who came hurrying up.

The newcomer, an individual slightly inclined to corpulence, fresh-faced, jolly-looking, shook his head. Apparently he found it warm, though it was early March and a keen wind was blowing, for he removed his soft hat, disclosing a mass of well-brushed, fair hair, and mopped his forehead with a silk handkerchief.

'Not a sign of him,' he proclaimed. 'He must know his way about these parts. Lawrence and Irving are still searching. He really did us in the traffic. How he got across without being knocked down beats me. This the interfering stranger?' he asked, looking keenly at Preston.

'He is,' nodded the big man. 'And now you've arrived, Hill, we'll take him for a little walk. Come along!' he added to the actor.

They ranged themselves on either side of him, and marched him along the Strand, across Trafalgar Square into Whitehall. Preston began to have visions of Scotland Yard, but they turned into a building almost opposite the Foreign Office. He was ushered into a lift, which took them up to the second storey. There Preston was left in a small, bare apartment, containing only a table and two or three chairs, with Hill to guard him while the big man went out. He was away a considerable time, but came back at last, and beckoned to Hill and the actor. They followed him along a corridor, passing several closed doors, until they came to one on which the leader knocked. A voice, that seemed far away, bade them enter. Preston had just time to observe that the door was of a remarkable thickness and padded on the inside as he was gently pushed into the room. The big man alone accompanied him.

By now the actor was becoming greatly interested. He knew he was in some government office, but the numerous men who seemed to be on watch in the corridors and at the entrance, the closed doors, the air of secrecy that prevailed, intrigued him vastly. He found himself in a large, lofty room, most of the walls of which were lined with bookshelves containing dry-looking volumes and paperbound documents. In one corner was a huge safe. The only wall not occupied by a bookcase was entirely covered by a huge map of Europe, while another of Asia hung over the fireplace. A large flat desk occupied the centre of the room. Behind it, his back to the two great windows, sat a fair-haired, good-looking man with blue eyes and a small, well-trimmed military moustache. He regarded the actor somewhat sternly.

'You are Mr Gale Preston?' he asked.

'I am,' replied the actor. Some of the self-confidence which formed a goodly proportion of his stock-in-trade began to evaporate. He felt that he had become mixed up in something he did not understand, and he disliked the feeling. He was so used to being regarded as a very important individual that the emotion, disagreeably like an attack of the inferiority complex, which came over him in the presence of the man at the desk and the big fellow standing by his side, was utterly distasteful. Nevertheless, it persisted. The blue eyes seemed cold, unrelenting, yet looked as though they could twinkle very attractively at times. Despite his unwonted sense of littleness, however, he endeavoured to assert himself. 'I must protest at the gross impertinence of this man,' he began, indicating his companion, 'who—'

'You can do that later on, if you wish,' he was interrupted in courteous tones. 'At present there are certain matters which you had better explain as much for our information as for your own peace of mind. I am Major Brien; this gentleman is Captain Shannon, and this building is the headquarters of the Intelligence Service. Need I say more?'

Enlightenment began to break on Preston, and his heart sank. He was quick-witted enough to realise that he had, innocently it is true, meddled with some Secret Service enterprise by accosting the man with the burning eyes and nervous manner. The last shreds of his self-assurance left him, his heart sank.

'Have I – er – inadvertently committed a faux pas?' he asked.

'You have committed more than a faux pas,' was the stern reply. 'Whether it was inadvertent or not remains to be seen. Sit down, will you?' He indicated a comfortable-looking leather armchair close to the desk. Preston sank into it. 'Now will you tell me,' went on Major Brien, 'what you know of the man you accosted in the Strand?'

'Nothing,' replied the actor promptly. 'I have never, to my knowledge, set eyes on him before.'

Sir Leonard Wallace's friend and chief assistant looked at him searchingly. He certainly seemed to be telling the truth.

'Then why,' he asked, 'did you put your hand on his shoulder and speak to him?'

Gale Preston told the story, describing the part of Stanley Ferrers in the play he had read, and his search for a man of similar temperament, in order that he could discover how he would react to a charge of murder.

'To you, sir,' he concluded earnestly, 'such an explanation of my behaviour may sound fantastic, but I give you my word that it is the correct one.'

Major Brien leant back in his chair.

'I see no reason to doubt you, Mr Preston,' he replied. 'I know how a keen actor likes to make a part he is playing seem convincing, and often studies a character from real life in order to obtain the correct atmosphere – I suppose that is the word, isn't it? But to actually go up to a man, pretending you are a police officer, and tell him you have a warrant for his arrest was going beyond all reason. Captain Shannon's statement that the fellow almost knocked you over and ran as soon as you touched and spoke to him bears out your story, otherwise I am afraid I should have been compelled to keep a watch on you. As far as we are concerned, you are at liberty to depart, and I hope you will take my advice – never attempt anything so foolish again. By all means study people, but refrain from pretending to be a member of the police force or, in fact, doing anything that may cause trouble to yourself or others. If the police cared to take the matter up, they could prosecute and cause you to suffer somewhat severe penalties. You may rest easy, however, we have no desire to make the affair public, and you will hear no more of it.'

Preston rose to his feet feeling exceedingly shamefaced and foolish.

'May I know who the man is, and how I have transgressed?' he asked diffidently.

Brien regarded him for a moment.

'I'll tell you this much,' he returned presently. 'He is a member of an exceedingly dangerous band of anarchists. We have been searching for him for weeks. Yesterday we at last found him, and have been trailing him ever since, in the hope that he would lead us to his companions. Your irresponsible action has caused him to take alarm – your very words, unfortunately enough, were calculated to give him warning that he was known and being trailed. He and his companions now, whether we find them or not, will no longer bask in the comfortable sense of security in which I have reason to believe they fondly imagined themselves. They will be very much on the alert, and our job will consequently be rendered a thousand times more difficult.'

'I'm terribly sorry,' apologised Preston.

'So am I,' returned Major Brien, dryly.

'It was a remarkable coincidence that I should choose that very man – the millionth chance in fact.'

'If you were a member of this service,' put in Captain Shannon, 'you would quickly learn that there are no such odds as a million to one against anything, or a thousand to one, for that matter. I should be beastly trite, but perfectly truthful, if I added that it is the unexpected that generally turns up.'

'That is true,' nodded Brien; 'to us nothing is unexpected. Perhaps it will help you in your future career, Mr Preston, if you remember that. Goodbye.'

Shannon escorted the actor to the lift. From there until he walked out of the front door he was passed on from one man to another, being hardly ever out of sight of at least two. He learnt more than one lesson that afternoon he never forgot. Perhaps that was one of the reasons why his acting improved so tremendously.

CHAPTER TWO

Carter and a Bootblack

Directly his visitor had departed Major Brien walked along the corridor to the room of Sir Leonard Wallace, and reported what had occurred. The Chief of the British Secret Service listened without interruption until the end. Except that he had frowned slightly at the information concerning the anarchist's escape, he showed no emotion of any sort. In fact, he appeared absolutely unconcerned.

'It is all very well to blame the actor,' he observed, 'but his action should not have been responsible for Pestalozzi's escape. Since yesterday afternoon, when Carter found him in Soho, he has been continually followed by two, sometimes three, today four men. "He has visited three houses, four restaurants, at which he has stayed for varying periods,"' he was quoting from a report on his desk, '"and slept the night in the Canute Hotel, in Waterloo Road." That is correct, isn't it?' Brien nodded.

'Well, in that time, the men who trailed him learnt that he was exceedingly jumpy, startled by the least happening out of the ordinary. He was, in short, on the *qui vive* and ready to bolt at a moment's notice. That being the case, why were they not more careful?'

Brien moodily took a cigarette from the box on the desk and lit it.

'It is going to be a devil of a job to pick him up again,' he remarked, 'and the king is due next week.'

'Not so difficult as it may appear, Bill.' Brien caught the glint in his friend's eyes, and all doubt or exasperation vanished at once. 'Send Carter to me if he's available, will you? If not Maddison will do.'

Warning had been sent to headquarters from the British agent in Vienna that a gang of international anarchists had grown very active in their meetings in that city of late. Certain information which had reached him suggested that they had determined to assassinate the king of a European country about to pay an official visit to Great Britain. Sir Leonard Wallace had hardly received the first report when a second arrived stating that three members of the band of anarchists had left for England – one of them, Pestalozzi, being known to have arrived already. How he had entered the country was a mystery, but there was no doubt of his being there.

Immediately an intensive search had commenced for him, while watch was kept on all ports and aerodromes for the other two. After nearly a month's heartbreaking disappointment, with scarcely a clue to suggest Pestalozzi's whereabouts, Carter, of the Secret Service, had traced him to a restaurant in Soho. From that moment he had been under almost constant surveillance until the unfortunate intervention by Gale Preston. Even when he had slept at the Canute Hotel, on the preceding night, a man had actually been in the lounge below, while another had watched the window from the street. It had been ascertained that he had not been staying at the Canute, having merely taken a bed for that night for some reason or other. Now he had been lost again, and the king was due to land in England within a few days. To make matters more serious, nothing had been learnt of the whereabouts of the other two anarchists. Beust, one of the most reliable men in the Secret Service, who had lived in Austria since he was a child, was certain they had left the country with the intention of reaching England. There was no information whatever regarding their movements after they had departed from Vienna. It was because of this that Pestalozzi had been so carefully shadowed. He had visited three dwelling houses in which were living compatriots of his, and taken meals in four different restaurants, as a result of which all the places, and the people who inhabited or frequented them, were now under surveillance.

It was certain that he must be lodged more or less permanently somewhere. He had taken no luggage with him to the Canute Hotel, and had paid in advance for bed and breakfast from a greasy pocketbook packed with banknotes. He was, therefore, not short of money. Sir Leonard Wallace felt certain in his own mind that he had found a retreat with people of his own breed living in a district devoted to foreigners, possibly Soho, and that the other two were with him. The difficulty of finding them was that the Secret Service possessed a description only of Pestalozzi. Beust had even managed, somehow, to obtain a snapshot of the man – it had been in Carter's possession when he had found and recognised him. He knew nothing about the other two, however, except their names – one was Zanazaryk, a Czechoslovakian, the other, Haeckel, a German – he possessed neither photographs nor description of them, and names were very easily changed.

When Major Brien had left his room, Sir Leonard telephoned through to the Assistant Commissioner of the Special Branch at New Scotland Yard, and suggested simultaneous raids that night on the three dwelling-houses which Pestalozzi had been known to visit. Two were in Kennington, not far from the Oval, the other was close to Vauxhall Station. He did not expect that either the Italian or his companions would be in any, but there was just a possibility that they might, or perhaps information regarding their whereabouts could be discovered. The Assistant Commissioner thought the idea a good one, declared he would make arrangements at once, and submit his plans to Sir Leonard that evening. As Wallace turned from the telephone a knock came at the door. In reply to his invitation there entered a young man who looked every inch an athlete from the top of his dark brown hair to the soles of his feet. His merry, laughing eyes, and altogether good-humoured as well as good-looking face suggested a happy-go-lucky disposition. He was one of the most efficient and certainly one of the most daring members of Sir Leonard's gallant band of assistants, although the youngest by two or three years. Wallace nodded to him.

'They've lost him, Carter,' he observed quietly.

'I've just heard about it, sir,' replied the young man. 'Shannon, of course, is taking it as all in the day's work, but I believe he is thoroughly fed up. He blames himself for not telling the SB men to keep parallel with Pestalozzi on the other side of the road.'

'Of course that should have been done,' commented Sir

Leonard, 'but it was not, and it is no use crying over spilt milk. It is essential that we get in touch with Pestalozzi again at the earliest possible moment,' he observed. 'King Peter arrives in this country next Wednesday. Today is Thursday. There is little over five days, therefore, in which to accomplish work that twenty-three have failed to bring to a successful issue. I am convinced that Zanazaryk and Haeckel are also in the country, and they, as well as Pestalozzi, must be in our hands or rendered impotent by next Tuesday. I am pinning my faith to one little incident connected with your finding of the Italian yesterday.'

'What is that, sir?' asked Carter quickly.

'You reported that after leaving the restaurant at which he lunched he walked to Leicester Square, and there had his boots polished by a shoeblack. That is so, isn't it?'

'Yes, sir.'

'You noticed, however, that his boots did not want cleaning, that they were, in fact, already very bright. Furthermore, he remained with the shoeblack longer than it would ordinarily take to clean a pair of dirty boots, and all the time they were engaged in conversation in low voices. In short, Carter, though you took little notice of it at the time, you believed that there was some connection between the two men.'

'That is true, sir,' nodded the young man.

'Well, I believe our opportunity lies in that shoeblack. Go to Leicester Square and, if he is still there, watch him and follow him when he leaves his pitch. Find out as much about him as you can; then report to me. We may be wrong, perhaps my instinct is leading me astray this time, but there is just a chance that he may turn out to be the key to the situation. None of the places which Pestalozzi visited has supplied us with any useful information yet –

they will be quietly raided tonight, but I am not anticipating any great result from that. If you find the bootblack hang on to him like grim death. Understand, Carter?'

'Yes, sir.'

The young man took a taxi as far as the Alhambra. Then, mingling with the numerous pedestrians, he strolled along to Leicester Square. A little sigh, expressive of exultation, left his lips when he observed the man for whom he was searching at the same pitch engaged in cleaning a lady's shoes. At first Carter felt a little troubled lest he should prove to be a different fellow, but on approaching closer his anxiety was allayed. He had taken particular notice of the bootblack on the preceding day, and it was undoubtedly he. The Secret Service man walked round the square, stepping into all the dust he could find, thereby causing his shoes to look badly in need of a polish. On returning to the bootblack he found that the lady had gone, leaving the man disengaged. He strolled slowly by as though he had not noticed him, reflecting that less suspicion would be caused if the man solicited his custom than if he went directly to him, and Carter wanted an opportunity to study him. As he had anticipated, so it happened.

'Will I clean it the shoe, mister?' asked a husky voice.

Carter glanced at the speaker, turned his gaze to his dusty shoes, and smiled.

'They do look as though they could do with a polish,' he admitted, and stepped up to the man, placing one of his feet on the little stand.

He felt a sense of disappointment. The bootblack's accent was Italian, Pestalozzi was Italian. It was quite possible that the only sympathy between them was their nationality. Then he remembered the shiny boots that did not need polishing, the conversation carried on in low voices. As the bootblack assiduously cleaned his shoes, he studied him. He was clad in the regulation uniform, and obviously was a member of the bootblacks' brigade. Carter took careful note of his number, storing it in his mind for further reference. Once or twice the man looked up, disclosing a lean, swarthy face, containing a pair of piercing, dark eyes, a somewhat broad nose and ugly mouth. He apparently possessed none of the sunny characteristics so typical of his countrymen; in fact, he appeared sullen and morose. Except for a casual remark about the weather, he made no attempt at conversation, and when Carter strove to get him to talk, either answered in monosyllables or did not reply at all.

When the shoes were cleaned, Carter tossed him a shilling and walked on to Jones' Restaurant. He ascended to the first floor and, finding a table by a window, ordered tea. It had occurred to him that it would be difficult to find a more ideal position from which to keep watch. He was correct in his surmise. He was able to look down on the bootblack without the slightest risk of being observed himself. He dawdled over tea, his eyes seldom far from the Italian, but nothing of interest occurred. Occasionally a man or woman stopped to have their footgear cleaned, but none of them aroused anything but the utmost indifference in the man. He entered into conversation with none, accepted payment without much apparent gratitude, and took no further notice of them.

Six o'clock came and went, and Carter remained at his table. At last, it was close on the half hour, the bootblack packed up his gear and prepared to depart. Carter was surprised that he had stayed so long, for dusk had fallen, and he could have had little hope of obtaining a client for some time past. Had he been waiting for anybody? This idea was supported by the fact that when his belongings were neatly strapped up in their box he still loitered, glancing about him as though in expectation of the arrival of somebody. Presently, however, he slung the box on his back, and set off along Coventry Street in the direction of Piccadilly Circus.

If the waitress who had attended to Carter's wants had wondered why he had tarried so long at the table by the window, she must have been vastly surprised when he suddenly started to his feet and darted out of the room. He was halfway down the stairs, when he remembered his bill, tore back, put half a crown into the girl's hand, and asked her to pay it for him. Then he was gone again.

Carter was one of the most expert shadowers in the Secret Service, and he was quickly on the track of the Italian bootblack. The latter led him to the Circus, crossing to Swan and Edgar's corner, where he stood waiting for a bus. Before long a number six arrived, and he boarded it, climbing to the upper deck. Carter went inside. Having no idea whither the man was bound, he took a twopenny ticket, and trusted to luck. He found he had to pay excess fare. The vehicle made its leisurely way along Regent Street, Oxford Street, passed Marble Arch, and turned up Edgware Road, and still the bootblack showed no signs of descending. At Warwick Avenue tube station, noting the conductor's suspicious frown, Carter took another twopenny ticket. Almost directly afterwards, he surprised that worthy by deciding to get off. The Italian had descended at the corner of Shirland Road. Directly the bus started again, Carter rose from his seat and jumped off.

'Why don't you make up yer mind?' came back to him in aggrieved tones from the puncher of tickets, as the vehicle disappeared into the darkness, which by then had fallen completely.

The young man chuckled to himself. He watched the bootblack cross the road and enter a dilapidated-looking house next to a school on the other side. He himself was quite hidden from view by a furniture van conveniently drawn up to the kerb. The bootblack unlocked the front door of the house, and entered. Obviously he lived there. Almost directly afterwards a light flared up in a room on the ground floor, and Carter had time to note the general disorder and tawdriness of the furniture before the man he had trailed crossed to the window and pulled down the blinds.

A little farther along, on the other side of the road, was a telephone kiosk. Carter waited ten minutes to make sure that his quarry had no intention of leaving the house, at least for the time being; then walked along to the box and rang up his headquarters. Sir Leonard Wallace was still in his office, and listened approvingly to his subordinate's report.

'I'll send someone to keep watch while you make enquiries,' he remarked, when he had heard all Carter had to tell him. 'That house must be kept under observation. It presents a slender hope, it is true, but still there is a hope.'

Carter returned to his post and, for the next quarter of an hour, kept his eyes glued on the building from a well-sheltered point. A crowd of ill-dressed, noisy children played round a lamp post in his vicinity, some of the inhabitants of the neighbouring houses stood at their gates chatting, every few minutes buses stopped close by, those coming from the West End being packed with men and women released from work for the day. It was not exactly a quiet region. At last a saloon car glided round the corner from Sutherland Avenue, and stopped by a chapel. A man got out; walked casually along towards Carter, while the motor turned, and disappeared. The newcomer was tall and thin, and, as he passed under a lamp, the watcher recognised the seemingly lugubrious, long, narrow face of his colleague, Cartright. He stepped from his coign of vantage.

'Hullo, Jimmy,' he greeted him. 'That's the house over there – the first from the school. You get a good view of anyone leaving or entering it on account of that lamp outside the front door.' He proceeded to give a careful description of the bootblack, and made certain that Cartright would know the man if he saw him. 'Any orders from the chief?' he asked.

'Only the same as those I believe he has already given you,' was the reply. 'He wants you to find out everything possible about the fellow and the house he is in. Sir Leonard will be along this way about nine.'

'Well, look here, I'll make enquiries round this neighbourhood first; then I'll rout out the secretary or manager or whatever he is of the Bootblacks' Association.'

'Right. The car is waiting in Sutherland Avenue, if you want it. I told West you probably would. You'd better have dinner before you return to relieve me.'

'It all depends if there is time. Cheer ho!'

Carter first went into a public house a little way along the road and ordered himself a whisky and soda. He began to chat with a large and voluble lady behind the bar, and adroitly steered the conversation in the right direction. They had discussed the general decrepitude of houses in that part of Shirland Road and a good many of their inhabitants, before they came to the one that interested Carter. She gave him his lead by describing a building on the other side as a perfect disgrace.

'It's such a shame,' she drawled, 'and this used to be such a nice neighbourhood. The landlord oughter be ashamed of himself – that he ought. I call it an eyesore, though the rest aren't much better.'

'Of course I don't know the district very well,' Carter told her, 'but it has struck me whenever I've been round this way, that the first house on this side – the one next door to the school – is about the most decayed of the lot. I suppose it is owned by the same landlord, isn't it?'

'Lord bless you, no! There's umpteen landlords own these houses and, if you ask me, they're all as bad as one another. Letting the places go to rack and ruin, that's what they're doing, but I don't suppose they care as long as they get their rent.'

'Still,' persisted Carter, 'tidy tenants can improve even dilapidated houses by growing flowers in the front, banging up clean curtains and that sort of thing. The people in the house of which I am speaking don't seem to have any of what you might describe as home pride.'

'Home pride!' snorted the lady behind the bar. 'I should think not indeed. Do you know who live in that house?'

He smiled.

'No; I'm afraid I don't.'

'Foreigners, all the blessed lot of them. And what can you expect from foreigners? An Eyetalian family used to rent the whole house, or most of it, and – it wasn't so bad then, but their circumstances improved, and they moved. They kept it on, though, and let it out in flats. An ice cream man lives in the basement with his wife and half a dozen kids – where they put them all I don't know. The ground floor is rented by a man who lives all by himself – he's a bootblack I think. The top was empty for a long time, but lately it's been taken by three brothers – nasty looking beggars all of them; they come in here sometimes and drink like fish. It's good for the house, of course, but I'd as soon they kept away. Now, mister, how can you expect people of that sort to try to make a house look nice?'

'No, I suppose they're hardly the kind to bother.' Carter answered somewhat absently, though he took care to hide the elation which had suddenly filled him.

It seemed to him that the unexpected had happened; that Sir Leonard Wallace's extraordinary power of intuition had once again proved correct. When Carter had first mentioned the bootblack to the chief the latter had seemed greatly interested even then. Although there had been nothing much to go on, he had at once assumed that the man was in some way connected with the anarchists. It was he who, by searching enquiry, had guided Carter's mind back to every detail of Pestalozzi's apparel, had ascertained from him that the Italian's boots had not needed cleaning, and had pointed out the importance of the fact. Now, having received instructions to follow the bootblack and learn everything he could about him, Carter had discovered the significant circumstance that the second floor of the house in which the man lived had lately been taken by three foreigners, who called themselves brothers. Were they brothers by blood or brothers by association? In short, were they the three anarchists for whom the men of the Secret Service and the Special Branch of Scotland Yard had been searching for so long?

Carter turned to the large lady behind the bar, hoping to get a description that would fit Pestalozzi, when the door of the saloon opened. Cartright entered; he was whistling a tune that Secret Service men often used to warn each other of their presence, and of the fact that they had news, or that there was danger about. At the same time Carter caught a glimpse of the bootblack in the public bar, and drew back for fear the man would recognise him. Next to the Italian was someone else, of whom he could only see an arm and shoulder. The landlady had a better view – she had half turned at the sound of the newcomers' voices and leaning towards Carter she whispered:

'Well I never! Talk of angels, they say, and you hear the flutter of their wings – not that these are angels by any means. It's the folk I was telling you about!'

At that moment Carter saw the face of the man next to the bootblack, and recognised it – he was Pestalozzi.

CHAPTER THREE

A Board That Creaked

Neither Cartright nor Carter took the slightest notice of each other. The former had entered the saloon bar in order to warn his colleague. That having been accomplished, he hastily drank a whisky and soda and departed. A few minutes later Carter took leave of the lady who had been so informative, and went out. He joined Cartright in a dark patch of pavement between two lamps on the other side of the road.

'Is any of them our man, do you think?' asked the latter.

Carter caught him exultantly by the arm.

'My boy,' he murmured, 'one is the bootblack and the other Pestalozzi himself.'

Cartright gave vent to a grunt which was intended to signify delight, but which might have meant almost anything. He was not demonstrative.

'There were four of them altogether,' he announced. 'I wonder if the other two were Haeckel and Zanazaryk.'

'I'd stake my life on it,' returned the exuberant Carter.

He repeated the conversation he had had with the landlady in the public house.

'I wouldn't stake my life on it,' observed his more cautious colleague, 'but it's a safe enough bet to plunk a couple of bob on.'

'That settles it,' decided Carter. 'When you are willing to bet two whole shillings, twenty-four pence, forty-eight halfpence on anything it must be a cert. Look here, Jimmy, it doesn't matter now whether I find out if the boot wallah is a pukka member of the association or brigade of bootblacks or not. He must be, anyway, or he wouldn't dare take up a pitch and wear the uniform and a number in Leicester Square. I'm going into that house.'

'It would be a good notion if one of us did,' agreed Cartright. 'Perhaps you'd better go. You're a more expert burglar than I am. I'll walk by and whistle the old tune, if they show signs of returning before you come back. I hope you get out in time.'

'Whistle it loudly,' enjoined the younger man. 'It would be a pity if my promising career was cut short, because you didn't whistle loudly enough.'

He crossed to the other side, and hurried along towards the house. It was an admirable night for his purpose. There was no moon, while a heavy cloudbank had blown up, and it had commenced to rain. The children had dispersed, and the chatterers had been driven in to their firesides. A bus came swinging round from Formosa Street, stopped to drop a single passenger, who went towards Bristol Gardens, and rattled on its way again. For the moment there was not a soul about. Carter slipped through the gate, up the steps to the front door. He did not worry about the lamp standard right outside the house. A bunch of skeleton keys which he carried about with him would provide the means of entrance. There would be no question of attempting to enter by a window, when he would be certain to draw attention to himself.

In a little over half a minute after trying a key in the lock, he was inside the house, the door closed behind him. He found himself in a dark, narrow hall, which contained an unpleasant odour of mustiness and decay. Making his way cautiously forward – he did not have a torch on him, and did not wish to risk switching on the light – he came to a staircase and, without making a sound, ascended. On the floor above was a passage narrower than the hall below. Two rooms opened into it, while there was a bathroom at the rear, down two steps. A door directly in front of him proved to belong to a cupboard, the staircase continuing upward to the left of it. He chose the back room in which to start his investigations as being the safer. His main object was to discover for certain, if possible, whether the two men with Pestalozzi and the bootblack were actually Haeckel and Zanazaryk. If he were able to ascertain that, there would be no reason for him to enter the front room at all. There was a great deal less risk in the back room, but would he hear Cartright whistle? A smile played round his lips at the recollection of his last remark to his colleague.

He pushed open the door quietly and entered. For a moment he stood listening; then feeling for the electric light switch, turned on the light. A quick glance round showed him a room in a state of awful untidiness. A double bedstead and a smaller one occupied most of the space, blankets, sheets and pillows being thrown on them in heaps. Shirts – dirty-looking objects – socks and collars covered the rickety dressing table and only chair, and overflowed on to the floor. A washstand in one corner of the room contained a cracked ewer and a basin full of black, soapy water. An expression of disgust crossed Carter's face, but he had no time for fastidious repugnance. The blind was already drawn down before the solitary window, therefore he could not be seen from the houses at the back. His eyes searched for and found what was of importance to him – three suitcases of varying sizes, all old and very much worn, pushed under the large bed.

Quickly he dragged them out. They were not locked, and rapidly but expertly he searched them, taking care to replace everything exactly as he found it. He was extremely disappointed when he had finished. He had failed to find a single article of any interest to him. At least he had hoped to come across the men's passports. Even if they were held under false names, as they were certain to be, he would have learnt something from them. He was particularly keen to know where they had been issued. Pushing the suitcases back under the bed, he set to work to search the rest of the room. The minutes passed quickly by, and still he failed to come across a single object that would have helped him to establish the identity of even one of the foreigners. The drawers of the dressing table contained nothing at all; none of the shirts or collars had a name on them. He was about to go into the front room when his eyes settled on a pair of high Russian boots thrown carelessly under the washstand. What innocent looking receptacles they would make, he thought, for anything the men wanted to hide that could not be carried about with them. Immediately he picked up one, finding it astonishingly heavy. Inserting his hand he found himself grasping a heavy automatic pistol. He drew it out and examined it. It had no name on it, but was of German make, a deadly-looking weapon, and was fully loaded. The other boot contained a similar pistol. At least he had found proof that the owner of the boots was not altogether a simple, guileless individual. Only a man who had sinister designs or was in fear of aggression would possess such weapons. Not expecting to discover to whom the boots belonged, Carter nevertheless turned back the tops and examined them. Then a low cry of exultation escaped from him. An attempt had been made to scratch out certain letters written on each. He carried them under the light and held them close to his eyes. The writing was practically obliterated. On one, only Y and K being visible, but on the other less success had attended the efforts of the owner. Carter was able to read Zan-za-yk – obviously Zanazaryk. He had established the fact that with Pestalozzi was, at least, one of his fellow anarchists.

He replaced the pistols in their unusual holsters, which he took care were put back under the washstand exactly as he had found them. That done, he switched off the light and left the bedroom; walked along the passage, and entered the apartment overlooking the street. The blinds were down, but, like those of the bedroom, were only flimsy things of linen, through which the light was bound to show. There were no thick curtains to draw across. However, Cartright was on watch. He would be bound to warn him of the approach of the men. Carter switched on the light, and glanced round the room which, though not in as disorderly a condition as the bedroom, was extremely untidy, as well as badly furnished. A large kitbag lying in a corner, under a rug which only partially hid it, immediately drew his eye. At once he was across the room and had removed the covering. A powerful-looking padlock secured the top of the bag, which on inspection, Carter decided would take some time to open –

probably far longer than he could afford. He felt several hard substances, the shape of them suggesting, as far as he was able to tell, large revolvers or possibly Mauser automatic pistols.

'They're well armed,' he muttered to himself. 'I wish to goodness I had the time to open that thing and look inside.'

There was nothing on the kitbag to indicate the name of the owner. After turning it over, he laid it down again, and drew the rug back over it. He then turned his attention to the rest of the room. An overcoat which he seemed to recognise was thrown over the back of a chair. Picking it up and holding it at arms' length, he decided that it was the one which Pestalozzi had been wearing when he had first come across the man. At first he thought there was nothing in any of the pockets, but on more careful investigation, he found a sticky lump in one. Taking it out he discovered, to his disgust, that it consisted of a half melted sweetmeat of some kind to which were adhering several torn scraps of paper. These he pulled away from the sweet one by one, placing them on the table. They were obviously all part of one small piece of paper, and he proceeded to put them together. It was an unpleasant job, as they were sticky and very dirty. However, he persevered. Presently he had succeeded in arranging the whole in one piece, and on it, to his delight, he found a message. It was written in German, and he quickly translated it to read:

Have brought instructions. Take room Canute Hotel, Waterloo Road, Wednesday night. Do not fail. Send S or H if you cannot come. Must return next day.

M

Carter gave vent to a grunt of satisfaction. The reason why Pestalozzi had taken a room in the Canute Hotel for one night was now explained. Somebody had met him there, and had given him certain instructions which, it was to be presumed, had been conveyed from the headquarters of the anarchists in Vienna. Who was 'M'? However, the identity of the messenger did not matter very much, as he had probably already returned whence he came. Carter had evidence now that Haeckel as well as Zanazaryk was with Pestalozzi, for the letter 'H' in the note could hardly refer to anybody else.

He copied the message into his notebook; then, replacing the scraps of paper on the sweet – a most distasteful task – replaced the messy lump in the pocket from which he had taken it. The coat was put back on the chair exactly as it had lain before. Carter had learnt, during his career, that to pay attention to the smallest details was a very necessary policy in the work of an agent of the Secret Service. He wiped his hands on his handkerchief until they no longer felt sticky; then continued his investigations. A folded map of the routes of London of the type issued by the London Transport Company lay on the mantelpiece, but he took no notice of it until he had completed his survey of the room and had found nothing further of interest. He picked it up casually and opened it. The next moment he gave an exclamation, spread it out on the table, and was studying it. On it a thin red line was traced from Victoria Station, along Victoria Street, across Parliament Square, thence up Whitehall, along the Mall by way of the Admiralty Arch to Buckingham Palace. It was the route King Peter would take on his arrival in London. A large red cross marked the spot about where the Cenotaph stood. It was expected that the king would place a wreath at the base of the memorial. Was it there that the anarchists had decided to assassinate him? Carter had little doubt of it. He carefully followed the route to make certain there were no other crosses.

He was thus engaged when he heard faintly the whistled notes of the tune British Secret Service men used as a warning to each other. At once, he folded up the map, replaced it on the mantelshelf and, darting across the room, switched off the light. A moment later he had run quietly down the stairs, had opened the front door, and was looking out. Cartright came by as he was about to close the door behind him, caught sight of him, and paused for a moment in his whistling.

'Back and hide,' came the low warning, barely reaching Carter's ears. 'Close behind!' And Cartright passed on, whistling louder than ever.

The lips of his colleague came together grimly, but he did not hesitate. Backing into the hall, he gently closed the door. He regretted now that he was not armed, but he smiled as he reflected that he knew where he would be able to obtain a weapon, if it became necessary and he was able to reach it in time. Where was he to hide? He knew nothing of the bootblack's flat. If he entered any of his rooms, the possibility was that he would find nothing in them behind which he could conceal himself; there was certainly no hiding place in either of the rooms above. He heard the sound of voices and footsteps outside; immediately ran back up the stairs; had reached the next floor as the door opened. It was his intention to ascend the next flight which led to an attic. As far as he knew the latter was unoccupied. There he hoped to be able to remain in security until the coast was clear. He heard the voices of the four men as they stood talking in the hall below. They were conversing in German, and Carter would very much have liked to remain where he was and listen to their conversation. Such a proceeding, however, would be, he realised, nothing but folly. The stairs above might creak, there might be obstacles in his way. While the three anarchists were ascending to their rooms they might hear him above, or reach the landing to find him vainly endeavouring to move from his path articles that had been left on the stairs. He had once before had a very narrow escape when, in order to avoid pursuers, he had darted up the stairs of a similar kind of house to find his way obstructed by a conglomeration of articles from suitcases and birdcages to brooms and dustpans. The tenants of the house had been in the habit of utilising the unused staircase as a handy place on which to store impedimenta, for which they otherwise could not have found room.

His experience was not repeated on this occasion, however, the stairs leading to the attic were quite clear, though uncarpeted and distinctly creaky. Before starting on the ascent he had stolen a glance at the quartette below. One of the men had switched on the hall light, and they were standing directly underneath it. There was no mistaking Pestalozzi and the bootblack, but the other two had their backs to Carter. All he was able to see of them was that they were both of average height, though one was a good deal stouter than the other. They had not taken off their hats. The shape of their heads and the colour of their hair, therefore, remained unknown factors to the Secret Service man.

Treading with the utmost caution, and feeling before him for obstacles, he crept step by step to the attic, but despite all his care, he could not prevent a creak occurring now and again. One in particular sounded to his ears almost as loud as a pistol shot, and he stood expectant, anticipating cries of alarm and the sound of men running up from below. However, nothing of an inimical nature took place; the murmur of voices went on. He continued his slow progress, and eventually reached the top. The atmosphere of mustiness was more pronounced than ever up there; the dust seemed to lie inches deep underfoot; he heard the scuttle of mice. It was certain that the attic had lacked a tenant for a very long time, and was almost, if not entirely, a stranger to fresh air.

There was a tiny little landing at the head of the stairs. Carter felt his way along until he came to a door. It was closed, but he found the handle, and turned it carefully. It squeaked a little, as did the door, when he slowly pushed it open. The farther it went the noisier it threatened to become. He desisted, therefore, as soon as he had assured himself that there was room enough to enter. Returning to the banisters he leant over, and stood listening. Up there it was quite impossible to distinguish what was being said, though he was still able to hear voices. The men remained where they were for some considerable time, but at last he heard the sound of heavy feet ascending the first flight of stairs; then walking along the passage. A light was switched on.

'Himmel!' grunted a voice in German. 'The fire has gone out. Zanazaryk, my friend, you will have to give us the benefit of your skill. Neither Pestalozzi nor I is much good at making fires.'

'One day it is certain you will be the fuel which will help to keep one going,' commented another voice.

'Ah! That is a Czechoslovakian joke,' was the retort, 'and therefore, not in good taste. If we burn, my friend, it is sure that you will do likewise, unless there is something worse than burning.'

Carter smiled to himself, as the three men entered the room, and closed the door behind them. He had feared they would leave it open, when it would have been utterly impossible to have passed without being seen. He decided to wait a little while; then attempt the descent. He dared not risk a light. There was not the slightest feeling of fear in his heart, though he knew very well his life would not be worth a moment's purchase if he were discovered. In taking precautions to escape detection he had not thought of himself at all. He had been altogether influenced by the necessity to avoid alarming the anarchists. Once they had him in their power they would kill him, and depart, at once, for another hiding place. Cartright was outside, but it was not certain that he would succeed in trailing them to a new refuge. They would expect another man, perhaps more, to be on watch, and would naturally take precautions accordingly. It was absolutely essential, therefore, thought the young man, that he must get out of the house unsuspected. Once Sir Leonard Wallace was in possession of the information he could give him, it is certain he would act quickly. The chief never allowed the grass to grow under his feet – he had a habit of acting with dramatic suddenness.

After waiting where he was for close on half an hour, it suddenly occurred to Carter that he probably could look down into the road from the attic window. He might be able to draw Cartright's attention, thus showing that he was safe. The thought had no sooner come to him than he squeezed into the room and, ascertaining where the window was from the square of faintly reflected light in the prevailing darkness, tiptoed cautiously towards it, fearful lest a board should creak or his footsteps be heard beneath. He had almost achieved his object when the very thing he was dreading happened. A loose board close to the window gave beneath his tread, and, as his foot was raised from it, returned to place with a loud squeak.

He immediately froze into immobility, hardly daring to breathe. His worst fears were realised when the door below was flung open, and there reached his ears the sound of excited and somewhat alarmed voices. They ceased after a few moments and a dead silence reigned. Carter knew the men were standing on the landing below listening.

'You are a fool, Pestalozzi,' remarked one of the anarchists presently. 'Upstairs there are many rats and mice. What else could it be?'

'It sounded to me,' replied a thin, nasal voice which spoke German indifferently, 'like a board creaking. Boards only creak when feet press on them.'

'That is nonsense,' put in the third man, 'a rat can make a board creak also. Since I came here I have often heard sounds like that. Once I went to see. There was nothing only dust and smell and the scampering of many feet. It seems to me, my friend Pestalozzi, that you are a coward.'

'Haeckel is right,' agreed the first man who had spoken – despite his peril, Carter gave a little sigh of triumph at this complete confirmation that Haeckel was the third member of the party – 'You are a coward, Pestalozzi. Why you were sent with us on such a mission I do not know.'

'You are fools, both of you,' replied the thin voice of the Italian. 'If you had the experience that I had today, you would not be so full of confidence. Are you not alarmed to know that the police have discovered that we are in this country, and nearly arrested me?'

'Bah! It was your imagination, my friend,' declared Haeckel – he seemed unable to leave the phrase 'my friend' out of a sentence, though his voice did not suggest friendship. 'A man rubbed against your arm and you immediately thought he was of the police. Your imagination did the rest.'

'But I tell you I heard him say the words, "I arrest you".'

The third man laughed.

'Your English is too bad to be certain of that,' he observed. 'It is more likely he was apologising to you. The police cannot know we are here. Our arrangements, and our entry into this country, were too well-planned, and English police do not look,' he laughed again, 'for people like us.'

'I tell you, you are wrong,' cried Pestalozzi. 'Why will you not be convinced?'

'Well, here we are quite safe,' decided Haeckel. 'We have watched well, and there has happened nothing to make us suspicious.'

Pestalozzi muttered something which Carter was unable to catch.

'Why don't you go up and look?' demanded Zanazaryk. 'At least you will convince yourself.'

Almost directly afterwards there came the sound of ascending feet, and Carter's body grew more rigid than ever; his hands clenched and his teeth gritted together. At the top of the stairs the approaching man stumbled, and swore in Italian. One of the others laughed.

'Have you fallen over a policeman?' he called mockingly.

The Italian came on towards the attic. Carter wondered if he knew the door should have been shut. He suddenly remembered the faint blur of light cast by the window, and quietly bent himself double for fear of being silhouetted. Pestalozzi pushed the door wide open and entered. Apparently he was not surprised or alarmed to find it was not closed. Carter heard his hand feeling for the switch, and little beads of perspiration broke out on his forehead. He had forgotten that the man would be bound to put on the light. This would be the end; there would be no chance of reaching the bedroom now, and obtaining one of the automatics concealed in the boots. One cry from Pestalozzi, and the others would rush to his assistance; then—! Carter's lips pursed in a soundless whistle. He waited calmly for the end.

The Italian's hand continued rubbing against the wall, searching for the switch. He was a long time finding it, and muttered to himself in exasperation. Carter thought he was rather a fool not to have brought a torch or a lamp with him. Ah! At last his fingers came in contact with it, and the Englishman braced himself for what he believed was about to happen. There was a click, but no light flared on to reveal the Secret Service agent crouching below the window. The latter, realising that there was no bulb in the socket or that, if there were, it was a dud, almost laughed aloud in his relief. But his ordeal was not yet at an end.

Pestalozzi stood by the door swearing softly to himself in Italian for a few moments, then he began to feel his way round the room. Carter held his breath, ready to grapple with him the moment the other's body touched his. Directly that happened, he would knock the fellow over, dash down the stairs, hoping thus to take the other two momentarily by surprise. There was just a chance that he would be able to reach the bedroom, snatch one of the pistols, and thus be in a position to obtain the upper hand. The plan was desperate, the chance of getting by Haeckel and Zanazaryk practically nil, but it was his only chance. He had no intention of being overcome without a fierce fight for liberty.

He heard the Italian's shuffling steps as he edged slowly round the room. Gradually the fellow drew nearer, was almost on him. Carter felt a slight puff of air above his head, realised that Pestalozzi's hand had passed just over him. The Italian moved on; he had missed him by what could hardly have been more than a fraction of an inch! A few moments later he left the room, walked along the landing, and descended the stairs. No voices greeted his appearance. Carter concluded that the other two had re-entered the apartment beneath. He straightened himself, and leant, breathing a little more deeply than usual, against the windowsill. He had experienced some very narrow escapes during his career, but this deserved to rank with the narrowest.

He heard the door close below, remained perfectly still for some time; then, certain that the three had by then settled down again, began to feel for the fastening of the window. His fingers soon found it, but were unable to move it. From long disuse it had jammed into place, and he was afraid to exert too much pressure lest, in forcing it back, it made too much noise. Eventually he was compelled to give up any hope of opening the window. With his handkerchief he wiped away some of the accumulation of dirt on the glass, and was able to look out. He could not see much, however. The room below possessed a bow window, the roof of which completely cut off his view of the road and, in fact, of the pavement on the other side. Carter was very disappointed. He had hoped to have been able to get into communication with Cartright. There was only one thing left to do. That was to endeavour to get out of the house as soon as possible. Jimmy, he decided, would be getting anxious. He turned to begin his stealthy creep across the unstable floor. Then suddenly a blinding flash of light shone full in his eyes, and he started back with a cry.

'Ah!' came a low, guttural voice, sounding more sinister to

Carter's ears, since he was unable to see the speaker. 'So mine friendt a fool vas not. He zinks that zomeone very quiet in zis room is, and tell me zo. Your hands put up, or shot you will get.' Carter's hands had been promptly raised at the order. The German, in his own tongue, called down to his companions, who quickly ran up the stairs to his assistance. Their exclamations were more forcible than polite when they saw Carter. 'Take him by his arms and go with him in front of me,' directed Haeckel. 'We will take him to our room, and ask him some questions before we kill him.'

The two entered the attic. Carter's arms were gripped roughly, and he was led down to the apartment below. On the threshold he made a fierce attempt to wrench himself free, risking a bullet from the gun carried by the German behind, but he was held too tightly. They hustled him into the room with brutal force. The door closed on them.

CHAPTER FOUR

The Raid in Shirland Road

Cartright had hoped that he would have been able to give his colleague warning of the coming of the anarchists in ample time to enable him to escape. He had watched them from the saloon bar, to which he had returned when Carter left him and, directly they showed signs of moving, had hurried out and made his way towards the house. Unfortunately, however, the four foreigners seemed to be in great haste also. They had left the public house soon after him, but instead of slouching along home, had walked rapidly. The result was that when Cartright passed the front gate, they had not been more than thirty yards behind him, and he had had no recourse but to advise his colleague to go back. Had Carter attempted to descend the steps, he could not have avoided being seen.

Knowing his friend to be in a house with four men who would not hesitate to murder him, if they discovered him,

Cartright was distinctly worried. For some time he considered the idea of entering in order to be able to go to Carter's assistance if necessary, but eventually decided against it. The chances were that he would do more harm than good. He had no idea how the rooms inside were situated, or, in fact, very much about the house. If he broke his way in, he might quite possibly blunder right into the anarchists, and thus give the whole business away. Carter, he knew was a young man of infinite resource and, in that knowledge he took a good deal of comfort. As time passed, however, and his friend did not appear he became definitely anxious. He dared not leave his post, otherwise he would have gone to the telephone and rung up for assistance. The driver of the car in which he had travelled from Whitehall was waiting out of sight in Sutherland Avenue. If he could only get hold of him! But the risk of walking even that short distance away was too great. The anarchists might emerge while he was up the road and depart for a fresh address, leaving Carter's dead body behind to testify to their desperation and contempt for the authorities. If they escaped, Sir Leonard Wallace would never forgive him. Cartright decided to remain where he was, every now and again casting glances along the road in the hope that West, the driver, would glance round the corner, when he might be able to signal to him to approach. West, however, like most of the drivers employed by Secret Service Headquarters, was an old soldier of exemplary character and a rigid sense of discipline. He had been told to take the car out of sight and stand by it until Carter or Cartright came to him, and there he would remain until Doomsday if need be. Cartright knew that perfectly well.

A neighbouring clock began to chime preparatory to striking nine. He looked across at the house. There were lights in the basement, on the ground floor, and the storey above. Once or twice shadows had been thrown momentarily on the blinds, but otherwise there was no sign of life. Everything seemed so utterly peaceful that it was hard to imagine violence taking place over the way. But nobody knew better than Cartright how deceptive appearances can be. He shivered a little, and it was not altogether due to the chill wind or the rain, which was now descending in a steady stream.

The last note of the hour was striking, when a large black car glided noiselessly round the corner from Formosa Street, passed him by, and stopped forty or fifty yards farther along. He recognised it as belonging to Sir Leonard Wallace, and a feeling of relief replaced the anxiety in his mind. A man of medium height, slim even in the raincoat he wore, with a felt hat pulled well down on his head, and his left hand in his pocket descended from the car, and strolled along the pavement towards him. There was no mistaking the chief. Cartright moved slowly to meet him.

'Anything of interest to report?' asked Sir Leonard, as he acknowledged the other's salute.

'We have discovered that Pestalozzi is in there, sir,' Cartright told him, 'and are pretty sure Haeckel and Zanazaryk are with him.' He proceeded to repeat the conversation Carter had had with the lady in the public house, described how he had followed the four men to the place, and Carter's recognition of Pestalozzi. A deep sigh of satisfaction was the only sound that left Sir Leonard's lips by way of reply. 'While they were in the pub,' went on Cartright, 'Carter decided to search their rooms. He was in there a considerable time, and had not reappeared, when they got ready to return. I hurried along and warned him by whistling, but they were too rapid to give him time to get out safely. He was opening the front door, when I passed, but they were so close behind me that I had to tell him to get back and hide. That was nearly three quarters of an hour ago, sir, and there has not been a sign of him since.'

'He may be hidden somewhere listening to their conversation,' commented Wallace. 'Is he armed?'

'I don't know, sir. I'm afraid I forgot to ask. I am.'

'H'm! I don't suppose for a moment that he is.' He stood in deep thought, his eyes fixed on the house across the way. 'The ground floor is occupied by the bootblack,' he murmured, presently, 'and the floor above by Pestalozzi and his supposed brothers. We needn't bother about the basement particularly, though we'll keep a watch on it. Have you a bunch of skeleton keys on you, Cartright?'

'No, sir.'

'Then take these, go across, and open that door. Not a sound mind.'

Cartright waited until a man and woman had passed by and a bus, going to the West End, had rounded the corner and disappeared; then he stepped from behind the tree which had sheltered him, and walked to the Formosa Street end of the road. A minute later he came back on the other side, slipped through the gate, and went up the steps to the door. Wallace strolled back to his car, put his head in the open window, and spoke to somebody within. One by one four men stepped out, immediately taking care to avoid any light, and, as far as possible, became merged with the darkness. They were all very expert at that sort of thing for, as the car went towards Sutherland Avenue, a casual observer would only have noticed one man – a slim individual in a raincoat, with one hand in a pocket – who walked across the road, and slowly approached the house next door to the school. Yet, when he had assured himself that the door had been opened and raised his right arm, apparently as a signal, the other four appeared as though from nowhere. As silently as shadows they all passed through the gate, up the steps, and into the house. The door closed gently behind them.

The light in the hall had been left on, and Sir Leonard's eyes quickly took in the narrow, untidy hall, the stairs covered with a worn and shabby carpet, which looked as though it had not been swept for years, and the three closed doors belonging to the bootblack's apartments. His five companions eyed him expectantly, waiting for orders. Besides Cartright, Shannon, looking bigger and more burly than ever in that confined space, Major Brien, his blue eyes glistening with anticipation, and two intelligent-looking men of the Special Branch of New Scotland Yard were present. All, except Sir Leonard himself held revolvers in their hands. He was about to whisper his instructions when, from far above their heads, they caught the sound of a voice; immediately afterwards the same voice, now raised commandingly, shouted: 'Come up! There is a man up here!' Followed hoarse exclamations, and the sound of feet pattering up uncovered stairs.

'We seem to have made our appearance at the psychological moment,' muttered Sir Leonard.

They stood listening intently to the noises above. Came the tramp of several feet descending; then a loud scuffling punctuated by more forcible exclamations. Even though the din above their heads was loud enough to drown all other sounds, Wallace heard a movement inside the room opposite him. He glanced at Shannon, and nodded to the door. It was flung open as the big man turned. On the threshold appeared the bootblack, whose eyes almost started from his head, and whose face turned a sickly yellow as he saw the six men standing in the hall. He opened his mouth to cry out, but before his lips could utter a sound an enormous hand closed them completely. He was lifted up like a babe, carried back into the room, and deposited in a chair.

'If you are in a hurry to find out what the next world is like, sing out,' remarked Shannon. 'If not, keep quiet, and remain quiet.'

Sir Leonard sent one of the Scotland Yard men to keep guard over the prisoner, and called Shannon out.

'We may want the use of your muscles,' he observed with a smile. 'Come on, and tread carefully, all of you!'

He led the way up the stairs and along the landing. The door of the front room had been closed, but he bent down and applied his eye to the keyhole. As the key was in it, he was unable to see anything, but he could hear the sound of voices raised angrily. Straightening himself, he turned to his followers.

'Ready?' They nodded. 'Shoot at the first sign of resistance, but be careful of Carter. I'm pretty certain it is he they took in there.'

He turned the handle, and opened the door almost quietly. Into the room he stepped, his four followers crowding in behind him. The surprise was complete. Zanazaryk and Pestalozzi, who had been holding Carter by the arms, let go of him and shrank away with cries of alarm, the Italian's face suddenly ghastly. Haeckel's mouth and eyes opened wide in an expression of blank amazement, but there was little fear on his face. He possessed far more courage than his companions.

'Hands up!' snapped Sir Leonard. 'And keep them up. Carter come here!'

Haeckel recovered himself marvellously. As Carter was about to obey his chief, the German grasped his arm and raised his revolver to within an inch or two of the young man's head.

'If he moves or anyone of you shoot,' he snarled, 'he quickly is dead.'

It looked as though for the moment Sir Leonard and his men were checked. They might shoot the German, but the shock, as the bullets entered his body, would, in itself, be sufficient to cause his finger to stiffen on the trigger and bring about Carter's death. Zanazaryk and Pestalozzi recovered their courage somewhat on seeing the German's defiance. They had obeyed the order to raise their hands; now they lowered them again, and ranged themselves on either side of Haeckel. Sir Leonard smiled a little, both his hands were in his raincoat pockets now.

'Lower that revolver, and stand back,' he ordered quietly in German. 'Resistance of this sort on your part can only have one result. If you surrender, you will face a fair trial, with a term of imprisonment only behind it. On the other hand, if you persist in this attitude, you will lose your lives. I will give you two minutes to decide.'

Haeckel actually laughed.

'And of zis man vat?' he sneered, persisting in his poor English. 'Is it zat you mind not if killed he is?'

'He will not be killed,' declared Sir Leonard. 'Hurry, and make your choice; nearly a minute has passed.'

His tone was so cool and commanding that all Zanazaryk's and Pestalozzi's fears returned. They did not like the assurance of this calm man with the steely eyes and confident manner. It occurred to them he was prepared to sacrifice the man they had captured, if need be, to gain his ends. Carter was no whit perturbed. He even smiled as he listened to his chief.

'I haf mine choice made,' proclaimed Haeckel.

'So be it,' returned Wallace shrugging his shoulders a little. He eyed Pestalozzi and Zanazaryk. 'If you two possess any common sense,' he continued in German, 'you will persuade your companion to forsake his absurd attitude. We know you are all here with the intention of attempting to assassinate King Peter. If you hope for any mercy from the English courts, it will pay you to acknowledge that you are caught and not make your case worse by attempting to resist.'

'Do not listen to him,' hissed Haeckel. 'We will make a bargain for this man's life.'

Still looking at Pestalozzi, Sir Leonard continued to warn the anarchists of the folly of their attitude, but in the middle of a sentence he suddenly spoke in Hindustani, a language with which Carter was fairly well acquainted.

'When I cough, Carter,' he ordered, 'duck like lightning. Understand?'

'*Jih,*' returned that young man promptly.

'What is it you say?' asked the puzzled Pestalozzi; 'I no understand.'

Sir Leonard ignored him, and turned again to Haeckel.

'The two minutes I gave you are up,' he stated. 'What is your decision?'

'I tell you I haf mine dezision made.'

'Very well.'

He coughed, and Carter went down to the floor as though he had been poleaxed. At the same moment Wallace fired at Haeckel through the pocket of his raincoat. His bullet hit the German in the elbow, and the latter dropped his revolver with a scream of pain and fury. Pestalozzi cringed back, making no attempt at resistance, but Zanazaryk seemed suddenly to regain his courage. He threw up his arm and was about to fire at the recumbent figure of Carter, but Brien was watching him, and promptly shot him in the right shoulder. The Czechoslovakian reeled back; sank cursing into a chair.

The fight was by no means over. Despite his wound, Haeckel flung himself, with a snarl like that of a wild beast, at Sir Leonard Wallace. The latter could easily have shot him again, but refrained. Instead he stepped neatly aside, and the German found himself in the iron grip of Shannon. He struggled desperately, but he might as well have attempted to wrestle with an orangoutang. The most powerful man in the Secret Service held him with ease, and grinned cheerfully into his face.

'Naughty, naughty!' he murmured. 'You'll hurt that arm of yours.'

He handed him over to Cartright and the Scotland Yard man, the latter deftly snapping a pair of handcuffs on his wrists. Presently the pain in the German's elbow proved too much for his courage, which oozed out of him rapidly now. He was pushed into a chair and crouched there moaning. Sir Leonard looked round approvingly.

'A nice clean-up, thanks to you, Carter,' he observed, as the latter rose to his feet.

The young man felt a glow of pleasure. Words of that nature from the chief were worth a great deal, for Sir Leonard was not in the habit of giving praise lightly. Brien stood complacently surveying the scene, his blue eyes twinkling with delight.

'That was as good a shot as I have ever seen you make, Leonard,' he remarked to his friend. 'I guessed what you were up to, you old humbug, but I don't mind admitting I had the wind up.'

'If you were as windy as I,' retorted Sir Leonard, 'I'm sorry for you. I was trying to get a correct aim at the beggar all the time I was talking, and it was a ticklish business, I assure you. If I had missed he would have killed Tommy, and I should have been to blame. I don't think I have ever been more nervy in my life.'

'Nervy! You?' scoffed Brien. 'Is that a joke or what? You never had nerves, you cold-blooded devil – I have yet to meet anyone to equal you.'

Wallace grinned cheerfully.

'How little you know me.' He eyed the pocket of his raincoat ruefully. 'This is practically a new garment, and look at that hole. Ah, well! It was in a good cause. Now, Carter, what have you to tell us?'

The young Secret Service agent plunged into an account of the discoveries he had made. Wallace and Brien listened attentively; were particularly interested in the London Transport Company's map with the red line traced on it and the large cross. The look which Sir Leonard shot at the anarchists when he realised the significance of the cross must have caused them to squirm inwardly. Pestalozzi, at least, showed his feelings in his face. He had been handcuffed to Zanazaryk, but, as Wallace's eyes met his, he started back so violently that he caused his companion to cry out with pain. Of them all, Pestalozzi was the most craven, without a doubt. He was of peasant breed, obviously, and the manner in which his companion, Haeckel, had been baulked had apparently roused a suspicious dread of Sir Leonard Wallace in his heart. He even groaned once when the Englishman approached close to him. Wallace summed him up as a man whom it would not be difficult to question. Once he was thoroughly scared he would be likely to betray even his own mother.

There reached the ears of the men within that room the sound of many voices raised excitedly. Brien went to the window, lifted the blind a little, and glanced out. The road was crowded with people all looking at the house, gesturing and chatting loudly. From the windows of the houses opposite also were other men, women and children leaning out in great excitement. He reported the fact to Sir Leonard.

'Their interest has been aroused by the sound of the revolver shots,' he commented, and, turning to the officer of the Special Branch, added, 'Go down, find some police constables, explain the position, and get them to clear the road. When you've done that visit the basement, and interview the ice cream man who lives there. I don't suppose he has anything to do with this business, but you will know how to make certain. If your suspicions are aroused in any way, arrest him, and bring him up here.'

The man saluted, and hurried away. Under the eye of Sir Leonard his assistants then commenced a search of the rooms on the ground floor and those occupied by Haeckel, Pestalozzi and Zanazaryk. Conducted as it was by men who were expert in such work nothing escaped notice. The furniture was moved and examined, even the carpets were lifted and the floorboards inspected almost inch by inch. The bedrooms were practically dismantled, the pillows and mattresses being opened out in several places. The rooms of the bootblack yielded nothing, except that he had become a naturalised Englishman and was a properly accredited member of the Bootblack Brigade. His name was Luigi Casaroli. The bedroom used by the three anarchists was found to contain nothing more than Carter had already discovered. It was the locked kitbag and the men's own pockets which produced the only items of note.

The kitbag, when opened, was found to contain quite an assortment of weapons. Three Mauser pistols – among the most deadly of weapons – four narrow-bladed, ugly knives with edges as keen as those of razor blades, half a dozen small bombs which could be timed to go off to a second were there. The latter were most carefully wrapped up, and Sir Leonard found it necessary to utter a warning, when he noticed Shannon handling one as though it were a cricket ball. There were other articles of even greater interest in the kitbag. One was a letter in German addressed to Haeckel, wishing him success in the first real blow to be struck against the so-called royal families of the world. On plain paper and signed by one Dimitrinhov, it caused Sir Leonard a great deal of thought. Was there, he wondered, a gigantic plot being hatched against all those unfortunate enough to have been born royal? Another article which interested him was a small notebook in which appeared a list of names and addresses of men living in various capitals of Europe. Among them he found the name of Luigi Casaroli, and concluded from that that the list was of those in union with or sympathetic to the anarchist organisation. For the first time he began to feel that he was dealing not with a remote plot to assassinate one king, but a gigantic scheme controlled by a powerful association.

A search of the pockets revealed the significant fact that each was supplied with a great deal of money, while hanging from their necks were small discs of silver on each of which was inscribed a number with the letters I. A. S. beneath. Zanazaryk's inner coat pocket yielded up a photograph of King Peter, while Haeckel's contained one of members of the royal family.

While the search was continuing, the faces of the three scoundrels were pictures of varied emotion. Haeckel's showed hatred pure and simple, Zanazaryk's was more sullen, but in it was also a tinge of fear. With Pestalozzi the emotion was predominantly terror, with a touch of fanaticism, supplied by his burning eyes. Brien reflected that it would take little to turn the fellow into a maniac. They all refused to reply to any questions put to them, maintaining an obstinate silence. The only time Haeckel opened his mouth was when the letter addressed to him was found in the kitbag. Then he gave vent to a roar which can only be described as of baffled rage. It was easy to see that he had intended to destroy a document which could be, as it had indeed turned out, only a danger to him. Somehow it had been overlooked.

Their investigations concluded, the men of the Secret Service prepared to leave the building. Everything that was of interest or could be used in evidence was carefully packed in the kitbag. Sir Leonard intended taking it back to headquarters in his own car. The police had been communicated with, and a van was expected for the prisoners. The wounds of Haeckel and Zanazaryk had been dressed as well as was possible under the circumstances, but they would be properly attended to later on. Casaroli had been brought to the floor above from his flat, when the search began. He had promptly thrown himself on his knees before Sir Leonard, declaring his innocence, but such protestations were of no avail. He was manacled like the rest, and thereafter maintained a sullen silence, casting malevolent glares from time to time at his companions in misfortune. His rooms had yielded nothing at all of an incriminating nature, while his pockets and his person proved equally innocent. It was when the policeman entered the room to announce that the tender was at the door, that his feelings got the better of him.

'It is you I have to thank for this,' he suddenly screamed at Haeckel in Italian. 'You who forced me to join the association because of what I did in Berlin. I curse you. I came to England to escape from the clutches of the society of the—'

'Be quiet, you fool!' shouted Haeckel.

'I will not be quiet,' shrieked the excited man. Cartright took a step towards him as though to stop him, but Wallace waved him away. He was interested in what Casaroli had to say. 'You followed me,' went on the almost demented Italian. 'I was happy. I had a good job. Now it is ruined. May God curse you and Dimitrinhov, and Modjeska, and all the rest of those fiends. May their secret hiding place in Constantinople be burnt down, with them in it. I will tell the police everything, do you hear, Haeckel, and you, Zanazaryk, and you, Pestalozzi? The cause will be ruined and—'

Afterwards Wallace blamed himself for what happened. His attention, like that of all his companions, was fixed on the shouting Casaroli. None of them noticed the sudden tenseness of Haeckel's attitude. Abruptly, with incredible swiftness, the German lunged forward and, despite the fact that he was manacled, snatched up an automatic which someone had laid down on the table. Then, in quick succession, he fired at Casaroli, Pestalozzi and Zanazaryk, crying in a loud voice as he did so,

'Let us all die; then none can speak. The cause is preserved. I—'

Two or three other revolvers barked viciously. He stood

swaying a moment on his feet, a curious, enigmatical smile on his distorted features, then he crashed to the floor, twitched a moment, and lay still. The acrid fumes of powder filled the air as Sir Leonard examined the three sagging bodies in their chairs. Casaroli and Pestalozzi were dead, Zanazaryk undoubtedly dying.

'Fetch a doctor – quick!' he shouted. Two men hastened from the room. Sir Leonard turned to Brien with a bitter smile. 'I thought we had achieved a triumph,' he murmured to his friend, 'but I am afraid this is one of the biggest failures of my career.'

CHAPTER FIVE

Major Brien Points the Way

The happenings in the house on Shirland Road naturally caused a sensation in the country. The newspapers made a great deal of the story, though a good many facts were not permitted to leak out. For instance, though it was generally known that the men who had lost their lives were dangerous anarchists, the reason for their presence in England was kept a profound secret. Neither was any mention made of the discoveries of the agents of the Secret Service. In fact, that very silent organisation controlled by Sir Leonard Wallace did not appear in the matter at all. As ever, the work of the man upon whom Great Britain depends for its security, to an extent never realised by the public, was concealed from all but those in very high and administrative places.

Zanazaryk lingered in unconsciousness for two days but, despite all the best surgeons in London could do for him, died at the expiration of that time. Thus Sir Leonard's hopes of obtaining the information he desired so keenly were disappointed. Haeckel he knew would never have spoken, but Pestalozzi, Casaroli, and possibly Zanazaryk might have been persuaded to betray the organisation which he had reason to believe existed for the purpose of ridding the world of royalty. Now they were all dead, and he would be forced to rely upon the little knowledge he possessed to carry him farther on his investigations. The raids carried out on the houses Pestalozzi was known to have visited had proved, as Sir Leonard had expected, entirely abortive.

'I am convinced,' he told Brien, 'that a great blow is being aimed at royalty throughout the world. We heard enough from the words spoken by Casaroli and from the letter to Haeckel, to gather that a society exists, with its headquarters apparently in Constantinople, which is pledged to the extermination of royal families. I am going to follow this through to the bitter end, Bill.' His eyes glinted fiercely. 'Do you realise that our own royal family is threatened? At the moment our knowledge is extremely vague, but think of it! God! The very thought is intolerable.'

Brien had seldom seen him so profoundly moved. Gone for the time being was the nonchalant-seeming, unruffled man; in his place a fiery, vehement individual who made no effort to cloak his feelings. The deputy chief nodded in full agreement.

'It's going to be as desperate a venture as you have ever undertaken,' he murmured.

Wallace laughed, perhaps a trifle harshly.

'What of it?' he returned. 'I'll wipe out this association somehow. It will be a change from the usual kind of job.'

'And even more dangerous, I'm afraid.' Brien sighed. He was

thinking of Sir Leonard's wife, the beautiful Molly Wallace, whose life was bound up with rare devotion in that of her husband to the exclusion of practically everything else. 'Once this society knows you are on its track, you will be in hourly peril. Obviously its ramifications are pretty extensive, since it has agents in nearly every capital of Europe – I suppose there is no doubt that the names in the book we found are those of agents.'

'The society will not know I am on its track, if I can help it. If it finds out, well, I'll have to take my chance.' He rose from his desk, and began to pace the room. 'Do you realise that of all reigning families ours has always been the most secure and free from threats of assassination until now? To think that a band of miserable, fanatic devils hidden away in some hole in Europe, should dare to plot against them! Heavens! If Providence is kind, and I get in touch with the leaders, I'll more than earn the title of ruthless which some people have bestowed on me.'

Brien watched him in silence for a few moments.

'We don't really know that there is a plot against our royalty,' he observed presently.

'Isn't that letter enough to convince you? The man Dimitrinhov, whoever he may be, speaks of the first real blow to be struck against the royal families of the world. And even if Great Britain was not included in the scheme, are we to stand by while attempts are being made to exterminate royalty in other countries?'

'How about passing on the information concerning the secret hiding place in Constantinople to the Turkish government and putting them in possession of the facts?'

Sir Leonard came to a halt and faced his friend.

'Great Scott, man!' he cried. 'What facts have we that we can pass on? Do you think any government would act on the meanderings of a terror-stricken man? And what else have we to offer? A book with a list of names and addresses in it that may mean anything; a letter written in German from one fanatic to another, which would probably be passed over with a polite shrug of the shoulders; two names, Modjeska and Dimitrinhov, of men, against whom we have not an item of proof, who might be in any part of Europe. Can't you see the Turkish government administering a well-deserved snub? No, Bill, nothing can be done in the way you suggest. I am going to investigate this affair myself. When I have my proof, then I can demand action.'

'How will you set about it?'

'First I shall go to Vienna and find out all I can from Beust. The information concerning the attempt to be made on King Peter came from him, remember. It was in Vienna that the gang of international anarchists held the meetings which resulted in Pestalozzi, Zanazaryk and Haeckel coming to England. Although Constantinople may contain their hiding place, their headquarters may actually be in Vienna. However, whether I afterwards go on to Constantinople depends a lot upon what I learn from Beust.'

'Do you intend to go alone?'

'I haven't made any plans yet. Probably not. I'm afraid it is going to be too big a job to tackle without an assistant handy.'

King Peter duly paid his visit to England. It passed off without an untoward incident of any kind. Although the royal visitor was quite unaware of the fact, extraordinary precautions were taken to safeguard his person. The three would-be assassins, who had travelled from Vienna for the purpose of murdering His Majesty, were dead, it is true, but their deaths had not been kept secret – that had been an impossibility. There was a chance, therefore, that the organisation which had been behind them would despatch other men to accomplish the deed; not that such a contingency was very likely. Wallace thought there was hardly time for adequate preparations to be made. Still, he took no risks. Everywhere that King Peter went he was guarded with the greatest care, while numbers of men of the Secret Service and Special Branch, as well as plain-clothes officers of the CID, mingled with the crowds anywhere in the vicinity of the king, watching keenly for any sign that assassins were lurking in them.

It was after King Peter had departed for his own country that Sir Leonard made his preparations to commence the investigations that he hoped would end in the extermination of the anarchist organisation. He first had an interview with the foreign secretary, which left that statesman considerably shaken. Knowing the Chief of the Secret Service very well indeed, the cabinet minister wasted no time in expressing disbelief that a plot could exist, the aim of which was to assassinate members of the British royal family. He knew Sir Leonard was no alarmist, and that his insistence that the matter should be discussed by the cabinet in secret and steps taken to guard the royal family more adequately, was actuated by a very real sense that grave danger existed. Wallace gave him a copy of the list of names and addresses of men in the various capitals whom he believed to be spies or agents of the organisation; urged him to hint to the governments concerned that they were possibly members of an anarchic society, and should be watched. The foreign secretary received the information with encouraging gravity; promised to ask for a meeting of the cabinet at once.

On Sir Leonard's return to his office after his interview with the statesman, he found Brien awaiting him with every appearance of impatience.

'Hullo, Bill,' he remarked, 'you look agitated. What's the trouble?'

'I'm not agitated,' was the reply, 'but an idea has occurred to me. Has it struck you that the people who sent Haeckel and company to London will possibly be rather alarmed at the deaths of the whole bunch – including Casaroli?'

Sir Leonard removed his overcoat and hat, walked across to his chair, and sat down.

'It has,' he nodded. 'What of it?'

Brien pushed some documents away, and planted himself on the edge of the great oak desk.

'Isn't it likely,' he asked, 'that they may be worried in case information concerning them will have fallen into the hands of the authorities?' Wallace nodded again. 'Well,' went on Brien, 'I am wondering if they have sent a representative over here in order to obtain information; that is, to try and find out what is known about them, and what we intend to do about it.'

Sir Leonard sat up, and eyed his friend with approval.

'By Jove, Bill!' he exclaimed. 'That's a notion. It's the very thing they would do. If they have, and we could find the fellow, he might be trailed when he returns, and lead me to their headquarters. The trouble will be to find him among seven and a half million people.'

Major Brien smiled triumphantly. It was not often that he was able to point the way to his chief.

'I don't think there will be much difficulty in it,' he declared, 'providing, of course, a man has come to London. The messenger who conveyed instructions to Pestalozzi stayed at the Canute Hotel, in Waterloo Road. It is fairly safe to assume that another emissary would put up in the same place.'

'Of course,' murmured Sir Leonard, 'of course. They would hardly be likely to know a great deal about London, and information obtained by one regarding hotel accommodation would be sure to be handed on to another. Bill, you're a genius. We'll act on the idea at once.'

He pressed one of the numerous buttons under the ledge of his desk. In a few moments there came a knock on the door and, in response to Sir Leonard's invitation, a small, grey-haired man with piercing eyes entered the office.

'I want a list of the people staying at the Canute Hotel in Waterloo Road, Maddison,' Wallace told him. 'No suspicion of any sort must be roused. The proprietor is an ex-service man and perfectly trustworthy, so you can take him into your confidence up to a point. Go yourself – he will probably let you have the visitors' book,' Maddison hurried from the room. 'Is Cousins available?' Sir Leonard asked Brien.

The latter shook his head.

'Not at the moment,' he replied. 'He has been in Dublin for the last ten days, as you know.'

'But he was due back this morning.'

'I had a telegram from him after you had gone to lunch, saying that he would be delayed another couple of days.'

'That sounds as though he is hot on the track of that gang of sedition-mongers. It will be a feather in his cap if he can run them to earth. Well, I'll have Carter for this Canute Job.'

He pulled a large bowl of tobacco towards him, and proceeded to fill his pipe. Although Brien had watched the operation many hundreds of times, it still fascinated him to observe the skill and celerity with which his friend performed it. The artificial hand was used in various little ways, it is true; was occasionally quite useful, but Sir Leonard could do most things with one hand. When he had lost his left arm he had immediately set to work to teach the remaining limb to do the work of both. His fingers had become so remarkably prehensile that their functions were almost akin to that of two or three ordinary fingers. In addition his upper arm and wrist were developed to the utmost. His arm was more powerful, in consequence, than the average man's two, and he was able to perform athletic feats which were astonishing to those who knew of his disability but were not aware of how he had succeeded in overcoming it.

His pipe loaded to his satisfaction, he carefully lit the tobacco until it was glowing evenly, then sat back, and puffed away contentedly.

Brien remained chatting with Wallace until Maddison returned less than half an hour later. The latter placed a large book, the covers of which were somewhat the worse for wear, in front of Sir Leonard and opened it.

'There are only eight guests staying in the hotel just now, sir,' he stated. 'As you know it is only a small, third-rate affair and when full, can only accommodate twenty-four or thereabouts.' He proceeded to point out the names of the people then residing there. 'I have been able to ascertain their occupations in all but two cases,' he went on. 'These – Mr and Mrs Curzon – are regular visitors. They come up from Devonshire half a dozen times a year. He is a farmer, and the proprietor assures me he looks like one.'

'They can be washed out,' murmured Brien, who was looking over Sir Leonard's shoulder. The latter nodded.

'Mr Spedding,' went on Maddison pointing to the name, 'has been there a month. He is a naval pensioner, and is undergoing some sort of treatment at St Thomas's Hospital. Wilmer Peregrine Huckleberry Hawthorne—'

'My hat! What a name!' ejaculated Brien.

'Is an American gentleman over from the States on business connected with steel cables.'

'Only an American would have a name like that,' observed Wallace, 'and he can also be removed from the list of suspects.' He looked up at Brien with a smile. 'No mid-European anarchist, even if he were using a false name, would have imagination enough to rise to Wilmer Peregrine Huckleberry Hawthorne.'

'There are American anarchists,' Brien reminded him.

'I doubt it – there may be anarchists in America, but that is a different thing. Go on Maddison!'

'This gentleman –' Maddison coughed slightly as he pointed to the name, Julius Carberry '– is a traveller in ladies' lingerie, and, if I may say so, sir, looks like it. He was pointed out to me.'

'As bad as that, Maddison?' queried Brien, his eyes twinkling humorously.

'Quite, sir. He combed back his glossy locks while I was looking at him, and I'll swear he uses lipstick. He's the kind of unnatural creature who would stand with one hand on his hip and speak with a lisp.'

'Oh, I say,' murmured Brien in an affected voice, and his companions laughed.

'Miss Veronica Simpson,' went on Maddison, pointing out another resident, 'is a retired schoolmistress spending her pension on seeing the sights, I believe.'

'The old dear's making whoopee,' commented Sir Leonard.

'I don't think we need consider her. Great Scott!' he exclaimed suddenly, as Maddison's finger fell on another name. 'Look what we have here, Bill. Modjeska-Ivan,' he read, 'from Warsaw – Pole of independent means.' There was a glint of excitement in his grey eyes as he looked up at Maddison. 'What did you find out about him?' he demanded.

'He arrived yesterday, sir,' was the reply. 'Was here a little over a week ago, and gave as explanation for his return that a friend whom he had not seen for many years was coming to England from America, and is to meet him in London. His passport and other documents are in perfect order and, according to the landlord, he is a quiet, gentlemanly sort of man.'

'You did not see him?'

'No, he was out.'

Wallace sat back in his chair.

'You were right, Bill,' he declared, 'they have sent over a man to investigate, and this is he. Modjeska was one of the names mentioned by Casaroli in his frenzy. The note which Carter found torn up in Pestalozzi's pocket and which he pieced together was initialled with the letter M. It was Modjeska whom Pestalozzi went to meet at the Canute Hotel ten days ago.'

'There can be no doubt of that,' agreed Brien, 'but it puzzles me why he did not change his name.'

'Why should he? He has no reason to think that he is suspected. Therefore, it is far safer to come here under his own name, especially as his papers are in perfect order. Besides, having come over here once, and so recently, as Modjeska, he could not very well appear as someone else unless, of course, he had taken a room elsewhere. Altogether I think he is a wise man. There's another guest, isn't there, Maddison?'

'Yes, sir. This one.' He pointed to a much blotted name, the last in the book. It looked like Beynon, but Maddison read it as Brown. 'He arrived this morning, is quite unknown, and, to quote the proprietor again, talks with a broad north-country accent, and looks a bit down on his luck.'

'I don't think we need bother about him,' decided Sir Leonard. He closed the book. 'You can send it back – or rather take it back yourself, and allay any suspicions that may have been roused in the landlord's honest breast. Let him understand that his guests are all quite unsuspected persons, and that the authorities you represent were barking up the wrong tree. I don't want him to expect any police activity or anything like that, because another guest will arrive tonight. Neither he nor anybody in the hotel must have the slightest notion that the newcomer is anything but what he professes to be. You understand?'

'Quite, sir.'

Sir Leonard handed the book back to him.

'Send Carter to me at once,' he directed. When Maddison had gone, he turned to Brien. 'Modjeska's appearance in London has greatly helped me to complete my plans,' he declared. 'It may not be necessary to go to Beust at all unless the trail leads to Vienna. A lot will depend on Carter.'

That young man, as cheerful as ever, entered the room presently. Wallace waved him to a chair.

'Does the name Modjeska convey anything to you, Carter?' he asked.

'Yes, sir,' replied the other promptly. 'It was one of the names shouted by Casaroli just before Haeckel shot him.'

'It was. Well, the individual in question is in London, staying at the Canute Hotel. He was there ten days ago, but has returned.

It seems fairly obvious that it was he whom Pestalozzi visited the night before his death. Major Brien suggested that an emissary of the anarchist organisation would be likely to come to London in order to discover if any information concerning them had fallen into the hands of the authorities. He also suggested that the Canute Hotel, having been used once, might be used again. As a result Maddison made enquiries. Modjeska arrived yesterday.'

Carter was leaning forward in his chair, his face alight with eagerness. At that moment he looked barely twenty-five, though he was in his thirty-second year.

'Is he there under his own name, sir?' he asked.

Sir Leonard nodded.

'Now listen, Carter. I am determined to root out the whole gang of anarchists. It presents, I firmly believe, a terrible menace to all people of royal blood. At the moment we know little about the organisation, except that it has agents or sympathisers in twelve capitals of Europe, and that two important members of it are Modjeska and a man named Dimitrinhov. Fortunately Modjeska is in London, and our trail will commence with him. You are to go to the Canute Hotel, and take a room there. I want you to alter your appearance sufficiently to make yourself look like a man to whom the world has not been too kind. Appear resentful, sullen, and a trifle reckless, as though your woes have driven you to it. In short, I want you to appear the type of young fellow who would be likely to appeal to a man of Modjeska's kidney. He is certain to be rather at a loss for help in acquiring the information he has, come to obtain. It would be a great step in our favour if he chose you. Don't force yourself on his attention, mind – in fact avoid him, but air your grievances to the other guests pretty forcibly, taking care that he hears you occasionally, especially when resentment at your hard lot causes you to utter revolutionary sentiments. You get the idea?'

'Perfectly, sir,' grinned Carter.

'For heaven's sake don't go there looking as cheerful as that,' commented Brien.

'Not on your life, sir,' returned Carter, and grinned more cheerfully than ever.

'You must do your utmost to find out as much as you can about Modjeska,' went on Sir Leonard. 'I don't want you to follow him when he goes out – we'll see that he is well looked after in that way – of course, if you become so intimate with him that he invites you to go out with him, all the better. If you can search his belongings when he is out, however, you will probably be doing us far more service. Once you take a room in the Canute Hotel don't visit any of your usual haunts – avoid this district entirely. Take care that there is nothing in your luggage to suggest that you are anything but what you appear to be, and let it be as meagre as possible. I will give instructions for either Shannon, Hill, or whoever happens to be available, to call in the buffet opposite platform number seven at Waterloo at nine every night. If you have anything to report, meet him there and deliver your message over a drink. You'd better not know each other, but you can stand by his side and whisper it or pass a written report to him. No doubt such precautions are not really necessary, but we must take no chances in this business, Carter. If anything happens which you wish to report at once, telephone, but use a public call box. Now are there any questions you want to ask?'

'Only this, sir. Shall I carry a revolver?'

'Don't go unarmed from now on,' returned Sir Leonard, 'until this business is over, and always retain your revolver on your person fully loaded. There is just one more thing, Carter. If it is possible, give me plenty of notice of Modjeska's departure from England, and do your best – always remembering that it is essential no suspicion against you must be raised in his mind – to discover his destination, his route and the trains he travels by. When he goes, I want to go with him. Almost everything depends upon you, Carter. Remember I am relying on you.'

As the young man walked from the room, he unconsciously squared his shoulders; his form seemed somehow to become more athletic than ever – more upright, if that were possible. Sir Leonard Wallace and Major Brien watched him go; then turned and smiled at each other. In their eyes was confidence.

CHAPTER SIX

Introduces Ivan Modjeska

The Canute Hotel, in Waterloo Road, was flattered by Maddison when he called it a third-rate affair. It is doubtful if it was really worthy of being called fifth-rate. Its one great advantage from its proprietor's point of view was that it was so close to Waterloo Station. People arriving by train late at night welcomed it as being very convenient, and the greatest trade was done with what the landlord called the bed and breakfast guests. Some visitors stayed for longer periods, but these were usually few and far between. There were others known as 'regulars', who, on their periodical jaunts to town from the country, were in the habit of taking rooms in the Canute. At the time when Carter booked a room there were, strangely enough, seven people there who could not be exactly described as bed and breakfast guests. Mr and Mrs Curzon, not being able to afford better quarters, always stayed there on their visits to London. Mr Spedding had put up for one night and remained a month, principally because it was near St Thomas's Hospital, and he hated moving about. Mr Hawthorne, the American with the lengthy name, had been recommended to the Canute by a porter who was pally with the proprietor. He announced his intention every morning of going, but always changed his mind. Nobody knew quite why he remained. He was obviously fairly well-off; could have afforded better quarters. Perhaps he, like Spedding, disliked moving. Julius Carberry, a commercial traveller, used the hotel because it was not only adjacent to the station, but quite close to the premises of the firm that employed him as well. He was waiting for fresh samples with which to go again on the travels that he fondly imagined were anticipated with delight by the females of the district he covered. Miss Veronica Simpson was timid, she was also a maiden lady who liked big, strong, protective-looking men. Mr John Fellowes, the landlord, was a big, strong, protective-looking man. Having arrived at Waterloo from the country, she had gone to the Canute Hotel with the idea of seeking other quarters on the following day. But when she saw Mr Fellowes she decided to remain in his hotel for the duration of her holiday in London. Ivan Modjeska, not being particular, not knowing London, had seen the words 'Canute Hotel' painted across a drab-looking building, and had sought it like a homing pigeon. That was on his first visit. It was natural that he should seek it again on his second.

Carter arrived at ten o'clock, carrying a large, worn suitcase, which seemed rather heavy, or perhaps he was tired. His overcoat had been good once, but had become shabby; his linen was clean, but not over-clean. He wore an aggressive red tie and a hat which, like the overcoat, had seen better days. On his face was an expression of sullen discontent. Entering the door, he found himself in a narrow passage, caught a glimpse of a small, uninviting dining room through an open door on one side, looked into a poorly-furnished lounge on the other. A stout lady of uncertain age wearing pince-nez returned his glance over the top of an evening paper. A tiny office was at the end of the passage, and he walked towards it. At the desk sat a big man with a round, red face, a bristly moustache and somewhat colourless, though friendly, eyes.

'Can I have a room?' asked Carter.

'Certainly, sir,' replied the red-faced man in a deep ringing voice. 'For the night only I presume?'

'No,' returned Carter; 'I shall probably be here a week. I suppose you reduce your price for weekly guests?'

'Are you weakly, sir?' asked Mr Fellowes in real concern.

'I mean, I suppose you reduce your terms for people who stay by the week?'

'Oh! Well – er – yes, we do.' He quoted a price.

'All right,' nodded Carter. 'I suppose that's as cheap as anywhere else. I can't afford a great deal these days.'

'Down on your luck, I take it,' sympathised Mr Fellowes.

'None of your business, is it?' snapped Carter resentfully.

'All right, young man,' boomed the proprietor, 'keep your hair on. If you have been hard hit, it don't help being uncivil. Write your name there, and where you've come from.'

He pushed the book which Sir Leonard Wallace had examined with such interest towards Carter, and handed him a pen. There were six other names in it now – 'bed and breakfasts' presumably.

Carter wrote down his name with a flourish, added Guildford as the town from which he had arrived. That was truthful enough, for he had been born there. Mr Fellowes eyed him thoughtfully, scratched his head, and suggested a deposit. Carter grudgingly paid him a ten-shilling note.

'Alfred!' called the landlord, 'come and take this gentleman's bag up to sixteen.'

A boy in a rusty-looking black suit with tarnished buttons appeared on the scene from the inner recesses of the office. Carter regarded him with a frown, but felt greatly inclined to laugh. He could not have been more than four feet eight inches in height, and was distinctly weedy. He took the key of the room from the proprietor, and prepared to lift the bag.

'All right, youngster,' remarked Carter, 'I'll carry that.'

The boy seemed relieved. He led the way up a narrow staircase to the left of the office – the Canute Hotel did not possess a lift. They reached a landing on which were half a dozen numbered doors. Carter's room was not on that floor, however; they ascended another two flights before number sixteen was reached. Alfred flung open the door with a flourish, and Carter peeped within. He found himself looking into a tiny chamber which was almost wholly taken up by a bedstead, dressing table, washstand, and miniature wardrobe. The furniture was of the cheapest variety, but one thing Carter noted with relief; everything looked very clean. Whatever could be said against the Canute Hotel, and there was a very great deal, uncleanliness was not one of its faults.

'My hat!' commented the young man. 'What a room!'

'What do you expect?' demanded the boy cheekily. 'A luxury sweet or wot?'

'Don't you get fresh with me,' scowled Carter, 'or I'll put you across my knee and spank you.'

'Garn! I'd like to see you try it, you big bully.'

'Oh, you would, would you?' Carter put down his suitcase and assumed a threatening attitude.

Alfred retreated to a safe distance. Then Carter smiled broadly, but not at the boy. It had suddenly occurred to him that Shannon would have had an uncomfortable time, if he had been sent to the hotel instead of him. He was tall enough, but the thought of the burly Shannon in that tiny bedroom was too much for his risible faculties.

'Blimey!' exclaimed Alfred. 'It can smile.'

Carter promptly frowned.

'Yes, it can still smile,' he rejoined. 'I wonder why? When you've been ill-treated by the bloated capitalists like a bit of dirt, trodden on, laughed at, pushed aside, it's strange that you can smile, isn't it, youngster? I hope you never have to put up with what I have.'

'What's 'appened to you, mate?' asked Alfred with interest and a certain amount of sympathy.

'Never you mind. Just you fight shy of capitalists, kings, and aristocrats. They're nothing but bloodsuckers, damn them all!'

He abruptly entered the little bedroom. He heard Alfred slowly descending the stairs as though deep in thought, and was satisfied. He knew the boy would set the ball rolling – everyone in the hotel would know Carter's sentiments, or rather pretended sentiments, before long.

At breakfast on the following morning he saw most of his fellow guests and, with the exception of two, they were exactly of the type he would have expected to find there. The small dining room possessed half a dozen tables, each seating four, situated at exact distances apart. The pictures on the wall, most of which advertised some commodity or other, were also placed at regular intervals and at the same height. It was easy to see that Mr Fellowes' military mind had directed the arrangement of the furniture. It was a pity, reflected Carter, that the service was not conducted in an equally precise manner. An untidy-looking waitress and a waiter with the doleful face of an undertaker looked after the requirements of the guests – when it occurred to them or some demand roused them to action. Carter was shown to a table in a corner, then left for ten minutes unattended. The pause certainly gave him time to study the other occupants of the room, and he became interested in two. One was a pale, effeminate gentleman with sleek, black hair, and eyes and lips that looked as though they had been made up. Carter shuddered slightly – he discovered afterwards that this was Julius Carberry, the traveller in lingerie. The other man who attracted his notice had followed him in, and taken a seat at the next table. He was lean and tall, with rather a gaunt face and deep-set grey eyes under large tortoise-shell-rimmed glasses. His mouth suggested a kindly nature and a great sense of humour. He looked about thirty-eight years of age. Carter decided that he was out of place in the Canute. His well-tailored suit, his linen, the air of distinction about him suggested that he belonged to a much higher stratum of society than the usual habitués of Mr Fellowes' hotel. He appeared to be as interested in Carter as that young man was in him.

'Guess they're not very slick with the eats in these parts,' he remarked suddenly.

Carter found his smile very attractive; decided that he liked him. But, true to the character he had assumed, he regarded him sullenly as though resentful at being addressed.

'It's a wonder they don't serve you at once,' he grunted. 'You look prosperous – I don't.'

The other raised his eyebrows a little at the churlish remark.

'It kinda looks as if something's got your goat. Anything I can do to help? My name's Hawthorne – Wilmer Peregrine Huckleberry Hawthorne.'

Carter felt inclined to laugh, but he maintained his morose attitude.

'Why the dickens should I want to know your name?' he snapped. 'And I certainly don't need your help, thanks.'

Mr Hawthorne's eyebrows rose higher than ever.

'Oh, well,' he observed, 'if that's how you feel, I guess I'm sorry for butting in. Waiter,' he called, 'how about breakfast? I'm tired of acting as part of the scenery.'

His requirements were supplied after that. Carter also received attention. He noticed that both the waiter and the waitress regarded him curiously, as did two or three of the guests. He concluded that Alfred, the boy in buttons, had been talking. There was no sign of Modjeska. At least, none of the people busily engaged in taking in supplies looked like foreigners, except perhaps the fellow with the sleek hair and effeminate manner. But he was so obviously of a type unfortunately too common these days that the Secret Service man quickly put him aside. He would not have the nerve to be an anarchist, or in fact anything but the invertebrate Sardanapalus he was. Of course he may have been playing a part, but Carter was certain he was not.

He had almost finished breakfast, when a stoutish man of medium height entered the room. For a moment or two he stood looking round him indecisively, and Carter studied him surreptitiously. He was well-dressed and prosperous-looking. A mass of black hair surmounted a broad forehead. His eyes were partially hidden by rimless pince-nez, but there was something piercing, almost hypnotic, in their brown depths. His nose was a trifle fleshy, his mouth thin-lipped. He had cheeks that sagged a little and a sallow complexion. Several rings adorned a pair of white, rather over-manicured hands. Carter noiselessly drew in his breath. He felt certain that the newcomer was Ivan Modjeska, proof positive coming when he heard the waiter address him by that name. Curiously enough he was conducted to Carter's table. Before taking his seat opposite the man who was there for the express purpose of getting acquainted with him, he bowed politely.

'You permit?' he asked.

'Of course,' replied Carter ungraciously. 'I haven't booked the entire table.'

The man frowned, but made no comment. The service of breakfast went on, and, though he continued to study his table companion, Carter took care not to appear to do so. He had picked up a copy of the *Daily Express*, and was apparently reading that go-ahead journal. After some time he allowed a look of disgust to appear on his face, and threw the paper on the floor. The chatty American at the next table noticed the action. His eyes twinkled.

'Read something you disagree with?' he asked, forgetful or unmindful of the snub he had previously received.

'I'm sick of all the King and Country stuff,' snarled Carter, rising to his feet. 'Perhaps if we had a revolution, England would be worth living in.'

'Say,' cried the American, 'sentiments like that seem to me to smack of treason. I guess I'm a citizen of the States, but I like this little old country, and think your king's sure the greatest asset you've got.'

'You're welcome to your opinion,' returned Carter, 'and I suppose I'm welcome to mine. Whatever else it may be, it's supposed to be a free country, and one can say what one likes.'

'In reason I guess, but there are some things that shouldn't be said.'

Carter took no notice of the rebuke, but walked from the room, followed by the curious, and, in most cases, hostile glances of those who had overheard him. He sat in the lounge for an hour or so after breakfast pretending to read the very ancient magazines which littered the table in the centre of the room. He had hoped that someone who had listened to his remarks in the dining room would have commenced an argument with him and thus enable him to continue to air his supposed revolutionary opinions. Nobody addressed him, however, though most of the guests crowded into the lounge for a time and sat about with the bovine expressions on their faces which so many people seem to acquire after a meal. Neither Hawthorne nor Modjeska put in an appearance and, when Carter calculated that his room would have been tidied and his bed made by the chambermaid, he went upstairs. Closing the door he threw himself down and considered the position.

One of the most resourceful and astute of Sir Leonard Wallace's assistants, Carter had one fault. That was an inclination to impetuosity. Fortunately for him, however, he knew that as well as anybody, and had learnt to control his ardour. All his instincts, as he lay there, urged him to commence at once investigating the contents of Modjeska's baggage. Caution warned him to wait. He had taken care to learn the number of the Pole's room on the previous night, when signing his name in the hotel book. It was on the storey below the one on which his apartment was situated, and almost directly underneath. There could be no more ideal time, he considered, for entering and searching it, than directly after the servants had completed their work in the bedrooms, providing, of course, that Modjeska was out. As far as he had been able to ascertain, there were only four chambermaids – one to each floor – who did not remain on their landings when their tidying was done. Other guests would be the only danger, as far as he could see, but, if he chose his time well, when most of them were out, there would be little risk of his being interrupted. That risk would only exist during the short space of time it would take him to open the door of Modjeska's room. Once inside he would be safe enough.

He decided at length to wait until he knew more of the Pole's habits, though he was reluctant, as he phrased it to himself, to let the grass grow under his feet. He put on his overcoat and hat, and descending the stairs strolled out, wandering round the unsalubrious neighbourhood for some time. There was a shop on Westminster Bridge Road where he knew he could purchase books and papers of a distinctly Bolshevik nature. Thither he wended his way before returning to the hotel for luncheon, purchasing several scurrilous journals which, at any other time, he would have been loath even to touch. Armed with these he returned, and planted himself in the lounge, until a cracked bell, and the clatter of plates and cutlery, announced that the meal was served.

He left his papers, titles upward, on the chair he had been occupying, and repaired to the dining room. Only four other guests besides himself turned up for lunch, but one of these was Modjeska. The man looked worried, and several times Carter caught him casting speculative eyes in his direction. He began to wonder if the Pole had grown suspicious, but reassured himself with the reflection that he had done nothing that could, in any way, have roused mistrust. Modjeska sat at the table which Hawthorne had occupied at breakfast. The American had not put in an appearance. They were halfway through the very indifferent meal when he leant over towards Carter.

'Pardon,' he remarked in careful but guttural English. 'This London is very deeficult for the poor stranger. I cannot find my vay mooch. Perhaps you vill afterwards be kind and help me?'

Carter regarded him sullenly.

'What do you want to know?' he asked grudgingly.

'Presently I vill tell you. It is a place I cannot find.'

'Why don't you ask a policeman? There are enough of them about.'

Modjeska raised his hands.

'Ah! I have asked many times, but always I go wrong. If perhaps you vill help I vill not go wrong.'

Carter grunted. Inwardly he felt a sense of triumph. Had his disparaging remark at the breakfast table regarding King and Country already roused Modjeska's interest in him? It was more than he dared hope; in fact it put him more on his guard than ever, if possible. Afterwards they entered the lounge together. Carter apparently accompanying his companion with great reluctance. He found the room deserted except for the maiden lady who was looking down at the papers he had left in his chair, a look of the utmost distaste on her face. As he approached she turned and eyed him more in sorrow than in anger.

'Excuse me asking, young man,' she observed, 'but are these papers yours?'

'They are,' returned Carter, frowning at her.

'Well, I suppose it is not my business, but I feel called upon to protest. It is disgraceful that such insidious literature should be brought into a respectable hotel.'

'You seem to have been reading them yourself,' sneered Carter.

Inwardly he felt elated. This was help from an unexpected quarter. Everything seemed to be conspiring on his behalf. He had not failed to notice the interest with which Modjeska had followed Miss Veronica Simpson's biting remarks.

'My attention was drawn to them as I was about to sit down,' the lady said in reply to Carter's remark. 'I thought for a moment the papers belonged to the hotel and I was astounded. I shall feel called upon to complain to the landlord.'

'Do, by all means,' sneered Carter. 'It is no business of yours what I read, or what my sentiments are.'

'Are you really admitting,' she demanded, 'that your sympathies are with people who denounce royalty and religion?'

'They certainly are,' Carter told her emphatically. At that moment he gave a very good representation of a fanatical communist. 'Who wants puppets with crowns on their heads dancing round with pomp and ceremony, and all the time robbing the people of money which is rightfully theirs?'

'Oh, you wicked young man!' she cried, her eyes almost

starting from her head in horror. 'How can you say such awful things? No wonder this gentleman – a foreigner too – is looking so upset.' Modjeska shrugged his shoulders and slowly shook his head, sighing the while. 'What must he think of you?'

'Madame,' put in the Pole, 'the young have strange ideas, is it not so? This gentleman is very young and I think hotheaded, no?'

'He is old enough to know better,' she retorted, 'but perhaps it is his upbringing. Poor boy! Poor boy!'

She stalked indignantly away, Carter watching her go with a scowl on his face. He threw himself into a chair. Modjeska sank into one close by.

'It is perhaps, as I say,' remarked the latter, 'you are a leetle bit hothead.'

'Look here,' snarled Carter, 'I've had quite enough from that old hag. I won't stand any preaching from you – understand? Tell me what part of London you want to find, and I'll help you, if I can. Afterwards I shall be glad if you will leave me to myself.'

A crafty smile appeared on Modjeska's face.

'I do not vish to preach to you,' he declared softly; 'Oh, no. It is perhaps that I have the sympathy vith your doctrine. Who can tell?'

Carter started; then regarded him fixedly for several seconds.

'What do you mean exactly?' he asked slowly.

'Perhaps later I vill tell you. Now I ask you my question. There is a road vich I vant to reach. A friend of mine – his name I have forgot – lives there. The road is called Sheerland.'

By not so much as the twitch of an eyelid did Carter betray

the interest he felt. Of course Modjeska referred to Shirland Road, where his comrades had lost their lives.

'Sheerland, Sheerland?' repeated the young man in doubtful tones. 'I'm afraid I don't know any road of that name, but you must know more about it than that. What district is it in?'

'Alvays I write on my letters to my friend the road name vith London and aftervards a letter and a figure. The letter W and the figure nine.'

Carter understood now why Modjeska had appealed to him. Unwilling to enquire too closely from a policeman about a road that had lately become so notorious, for fear of arousing suspicion, the Pole had not dared to show the address in writing. He had, therefore, in all probability done his best to find the place himself, thinking that there he would be most likely to obtain the information he required. Having heard Carter's revolutionary remarks at the breakfast table, he had formed the opinion of that young man which it was intended he should form. The idea had occurred to him that here was one from whom he might ask for help without risk. He need not commit himself. Once again Carter felt a warm glow of admiration for the astute brain of his chief who had foreseen that such a situation would arise. No doubt the incident in which Miss Veronica Simpson had figured so prominently had done a great deal to cement the Pole's opinion of his companion, and raise his confidence in him. Carter reflected that he was making progress.

'Sheerland Road, W. nine,' he repeated. 'That should not be difficult to find. West nine is Maida Vale way I think.'

'Ah! You know London vell?'

'Fairly well. I spent a lot of time up here once. Why don't you get into a taxi, and ask to be driven there?'

'I have done it, but the so-stupid men say they know not of Sheerland Road.'

That was not to be wondered at, thought Carter, since the name was mispronounced, though London taxi drivers are generally cute enough to discover where their fares wish to go, no matter how they mispronounce names.

'I'll tell you what to do,' advised Carter. 'Go to Waterloo Underground Station and take a train by the Bakerloo line to Warwick Avenue or Maida Vale. Then you can ask. Someone will be sure to put you right – it is bound to be near either of those two stations.

Modjeska still looked doubtful. His companion could understand how he felt. Alone in London with the object of obtaining information, unable to ask outright for assistance, for fear of the risk he might incur by doing so, he was certainly in an unenviable position. To him Carter, with revolutionary doctrines akin to his own, must have appeared a regular godsend. The Secret Service man was now certain of one thing – that Casaroli had been the only agent of the anarchists in London. Since he was dead, Modjeska had no one to look to. It was rather a puzzle to know from whom he expected to obtain the information of which he was in search. Then Carter remembered the ice cream man living in the basement of the house in Shirland Road. No doubt Modjeska knew of his existence, and would go to him with some specious story, hoping thereby to learn a good deal about the raid. It was doubtful whether the Italian would possess the really important knowledge which the anarchist emissary wanted. He was not likely to be aware of the results, if any, of the police search, and obviously Modjeska's greatest anxiety was to know if they had found anything that would lead them to suspect the existence of a vast anarchist organisation. The Pole leant towards Carter.

'Could you not take me to this Sheerland Road?' he asked.

'Don't you think I have anything better to do than wander round London looking for obscure roads?' returned the Englishman disagreeably.

'It vill be a kindness that I vill mooch appreciate.'

'Why should I do anyone a kindness? No one has ever bothered to be kind to me.'

'Ah! Perhaps then I vill have the pleasure of repairing that so-sad omission.'

Carter laughed harshly.

'You!' he exclaimed. 'I suppose you are saying that to get me to find this Sheerland Road of yours. Well, look here, Mr – I don't know your name—'

'It is Modjeska – Ivan Modjeska.'

'Well, Mr Modjeska, let me tell you that I don't want your help – see! I'll assist you to get to Sheerland Road, if there is such a place. After that, I don't want to have anything more to do with you. That's plain, isn't it?'

'You grieve me, my friend. You are too vat you English call John Blunt, is it not? And for you I have conceive the liking.' He leant forward again. 'Vat vould you say if I told you that I might be able to get you a job in vich your hatred of kings and governments vould be of mooch use?'

Carter sat bolt upright. Had he deceived the Pole so completely and gained his trust so absolutely that he was about to take him into his confidence? It certainly looked like it. He glanced round uneasily towards the door, as though fearful that they might be overheard. They still had the lounge to themselves.

'You mean—?' he muttered, looking his companion full in the eyes.

'Never mind what I mean – now,' was the significant reply. 'Afterwards ve vill talk – yes? Come now, ve vill find this Sheerland Road.'

CHAPTER SEVEN

The Mysterious Wilmer P. H. Hawthorne

Carter was on his guard more than ever now that Ivan Modjeska seemed to have accepted him as the discontented, sullen seditionist he appeared to be. They walked to the Underground station, and went by the Bakerloo line to Warwick Avenue. On the way the Pole asked his companion several searching questions concerning his family, his upbringing, what employment he had had and why he had lost it. To all Carter replied with apparent frankness, though still maintaining his sullen, resentful attitude. He had been prepared for such a catechism and had, therefore, no need to search for convincing answers. Stealing a glance at his companion, shortly before they reached their destination, Carter was gratified to observe that he wore a thoroughly pleased air, as though satisfied that, in the young man by his side, he had found an unexpected but very welcome associate.

On arrival at Warwick Avenue, Carter went across to a taxi rank outside the Underground station, and asked if there was a Sheerland Road in that neighbourhood. Two or three drivers, standing by their shelter gossiping, shook their heads; then one asked him if he meant Shirland Road. He turned to Modjeska; repeated the question.

'Perhaps it may be so,' replied the Pole. 'It is spell S–ach–e–air–l–a–n–d.'

'Blimey!' commented the driver, 'sounds like a foreign lingo to me.'

'He means S–H–I–R–L–A–N–D, I think,' corrected Carter.

'Then that will be Shirland Road he wants. Go along till yer comes to Formosa Street – second turning on the left – then take the second to the right.'

True to the character he had assumed, Carter turned away without thanking the man, but Modjeska made ample amends. They walked on together until they turned into Shirland Road.

'This is it,' announced Carter briefly.

'Ah! You have indeed been the friend in need. Now vill you go to a saloon and have a drink at my expense? Aftervards ve vill go back to the hotel.'

He held out some money to his companion. The latter scowled angrily.

'I don't want your money,' he snarled. 'If I want a drink I'll pay for it myself. Anyhow it's too late – the licensing laws make pubs close at certain hours in this free country. I've brought you here, you'll be able to find your way back. I'm off.'

He strode away without another glance at Modjeska. The latter stood looking after him until he had turned the corner. There was a smile on his face, a light in his dark eyes. Modjeska decided at that moment that he had found a most useful man to take the place of Casaroli. Carter had done his work well.

The Englishman allowed his features to relax once he was out of the Pole's sight. He suddenly became his own cheerful self once more, and felt it a relief. Nature had certainly not intended that he should look gloomy or sullen. It had almost given him a physical pain to wear an expression of ill-natured sulkiness.

As he turned into Warwick Avenue, he glanced back more by habit than because of any thought that he might be followed. A tall, thin man was walking across the road from the direction of Bristol Gardens. There was something familiar about him. Carter suddenly whistled to himself. Was it Hawthorne, the American? It looked very much like him. He felt inclined to retrace his steps to make certain, for the man had disappeared along Shirland Road by then, but the possibility of being seen by Modjeska, and thus spoiling everything by rousing that worthy's suspicions, restrained him. He walked on to the Underground station pondering deeply. Of course it may not have been Hawthorne at all, but Carter thought it was. At all events the American may have been in that district on business and his appearance at that moment a coincidence. But was it coincidence? Carter felt convinced it was not.

In the train on the run back to Waterloo he continued to cogitate on the circumstance. He felt it impossible to associate the clean, frank-looking American with anything so vile as anarchy. He impressed one as being so utterly straight, the type of man who could do nothing underhand. Yet it was unwise to trust to one's impressions too much. Despite his appearance he may have been an associate of the anarchists. Directly he thought of that, however, Carter dismissed it from his mind. If he had been in any way a confederate of Modjeska's, the latter would not have needed Carter to take him to Shirland Road. Hawthorne, if indeed it were he, had apparently had no difficulty in finding his way there. Possibly he was of a curious turn of mind, and having read or heard of the tragic affair in Shirland Road, had gone, like so many hundreds of other people, to gaze at the house. That was a likely solution of Carter's little problem; yet he was not satisfied.

On his return to the Canute Hotel he found most of the guests present. The lounge was uncomfortably packed. He walked in, and immediately there was a hush. All eyes were turned on him, their expressions being distinctly unfriendly. Miss Veronica Simpson sat bolt upright in the centre of the room – apparently she had been holding forth. She gave the impression of being president or chairman of a meeting; the meeting, Carter thought with great amusement, having been called to condemn him. He caught sight of the journals which had roused the indignation and ire of the spinster, lying in a heap on the floor. Deliberately he went towards them, bent down, and picked them up. He was about to leave the lounge when a grey-haired, wrinkled old man, apparently unable to control his feelings, sprang up from his chair; walked up to Carter, and glared at him.

'Sir,' he stormed, 'we are all respectable people here, with a proper sense of duty and reverence to our country and the king. Your doctrines are obnoxious to us.'

'So are yours to me,' retorted Carter icily, 'but I'm not ramming them down your throat, am I? I don't care what you think. Why should you bother what I think?'

'Because it is shameful that a man with a good old English name, and one who looks English, too, should think as you do. Why don't you go elsewhere, where you can find others of your

THE MYSTERIOUS WILMER P. H. HAWTHORNE 101

own breed and relieve us of the disgrace of harbouring a man of Bolshevik ideas in our midst?'

'Because I choose to stay here, where I have as much right as you.'

He turned on his heel, and walked out, followed by murmurs of opprobrium. He was passing the office, when the proprietor stepped out, his ruddy, good-humoured face now stern and a trifle perplexed.

'Look here, Mr Carter,' he remarked, 'I don't want to appear officious, but people have been complaining. I'm an old soldier, and loyal and patriotic I hope, but I don't interfere with the sentiments of others, if they're kept in bounds. You've got a grouse, and it's turned you Bolshie. Well, be Bolshie if it pleases you, but keep your thoughts to yourself, and don't offend others, if you don't mind. Otherwise I'll have to ask you to find a room elsewhere.'

'All right,' growled Carter. 'I won't say anything that's likely to offend your milksops, if they will not attempt to preach to me.'

He went on up to his room; threw himself on to the bed. 'Lord!' he murmured. 'What a little blue-eyed angel I have become!'

He did not go down to tea, a report he was writing taking a considerable time, but appeared for dinner. He was greeted with stony stares, but nobody addressed him. One woman, whom he passed closely, drew her skirts close to her figure as though afraid he might touch and contaminate them. Modjeska was sitting at his table again; there was still no sign of Wilmer Peregrine Huckleberry Hawthorne. The Pole had sensed the antagonism against Carter in the atmosphere, and had responded to it, deeming it best, no doubt, to seem in accord with the other guests. He eyed his table companion coldly, but when he knew he was unobserved, a friendly smile appeared fleetingly on his lips. Carter made no attempt to speak to him, not even asking if he had found the friend he had gone to seek. It occurred to the Englishman that Modjeska had deliberately placed himself at his table in order to answer any question he might ask regarding his visit to Shirland Road. There would be little fear of being overheard when they were in such close proximity, while a question asked from one table to another would be bound to be heard. Modjeska naturally would not desire the other guests to know that he had any interest in a neighbourhood that had become as notorious as Shirland Road.

After dinner Carter went out for a stroll. He wandered about aimlessly for a time; then, when he felt certain he was not being followed by Modjeska, made his way by a circuitous route into Waterloo Station. He entered the buffet opposite platform number seven just as the hands of the clock pointed to the hour of nine. Lounging against the bar was the unmistakable figure of his colleague, Hill. Carter walked up to the bar and squeezed himself in between Hill and another man. The former turned languidly, and regarded him for a moment, but there was no sign of recognition in his jolly face.

Carter called for a whisky and soda. While the barmaid, with whom Hill had been chatting merrily, was away attending to his order, Carter placed his closed left hand on the counter close to Hill's right which was already resting there. For a moment they touched; then the latter moved his hand away. He glanced at his watch.

'Jove!' he exclaimed to the girl, who had now returned. 'I must be off. See you again tomorrow night about the same time, miss.'

She simpered, but Carter knew the last remark was intended for him. Hill raised his hat to the girl, and walked quickly away. With him went Carter's written report of the day's events for Sir Leonard Wallace. The pseudo-communist turned and watched his friend's departure with a slight smile on his lips; then, despite his self-control, he started. Outside, just about to pass behind a bookstall, was Wilmer P. H. Hawthorne!

Carter drank his whisky and soda very thoughtfully, his brain exceedingly busy. It could not be coincidence that the American had twice that day turned up under somewhat peculiar circumstances. The young Englishman began to believe that Hawthorne was watching him. If so, for what reason? Was it because of his supposed seditious doctrines? No; it could hardly be that. If the man with the extraordinary name had been British there might be a certain amount of reason in such a thought – he could be a detective whose suspicions of Carter had been roused by his utterances. But there was no mistaking the fact that Wilmer Hawthorne was a bona fide American. Carter decided that it might pay him to investigate the luggage of Hawthorne as well as that of Modjeska.

He drank his whisky and soda, and walked out on to the platform. There was no reason why he should not be open about it. Of one thing Carter was perfectly certain. That was that, whether the American was spying on him or not, the man could not possibly have any notion that he had had any communication with Hill, or that a letter had passed between them. Sir Leonard Wallace had been wise in advising that his messenger and Carter should not appear to know each other.

For several moments he was unable to find Hawthorne, and had begun to think that he had left the station, when he caught sight of him standing between a mail van and a taxicab in the road that divides Waterloo Station into two parts. His back was towards Carter, and he appeared to be watching someone at the other end of the huge station. The Secret Service man became greatly interested. It was a certain relief to find that he was not, after all, the object of Hawthorne's curiosity. He resolved to find out, if possible, who was. Approaching cautiously, he was able to get within a few yards of the American, and took up his station behind a platform ticket machine. At first he was unable to satisfy himself. Hawthorne might have been watching any one of a score of people. Then he saw Modjeska, and whistled softly to himself. The Pole was standing by the gates of platform number fourteen, as though awaiting the arrival of someone by train. Maddison had told Carter of Modjeska's statement to the proprietor of the Canute Hotel that he had returned to England to meet a friend whom he had not seen for many years, who was due to arrive from the United States. It looked as though his announcement had been true. A boat train was due in from Southampton – Carter had casually noticed that fact when he had first entered the station. Things were certainly becoming intensely interesting.

Apparently Hawthorne knew of the expected arrival. Who was he? Carter wondered. He was certainly not the man he had represented himself to be. It had become evident that he was in England on less innocent business than one would suppose to be connected with steel cables. Suddenly Carter thought he saw light. Was he an American detective, who was on the trail of Modjeska's friend, and knew that the two had arranged to meet in London? The idea opened up all kinds of possibilities. A friend of Modjeska would in all likelihood be an anarchist. Perhaps the man expected was the agent of the organisation in the United States; had come to England for a consultation with Modjeska. It was strange that, if Hawthorne were a detective and was watching him, he had arrived in London several days ahead of him. Still that was capable of very simple explanation. Carter felt convinced that he was on the right track.

The boat train ran in, and immediately disgorged its load of humanity. The scene became very animated. Carter lost sight of Modjeska in the crowd of people pouring through the gate. Hawthorne approached closer, taking advantage of cover very expertly; the Englishman followed him with equal caution. Presently he saw the Pole again and at that moment the latter met and shook hands warmly with a tall, burly man who had passed through the gates followed by a porter carrying a couple of large suitcases. They stood talking for some minutes; then walked to the steps which descend to Waterloo Road. Hawthorne followed them, and Carter followed Hawthorne. At the bottom of the steps the bags were handed to an outside porter, and the party continued on its way, Modjeska and the stranger walking arm in arm. It became evident that they were bound for the Canute Hotel.

Hawthorne and Carter, from different coigns of vantage, watched them enter the drab-looking place. The American did not, at once, follow them in. He lounged about for nearly half an hour, before approaching the door and glancing cautiously in. Apparently satisfied, he then entered without any further attempt at secrecy, and went straight upstairs to his room. Carter gathered that Modjeska's friend knew him, and that the American wished to avoid recognition.

The Secret Service man waited about in the vicinity for a few minutes longer, after which he walked into the hotel, and, obtaining his key from a stout lady sitting at the desk – he presumed she was

Mrs Fellowes – who eyed him coldly, ascended to his bedroom. He undressed and got into bed, but had no desire for sleep. He filled and lit his pipe; then lay puffing contentedly, while he reviewed the events of the day, dwelling particularly on the arrival of Modjeska's friend, and the great interest Wilmer Hawthorne seemed to be taking in both of them. An hour went by, a clock in the neighbourhood struck eleven and still he was wide awake. Suddenly came a soft tap on the door. Carter was surprised and a little startled. His hand involuntarily sought the revolver under his bolster.

'Come in,' he called – the door was not locked. Unlike most hotel doors, none of those in the Canute were self-locking.

Immediately Modjeska entered, a finger raised to his lips to enjoin silence. Carter sat up, wondering what such a visitation could portend. Remembering his role, he set his face in a scowl. The Pole softly closed the door and locked it. That done, he walked quietly to the bed, and sat on the end.

'Here ve can talk,' he remarked, 'vith the perfect safety. The room next to this vone is empty, and it is the same vith the vone opposite. Ve vill not be overheard.'

'What do you mean by coming into my room like this?' demanded Carter. 'What do you want?'

'Do not be angry, my friend, but listen to me. Today you told me no vone vanted to be kind to you, and I answer that it vould be a pleasure for me to repair the so-sad omission – yes?'

'You did say something to that effect,' agreed Carter in grudging tones. 'What about it?'

'Also I visper to you I might be able to get you a job in vich your hatred of kings and governments vould be of mooch use – vas it not so?'

Carter decided that the time had come for him to drop a little of his sullenness and show interest. The piercing eyes of the Pole were watching him closely – it would not do to show too much eagerness all at once. The Englishman's face registered an expression in which curiosity and suspicion were equally blended.

'What are you getting at?' he asked.

'I vill tell you. First I must say that I am so sorry you feel insulted that I offer you money for the drink. I did not mean to insult you. To me you vere kind – it vas right that I offer you the drink. You forgive me – yes?'

'That's all right,' grunted Carter. 'Get on with what you came to tell me.'

'Vell listen, my friend. I am going to tell you mooch that vill surprise you. Listen to me with care of the greatest. I am a member of a most great society vich for its object vishes that in this vorld should be no kings or families vith vat is called royal blood.'

Carter's eyes opened wide, he glanced round uneasily. Modjeska noticed his apparent disquietude, smiled approvingly.

'There is nothing to fear,' he assured the man in the bed. 'Ve are unheard, and no vone have seen me come here. Besides every vone think I am the man who loves mooch the kings and crowns. After dinner I sit in the lounge vith those so-great fools and ve talk vith mooch sorrow of you. I say it is peety and mooch to be regretted, for I have such big respeck for the King of England. They all say I am fine fellow – the big fools.' He laughed at the recollection.

'If you are in sympathy with my sentiments,' growled Carter, 'why did you want to make it appear otherwise?'

'Because, my friend, it is not good that anyone think I am – vat I am. You are too hothead. You are too mooch John Blunt. If you speak not of hating kings and governments and say nothing of revolution, you can do very mooch more for the cause. Understand?'

'Why are you telling me this? How do you know I won't give you away?'

Modjeska laughed again softly.

'Because I am judge of the face. It is not vat you say that convince me but the light in your eye, the look in your face. It speak of your feelings too mooch. It is good for me to read, but is not good for other people. You must learn not to be so hothead, and to hide vat you think. Anyvone can see at vonce you are communist of the most fanatic, if he is not fool.' Carter did not exactly feel flattered, but he was certainly delighted to find that Modjeska was so convinced of his bona fides that he did not hesitate to talk openly to him. 'I know,' went on the Pole, 'that you vill, therefore, not betray me. But think a leetle. Even if I am wrong, vat could you do? Everyvone think me a lover of kings, everyvone know you hate them. If you say I am member of society that vishes to vash out all royal families everyvone vould laugh at you. There is no proof, not even a leetle bit. In my country I am mooch respeck – I am important man and good citizen. Nobody know I am member of the society but my comrades and now you. But you vill not give me avay – I have study you too vell, my friend.'

'All right,' nodded Carter, 'we will take that for granted. Go on.'

'Ah! You are eager to hear more. Vell, listen! I say perhaps I can get you job after your own heart. It is this: if my comrades approve you vill be appoint agent of the society in this country. Ve have none here, and it is necessary that there must be vone. Vat you say? Vould you like become member of the society? – Tell me!'

Carter's face was a study in emotions. He would have probably been very successful as a dramatic actor. The sullenness had departed, leaving it alight with eagerness, though a shadow of distrust lurked still in the background.

'You say that the object of this society is the abolition of all royal families,' he commented. 'How is it intended that this should be done?'

Modjeska laughed, and Carter noticed for the first time how cruel his face could look.

'There is only vone sure vay,' he replied in tones that made the Englishman long to take him by the throat, and his hypnotic eyes bored into those of Carter as though endeavouring to search his very soul.

The latter succeeded in looking a thorough fanatic. His mouth half-opened, exposing the teeth, his nostrils dilated, a wicked-looking gleam came into his eyes.

'Assassination!' he breathed.

'Exactly so, my friend,' he returned, 'assassination.'

For some minutes Carter lay back looking at the ceiling, the gloating expression on his face apparently giving great satisfaction to the Pole, who continued to nod his head and smile.

'It vill take a very long time – oh, yes, a very long time. But ve are very powerful – vat is it you say? Ah! organeesation, is it not? – Ve are very powerful organeesation. Some of our comrades vill fail, and perhaps die in the cause, but others vill take their place. At the head are ten great men with mooch money and clever brains. Vat you say? You vish become member of this so-powerful society? You vill have very good pay and the vork you like.'

Carter sat up and, leaning forward, grasped the other by the arm in a grip that hurt. But the Pole did not mind. He understood that it was caused by the deep emotion of the young Englishman.

'Do you mean it?' demanded Carter. 'You are not fooling me? You are not leading me into a trap?'

'My friend, there is no trap vich I am causing you to enter. If I vas English you might think that – you might think I vas of the police in disguise to deceive you. But you know vell I am not of your country. Vat objeck could I have, therefore? No; I am very mooch sincere. I think you vill be of great use, so I tell you all this. Look!' He undid his shirt and vest at the neck and drew forth a silver disc on which was engraved a number and three letters. It was similar to those found suspended round the necks of the anarchists who had died in the house in Shirland Road. 'All of the society vear these,' Modjeska stated. 'Ven you become a member, you vill vear vone also.'

'What do the letters mean?' asked Carter.

'That you vill know if the committee of ten approve of you.'

'When can I join?'

Modjeska laughed.

'It is good to see eagerness so great,' he declared. 'Listen! In two, three days I vill return to the place vere ve have our headquarters. You vill go vith me, and to the ten I vill show you. They vill decide. But have no fears, my friend, that they vill not approve. In me have my comrades great trust – they know I am man of great judgement. And, in your ears I visper, Mr Carter, I am vone of those ten. Sleeping downstairs now is vone more. Today he comes from America, vere he has big business. He has come because it is necessary that all the ten meet together for consultation – one blunder has been made.' Carter guessed he was referring to the Shirland Road affair. 'Tomorrow, Mr Grote vill see you – I have already told him about you, and he takes my vord for you. Ven you are seen by the others, I have no doubt they vill take my word also.'

Carter suddenly looked despondent.

'I'm afraid I shall not be able to go with you,' he remarked in disappointed tones. 'I only have a little money, and that—'

'Ah! Bah! Your expenses vill be paid of course. I vill arrange that matter.'

The Englishman's eyes lit up.

'That's splendid,' he cried. 'Lord!' he added vehemently. 'To have the chance of striking one blow – just one blow at royalty.'

'Such enthusiasm is good to see,' smiled Modjeska, 'but you must learn not to show so mooch your feelings. It is not vise.'

'I'll remember,' promised Carter.

'Good. I hope you vill for your own sake. Now, before I go, there is vone more thing I vish to say. Today my friend in Sheerland Road was out – tomorrow I go again to see him by the appointment at ten of the clock. Perhaps I finish my business quickly perhaps it take two, three more days. Until I go avay, speak not to me mooch in this hotel; I must pretend I am not approving of you like those other fools. Understand?' Carter nodded. 'Also I think, it vill be better that you do not travel vith me and Mr Grote ven ve depart. Ve vill meet you in Vienna. I vill buy your ticket, and tomorrow night vill come here at the same hour and give you instructions and money.'

'Thanks,' returned the now exuberant Carter. Modjeska pushed the silver disc out of sight, and stood up.

'I think,' he declared, 'that you vill be a very most useful member of the society.'

'Supposing,' queried Carter, 'that, by some chance, the other members of your committee do not approve of me – what then?'

'Ah! Vat then!' repeated Modjeska. 'You vill come back to England and become discontent man again – no?'

But the manner in which he spoke and the cruel gleam in his weird eyes was quite enough assurance to Carter of what would happen if he were not accepted. He would never return!

CHAPTER EIGHT

Carter and Hawthorne Surprise Each Other

It was a long time before sleep came to Tommy Carter that night. His mind was so full of the interview with Modjeska, and the manner in which the latter had been deceived in him, that he remained very wide awake indeed for two or three hours. He can be forgiven if he felt elated at the success which had attended him. In one day he had accomplished all and more than Sir Leonard Wallace had hoped he would achieve. His gratification was, it is true, slightly tempered by the reflection that possibly there was a trap somewhere, but, search as he would into every word that had been spoken or incident that had happened since he had arrived at the hotel, he was unable to find any reason whatsoever why Modjeska should regard him as a danger that must be removed. Although it seemed too good to be true, the Pole, he was convinced, was thoroughly hoodwinked, and to such an extent that he had decided Carter was the very man to be useful to the society of which he had spoken. Even then he seemed to have acted with dangerous precipitation, but doubtless he was so convinced of the infallibility of his judgement of men, and the society was so anxious to have an agent in London, that the risk had, to his mind, been very small. Again, Carter would have to face rigid scrutiny from the other members of the committee of ten. If they were not entirely convinced that he was quite the individual Modjeska represented him to be, he would not only be rejected, but would be assassinated. He would not be permitted to return to England, possibly to divulge what he had learnt concerning the organisation. That was quite certain. The thought of being murdered in some remote part of the continent of Europe did not bother Carter, however. He knew that when he left England he would be closely followed by Sir Leonard Wallace and probably other members of the Secret Service as well.

He rose the next morning feeling very bright and cheery despite the little sleep he had had. He was still resolved to search Modjeska's belongings, though the Pole had admitted so much to him that it seemed unnecessary. Still there was a possibility that he might find something of value. It would be a good idea, too, he thought to find out what was the number of the newcomer Grote's room, and search that also. If the latter accompanied Modjeska on his visit to Shirland Road, he would be presented with a splendid opportunity to enter both bedrooms.

On entering the dining room for breakfast he was again subjected to a battery of hostile glances, but he took no notice whatever of his fellow guests. The sullen expression was again on his face, though he had allowed it to appear less aggressive and discontented. Modjeska and Grote sat at a table in the opposite corner of the room. Carter noticed that the latter subjected him to several sharp glances; was doubtlessly weighing him up. He surreptitiously studied the man, finding him to be a big, beefy-looking person with small, piglike eyes, broad nose and loose mouth in a countenance that can only be described as bloated. Carter decided he was a German, though his name might have been common to half a dozen races. There was no sign of Hawthorne, his absence supporting the view Carter had already formed that he was known to Grote and wished to avoid recognition.

After breakfast the Secret Service man planted himself in a corner of the lounge with some of the papers that had caused such a commotion the day before. He noticed with amusement that the Curzons, Spedding and Miss Simpson entered with the object, no doubt, of sitting there, but, on seeing him, departed again. He wondered if anybody else had ever made himself so thoroughly unpopular in such a short space of time. Modjeska and Grote came in and sat down for a little while within a few yards of him. The lounge then being occupied by the three only, Modjeska took the opportunity of whispering an introduction. Carter half rose, but the other motioned to him to resume his seat.

'It is best you stay vere you are,' he murmured, 'in case anybody come in. Ve must not be seen talking to you like friends.'

Grote smiled, and Carter thought he preferred him without such a grimace. It caused him to look more brutal and uglier than ever.

'I am glad to make your acquaintance, Mr Carter,' he remarked in perfect English. 'Ivan Modjeska has told me all about you, and I may say that I trust his judgement implicitly.'

'He knows me vell, you see,' put in the Pole with a self-satisfied smirk.

'An agent of our great association is badly required in London,' went on Grote, 'and, if you are selected, you will find it a very good job, I assure you. But we require entire fidelity and obedience.'

'You will get it,' returned Carter. 'You can trust me for that.'

'Splendid. I feel already I am in agreement with my friend Modjeska about you.'

'Thanks.'

They ignored him after that, and Carter took up his papers again. Before long they went out, Grote nodding to him as they passed by.

'Tonight at eleven you vill expect me – yes?' asked Modjeska.

'I will be waiting. Don't knock. Come right in. The door won't be locked.'

Carter sat on until long after half past ten; then walked along to the office. Just outside hung a railway advertisement. Pretending to study this, he managed to glance at the open visitors' book close by. Grote's name was the last, and the number of his chamber nine. Satisfied, he ascended to his room. On the way up he had met no one. The doors of all the bedrooms were shut, which was fairly good evidence that the chambermaids had finished their work. They invariably leave doors open while engaged in tidying rooms. Of course one or more of the guests may have been inside, but Carter decided that it was unlikely. The weather was glorious, and it was hardly to be expected that people, the majority of whom were in London on pleasure, would be in their tiny bedrooms at eleven

o'clock on such a morning. In any case he would have to risk
the sudden appearance of one of the inmates. After all, it would
not be much risk – he could always pretend to be knocking on
the door he was endeavouring to open. Grote had accompanied
Modjeska. He had seen them go out.

He remained in his apartment for ten minutes or so; then
descended to the floor beneath. Modjeska's room, number
ten, was exactly opposite number nine, which was a fortunate
circumstance. No doubt Modjeska had arranged it in order
that his friend would be conveniently close. Carter smiled
at the thought that Modjeska had little realised that he was
also making it more convenient for the Secret Service man's
investigations. He stood on the landing listening for a few
seconds; then went swiftly along to number ten, a bunch of
skeleton keys held ready in his hand. Nobody disturbed him,
and in less than a minute he was inside the room, closing
the door behind him. He wasted no time, but set to work at
once to make his investigations. Although locked, Modjeska's
suitcases presented no difficulty to him at all. They were
quickly lying open, while he examined the articles within
with the greatest care, always noting the exact position in
which each lay in order to replace it as he found it. There
was absolutely nothing to associate the Pole with an anarchist
organisation. Carter drew a complete blank. As a matter of
fact he had not expected to find anything, though he had
hoped that there might have been a letter or document,
which would perhaps give some indication of the society's
headquarters. The cases were locked again, and pushed back
under the bed where they had previously been lying. He then
turned his attention to the rest of the room. A suit of clothes

and a dressing gown were hanging in the wardrobe, but the pockets were empty. There were some shirts, collars, and socks in the drawers of the dressing table, toilet articles on the top – nothing else. Carter gave one last look round to make certain that he was leaving no evidence of his presence about; then crossed to the door, and gently opened it. A cautious glance along the corridor assured him that he still had it to himself. He closed the door quietly behind him. Two or three minutes later he was safely inside Grote's room.

The man from America had not troubled to unpack anything, apparently, except toilet articles and pyjamas. There was nothing in the wardrobe or the drawers. Carter found one suitcase difficult to open, but he managed it at last. To his surprise it was steel-lined; must have been very heavy. It contained bundles of American banknotes each of large denomination. After examining them, Carter calculated that there must have been at least three hundred thousand dollars in the bag. Was Grote leaving America for good, or was he carrying a contribution to the society's funds from anarchists and communists in the United States? He was standing gazing down at the packages of notes when his whole body stiffened with consternation. Someone was inserting a key in the lock. As quick as thought Carter closed the case, pushed it under the bed and followed it himself, his revolver in his hand. There was no other hiding place in the room. The chances of his escaping detection were very small indeed, unless the person now opening the door happened to be a chambermaid. If it turned out to be Grote—! Carter almost groaned at the thought. All he had accomplished would be utterly thrown away, his efforts entirely wasted. Worse still, the anarchist organisation would be warned that efforts were being made to unmask it.

The door closed softly. Carter saw a pair of neatly shod feet – a man's. Grote must have returned, though the Englishman felt that the feet hardly seemed to suit him. They were too small, too elegant. He would have expected the anarchist to have possessed rather ugly extremities – his hands were large and coarse-looking, Carter had not noticed his feet. A hand appeared and, catching hold of the case the Secret Service agent had opened, commenced to pull it out. It was a white, well-shaped hand, with well-manicured nails – most certainly not Grote's. Who on earth, wondered Carter, could the intruder be? He was quickly to learn. The second suitcase was dragged out; then a face appeared, eyes glancing under the bed. It was the face of Wilmer Peregrine Huckleberry Hawthorne.

'Well, this sure is a surprise!' exclaimed the American coolly. 'Guess you'd better come out, young man.'

Carter saw no point in remaining where he was; he was at a very big disadvantage under the bed, even with a revolver in his hand. He obeyed the American's command, therefore, crawled out, and rose to his feet. Immediately he discovered that Mr Hawthorne also possessed a weapon, the barrel of which he pushed into Carter's ribs. For the life of him the latter could not forbear a broad grin. Hawthorne's eyes widened behind their large glasses.

'We both have revolvers,' chuckled the Englishman, 'but neither of us dare use them. I don't particularly want to use mine.'

'Guess you're right,' commented the American. 'They're no darn good here – we'd sure bring the whole block along, anxious to see the body. We can't fight it out either, that would make almost as much noise. I kinder feel we'd better talk this thing out.'

'I suppose we'd better,' agreed Carter. 'But this is hardly the place for a confidential chat, is it? We might be disturbed just when we were getting interested in each other.'

'You've said it,' nodded Mr Hawthorne. He put his revolver away, an action that was copied by the other. 'Say,' went on the American, 'what's happened to you? You sorter look different.'

'How do you mean – different?' asked Carter.

Mr Wilmer P. H. Hawthorne scratched his head. 'You don't look the same guy as the one I tried to talk to yesterday morning.'

'I am he,' returned Carter, but he knew what the difference was. He was no longer cloaked in a disguise of sullenness and gloom. Somehow he felt vastly relieved that the intruder had turned out to be the American. He felt instinctively that he had little to fear from Hawthorne. 'Where shall we go?'

'I guess my room would do for a little pow-wow. It's sure quiet, and I can mix you a highball. A drink is indicated, I reckon. This surprise meeting with you has perturbed me some.' Carter smiled again. Hawthorne looked the least disconcerted of mortals as he stood there regarding his companion. The Englishman bent down, and was about to lock the suitcase, when the other stayed him. 'So you've already opened it!' he commented. 'You've a nice, handy, little instrument there. Guess I'd like to take a peek inside that case if you've no objection.' Carter opened it without hesitation, and the American gazed at the contents silently for a few seconds. 'Gee!' he remarked presently. 'He sure has made a nice little collection of plunks. All right, Mr Carter, shut it up.'

The Englishman locked the case; then pushing it, with the other, back under the bed, rose to his feet. Hawthorne went to the door, opened it slightly, and glanced out. The way was clear, and he left the room, followed by Carter. The latter shut the door, making certain that it was properly fastened. The American led the way down the stairs, and walked to room number two on the first floor. He unlocked the door and stood aside for Carter to enter. The latter was surprised to find the apartment a good deal larger than his own. It was also better furnished, even boasting an armchair, and possessed two windows, which looked on to Waterloo Road, not that that was a very great asset. The view from Carter's window, however, was distressingly bleak. A wilderness of drab walls, roofs, and chimney pots was his portion. Hawthorne opened the wardrobe, produced there from a bottle of John Haig, a soda siphon, and a glass. He mixed a drink for Carter according to the latter's requirements.

'What about yours?' asked the Englishman, as he took the glass. 'You want one more than I. You're so perturbed you know.'

Hawthorne's eyes twinkled as he looked at him.

'I sure am,' he replied. 'Aren't you?'

'Not a bit.'

'Well, I guess you oughter be.' He crossed to the washstand, picked up the tooth glass, and examined it critically. Passing it as satisfactorily clean, he returned to Carter and poured himself out a liberal dose of whisky, splashing in a little soda. That done, he sat on the bed, indicating to Carter to take the armchair, an invitation promptly accepted by that young man. 'Here's how,' remarked Hawthorne by way of a toast, and proceeded to reduce his drink to a negligible quantity. 'Now,' he observed, 'I reckon it's up to you to explain a few things, Mr Carter. It will kinder clear the air.'

'Oh,' returned the Secret Service man, 'how about your commencing the explanations?'

'Yes; I daresay you have as much right to ask me as I have to ask you. We're both in a darn predicament, I guess, like a couple of guys trying to spar with our eyes blindfolded. Perhaps you'll start by putting me wise about one thing. What's the big idea of the Bolshie stunt? You sure took me in, and, to judge from what I've heard, you've taken in everyone else in this all-fired joint. But you're no more a communist than I am.'

'Are you sure of that?'

'Of course I'm sure. There's a subtle difference in you now, your face is different, though your clothes aren't. But I reckon, looking at you now, that you're not in the habit of being so slovenly, in your personal appearance. And, gee! That tie! Say, Mr Carter, it gives me a pain.'

'I feel ill myself when I look at it,' admitted Carter. 'Luckily, once it's on, I don't have to look at it.'

'Well, what's the answer?'

'I'm afraid there is none – at least, not until I know something more about you.'

'And, as I can't tell you anything about myself until I know you're on the level, we sure are the world's pet dumb oysters, aren't we?' He sat regarding Carter quizzically for a few moments. 'Well, I guess there's no more to be said. Yes, there is,' he added quickly, 'there's one question you won't mind answering, I think. Were you in Grote's room for the purpose of lifting the dough in that bag?'

'No; I didn't know it was there until I saw it.'

'When you saw it, was it your idea to lift it? I mean, would you have helped yourself to it, if I hadn't happened along?'

'No, certainly not.'

'Well, that's good enough for me. You're not a Bolshie and you're not a crook. I didn't think you were the second, anyway.'

'I am going to ask you the same question. Not that asking a question of that sort is a great deal of good anyway. We may both be lying.'

'But we're not,' observed Hawthorne.

Carter eyed him steadily.

'No, we're not,' he decided after a slight pause. 'Do you happen to be an American crook who, knowing that Grote was carrying all that money about with him, was waiting for an opportunity to rob him, and did you enter his room with that purpose?'

'No to both questions,' replied Hawthorne promptly. 'I admit, though, that I knew he was packing a mighty large wad.'

'It amounts to about three hundred thousand dollars.'

Hawthorne nodded his head.

'I calculated it would be about that figure,' he admitted. 'I'll tell you this much, Mr Carter – it's not clean dough, not one darn plunk of it.'

'Then I have guessed right. You are a member of the United States police force?'

Hawthorne had a most attractive smile. Carter thought so, as he observed it now.

'I am and I'm not,' was the American's paradoxical reply.

'That's exactly what I expected you to say, somehow,' commented Carter. 'I don't quite know why. Well, as neither of us can tell the other much, suppose we both agree not to give each other away? I remain a red-hot communist, you continue to be a businessman interested in steel cables.'

'That goes with me,' agreed Hawthorne; then added in regretful tones, 'though I guess if we could get together we could help each other some. Have another drink?'

Carter accepted.

'I believe,' he remarked, 'that I have the advantage of you to a certain extent. I know that you were watching Modjeska when he went to Shirland Road, Maida Vale, yesterday. I also know that you were at Waterloo last night and saw him meet Grote.'

Hawthorne paused in the act of pouring whisky into his companion's glass. He frowned a little.

'Say,' he demanded, 'have you been trailing me?'

'No. As a matter of fact I thought you were trailing me. Didn't you follow Modjeska and me to Maida Vale yesterday?'

'I did not. Say when!'

Carter obliged, the American added a little soda to the whisky, and handed the glass back. He proceeded to replenish his own tumbler.

'It was sheer coincidence then,' pursued the Englishman, 'that you happened to be on the spot yesterday afternoon?'

'You're asking questions again, but I don't mind answering that one. It was not coincidence. I expected Modjeska to turn up in Shirland Road sooner or later. I was on the watch for him.'

'I wonder why,' murmured Carter.

'Go on wondering,' grinned Hawthorne. 'It don't cost anything. But say,' he added, looking really perturbed this time, 'I didn't see you. Have you told Modjeska you saw me?' Carter shook his head. 'That's a relief. You'd sure queer my pitch, if you did. Have you any objection to telling me why you went with him to Shirland Road, and why you were keeping watch?'

'I wasn't keeping watch. He had had some difficulty in finding the place, and asked me to help. I think he was rather shy of asking, and besides he pronounced the name wrongly. I left him there, and was about to return when I glanced round, and saw you.'

'And you say you were not trailing me when I went to Waterloo last night? I guess you were trailing him then.'

'No, I happened to be there, and saw you. Naturally I wondered what you were up to, and watched. In consequence I also witnessed the arrival of Grote and his meeting with Modjeska. I also discovered that, for some reason or other, you were greatly interested in their movements. Your obvious desire not to be seen convinced me that you were known to Grote and had no wish that he should meet you.'

Hawthorne groaned.

'I guess I've been a darn fool,' he declared. 'There was I thinking I was so mighty slick, and all the time my movements were being observed by you. Gee! If you'd been in with them—' The thought seemed to give him very great concern. His lips pursed together, and he lapsed into silence. Presently an expression of perplexity settled on his face. 'I wish I knew where you and I stand in relation to each other in this business,' he observed. 'We both seem to be on the same lay, and it looks like we might be allies. Yet, on the other hand, it is possible our objects may be in opposition. We can't find out, because neither you nor I are going to spill the beans about ourselves. You think I'm connected with the USA police – I've got a hunch now that you're not unconnected with little old Scotland Yard.'

'New Scotland Yard,' corrected Carter with a smile.

'Anyway, I guess you're on the level, but I daren't take a chance.'

'Same here,' nodded the Englishman. 'But why worry? We have agreed not to give each other away. You can rely upon me, and I jolly well know I can rely on you.'

Hawthorne smiled.

'That's so,' he agreed, and held out his hand. 'Shake!'

They solemnly and firmly clasped hands. Carter finished his drink and rose.

'I'd better go before people commence to return for luncheon,' he remarked. 'It won't do your character any good, if it becomes known that you are friendly with a fiery communist.'

'I guess not,' returned Hawthorne, his eyes twinkling humorously. 'You won't see me at lunch, tea, or dinner. It's as much as I can stand to sleep in this darn joint, and have breakfast here.'

'You weren't at breakfast this morning.'

'Nope. I had it up here. While Grote stays, Wilmer P. H. Hawthorne keeps coyly out of sight. I guess that guy would have a mighty bad fit if he knew I was here.'

'He might see your name in the book, or Modjeska may mention it to him.'

'That won't cut any ice.'

'You mean the name is false?'

'Well, I reckon I should hate like hell to be attached to a name like that, if it was real.'

Carter laughed.

'It certainly proves that you possess a fertile imagination.'

'I chose it because, nobody would suspect it to be an alias. What guy, who was travelling under false colours, would choose Wilmer Peregrine Huckleberry Hawthorne? Anyone who heard it would reckon that such a name could only have been given by misguided parents. Now if I had called myself William Brown or John Smith or—'

'Or Tommy Carter,' interposed that young man, 'you would expect people to think that your name was adopted.'

'Is yours an alias?' asked Hawthorne.

'No; it's my very own.'

'I calculated it was. You don't look as though you lack intelligence.'

At that Carter laughed outright.

'You mean that it is too obvious sounding an alias to be an alias?' he chuckled.

'Sure. I guess you get me. Well, Tommy, I seem to have said a good deal more than I should, but I'm not worrying. You and I are far more likely to turn out to be allies than enemies. By the way, have you any objection to my calling you Tommy? It's a habit of mine to use first names, when I know them. I reckon that's what they're for anyway.'

'I don't mind at all,' Carter assured him. 'Most of my friends call me Tommy, and I believe you and I are going to be friends.'

'We sure are.'

'May I know your real name?'

Hawthorne regarded him with a whimsical smile.

'I guess not – not just yet. If you don't mind, I'll remain Wilmer Peregrine and the rest to you for the present.'

There came a knock on the door. The two men looked questioningly at each other. Carter quickly stepped out of sight, while the American opened it. Outside stood one of the chambermaids.

'Cable for you, Mr Hawthorne,' she announced.

'Now isn't that nice? You're sure a kind-hearted girl to bring it right up. How did you know I was in?'

'Your key wasn't hanging with the others.'

'But I might have taken it out with me. I often do. Anyhow it's swell of you.'

He tipped her, and closed the door. Taking care that Carter was not near enough to be able to read the cable, he quickly tore open the envelope. At once an expression of beatific happiness spread over his face. Carter gathered that the message had nothing to do with his work.

'Bless every hair of her lovely head,' murmured the American, and his companion felt as though he were intruding. He walked towards the door, and was about to go out. 'This is from my wife,' announced Hawthorne, putting out a hand to stop him. 'She's a great girl, Tommy; you'd love her. Don't go for a moment. It's good to be able to talk to someone about Joan. It's mighty lonesome without her. She and I have been married nearly four years, but I hate like hell being parted from her. Guess we'll have another drink to toast her.'

Carter was not particularly anxious for any more, but he could not very well refuse with such a purpose in view. Their glasses replenished, they raised them with great solemnity.

'Joan!' murmured the American.

'Mrs Hawthorne,' said Carter.

The toast was drunk; then Hawthorne laughed.

'You startled me with that name for a moment,' he remarked. 'Gee! I don't like it attached to Joan somehow. It don't fit. She's a swell kid to send me a cable, don't you agree, Tommy?' Carter assured him that he certainly did. 'She's English,' went on the American, 'and every year spends a holiday over here. I have never been able to accompany her yet, but she's going to join me when – when my job is finished, and by heck! We're going to make little old England sit up and take notice. I have a picture of her with me. Like to see it?'

Carter nodded with an eagerness not altogether assumed. He

felt he would be interested to see what kind of a wife Hawthorne possessed. The latter took a photograph – postcard size – from his pocket book; handed it almost reverently to the Englishman. Carter gave one glance at it; then sank weakly into a chair.

'Good Lord!' he exclaimed. 'Shannon's sister! Then you must be Oscar Miles, the Chief of the United States Secret Service!'

CHAPTER NINE

Carberry Takes a Hand

The man who called himself Wilmer Peregrine Huckleberry Hawthorne stood looking down at his companion as though dumbfounded. There was silence for quite an appreciable period.

'Do you mean to say,' he demanded at length, 'that you know Hugh Shannon?'

'I do – very well indeed,' Carter assured him. 'In fact he is one of my best pals. Furthermore, Joan and I are excellent friends also.'

'Well, can you beat that?'

'You and I have never met before, because Joan has always come to England without you. Nevertheless, I know all about you, of course. I hoped one day to meet you – now I have.'

'I guess this is the strangest thing ever, Tommy. Now I think about it, she has spoken of a guy called Carter. He, like her brother, is in the Secret Service.'

'Useless to deny it,' smiled Carter. 'At least we do know where we stand now.'

'Fancy little Joan, thousands of miles away, sending a cable which was instrumental in removing our impasse. Gee! This is a funny world. I guess I'd better tell you right now that I'm not over here on any stunt likely to be of disadvantage to Great Britain. If it wasn't that my mission was confidential, I'd have gone right along to Sir Leonard Wallace, and let Hugh know I was across just as soon as I had stepped out of the train. At any rate I meant to look the old firm up before I went back. Now I know who you are, I don't mind telling you what I'm doing over here – I understand, also, a whole lot that was puzzling me before.' He took back the photograph which Carter was holding out to him. 'Gee!' he murmured. 'Isn't she just the cat's whiskers?'

He put the picture away; then, unbuttoning his waistcoat, opened it out in order to show Carter a badge pinned inside. The Englishman immediately recognised it as the emblem of the Federal Secret Service worn by all officers of that important branch of the United States Department of Justice. Appreciating the act, Carter, in return, produced his warrant.

'Guess any lingering doubts are plumb removed now,' commented the American with a smile, as he buttoned his waistcoat. He pulled up a chair close to the one in which Carter was sitting and, placing himself firmly in it, leant forward. 'I am going to put you wise right now to the reason why I'm so darn interested in Grote and Modjeska. For the last year communists have been almighty active in the USA in a secretive kind of way, a way which I decided was a great deal more dangerous than spouting hot air at meetings. A lot of fiery rhetoric does nobody any harm; it lets off steam and that's all, which is all to the good. But I sure didn't like the innocent, secret business. It seemed to me to mean trouble. I put on all my best men to investigate without much result. One of them, however, got wise to the fact that Hermann Grote, who was in business in a big way in New York City, was somehow connected with the activity. After that we just kept our eyes peeled and everything Grote did was noted. But was that guy coy? I'm telling the world that he's as bashful as a girl at her first party; that is, where his underground operations are concerned. We couldn't get a real line on to what was happening for a mighty long time. We opened both his incoming and outgoing letters, went through his office and his home with a small tooth comb, practically without result. All we did find, and I guess it was useful enough, as it turned out, was a very innocent document signed by a man called Vladimir Dimitrinhov saying that the society was badly in need of funds, and that operations would shortly commence. There was no address on the letter, not even a date. But the envelope was postmarked "Vienna".

'An agent was sent to Austria to find out all he could about the guy Vladimir. He has not been heard of from that day to this, and he left the United States three months ago. I guess they got wise to him over there. Since then two other agents of ours have been found mysteriously murdered – one in Cincinnati, the other in Boston. The second was not quite dead, when he was picked up, and he had just time to gasp out, "Anarchists – extermination of royalty – collecting funds – devilish plot" before he croaked. After that I took an active hand in the game. A cable arrived for Grote a couple of weeks back. Of course it was in code, but we didn't need wet towels round our heads to decipher it. We have a department like yours which is pretty slick at figuring out things like that. It was from a guy calling himself Ivan Modjeska. He said it was imperative for Grote to cross to Europe bringing supplies with him. Modjeska would be staying at the Canute Hotel, London, and would meet him if he would cable the date of his arrival. Grote promptly sent back a reply, also in code, indicating that he would arrive on March the twelfth. Well, I guess I just packed my bags, and came right over. I reckoned it would be a fool's game to travel with a man who knew me by sight; besides, I wanted to get wise to Modjeska before Grote turned up. That's about all, I guess.'

'Thanks for telling me,' acknowledged Carter. 'There's no doubt now that, as you would put it, we are on the same lay. There's only one thing you haven't explained.'

'Shoot!' invited the American tersely.

'What made you anticipate that Modjeska would go to Shirland Road, and what did you expect to learn there?'

'I knew all about that anarchist affair, and when I heard Modjeska enquiring from the boss of this joint where Sheerland Road was, I just naturally guessed he meant Shirland Road, and put two and two together. It hadn't occurred to me before that the house your police raided and Modjeska had anything in common, but I knew then. I was darn curious to know what he expected to find there. He went down to the basement, and a woman answered his knock. He was only there a few minutes, so I reckon he didn't get what he went for.'

'An ice cream vendor and his family live in that basement,' explained Carter. 'Between you and me, Modjeska and his pals are exceedingly worried. As all their emissaries were killed, they have no means of knowing what roused suspicions, or whether the authorities are in possession of any information regarding the society. Modjeska apparently thinks the ice cream merchant might be able to tell him something, as he lives in the same house.'

'Is he connected with the gang?'

'No; and I don't suppose he can help Modjeska in the slightest degree. Poor Ivan; I can sympathise with him in his troubles. His only alternative is to enquire of the police, and somehow I don't think he will do that.'

The American chuckled.

'Not on your life, even if he were the cutest guy on two legs, with a cast-iron story about an erring brother and a dying mother. There's not a great deal in Ivan except his admiration for Modjeska. Say,' he added, 'what did rouse police suspicions against those anarchists?'

Carter smiled enigmatically.

'Ask Sir Leonard Wallace,' he returned.

His companion clicked his tongue a trifle impatiently.

'Gee! Open out a bit, Tommy. I've spun my yarn to you, and I guess it's up to you to respond some.'

'I'll tell you this much. The anarchists were here with the purpose of murdering King Peter when he visited England recently. It was to be the first step in their proposed extermination of all royalty.'

The American whistled.

'Then I guess poor Hamilton was not raving when we found him dying. Well, I've got to admit that you've handed me one item of information, you darn clam.'

Carter regarded him seriously.

'There's no reason,' he observed, 'why your department and mine shouldn't run in double harness in this affair, Mr Miles. I suggest—'

'For the love of Mike,' interrupted the other, 'don't Mister me. My name's Oscar, and if Tommy's good enough for me, surely Oscar's good enough for you.'

Carter nodded with a smile, and rose.

'I'd better go. If I may make a suggestion, I think you will be well-advised to see Sir Leonard Wallace as soon as possible. I can't tell you much – I haven't the right – but I've no doubt he will. In this business there's no reason, as far as I can see, why the two departments should not join forces. You once helped our men in India, and you may be sure Sir Leonard will be only too willing for us to work together now, especially as our aims are more or less identical.'

'I guess you're right, Tommy. Where do you think I'd better see him?'

'Ring him up from a public call box. He'll arrange the appointment. He will probably have you shadowed to his office to make certain that nobody suspicious is shadowing you, so you needn't be worried on that score. I don't think it is likely anybody but Grote would be interested in your movements, and he, we presume, does not know you are here; still there's no knowing. You might have been trailed from New York.'

'I'm darned sure I wasn't.'

Carter managed to leave the room without being seen by anybody, though he had a narrow escape. He was going up to his bedroom when he heard footsteps on the first flight of stairs. Glancing over the banisters he observed Modjeska and Grote walking towards their rooms. It would have been distinctly awkward had they caught a glimpse of him emerging from Miles' room; not that they had any suspicion of the man who called himself Hawthorne, but knowing Carter to be ostracised by the hotel guests, it would naturally strike them as strange that he was so friendly with one that he visited him in his room. Their surprise and consequent curiosity might then lead them to take an interest in Miles that could only end by being disastrous to him and to Carter as well.

That afternoon the Secret Service man locked himself in his room, and wrote a long and detailed report for Sir Leonard Wallace. He repeated almost word for word his secret conversation with Modjeska, told of the arrival of Grote, and his surreptitious introduction to the German-American. He then went on to describe the discovery he had made in the newcomer's room, the appearance of the man calling himself Hawthorne, and the subsequent revelation that he was Oscar J. Miles, the Chief of the United States Secret Service. He concluded by assuring Sir Leonard that if anything urgent came of his coming conversation with Modjeska, he would telephone him in the morning.

It was teatime long before he had finished, and, in consequence, he missed the meal beloved of ladies, curates and government clerks. That did not worry him, however. The anaemic-looking liquid served as the beverage at the Canute Hotel was extremely unpalatable – enough, as Carter mentally phrased it, to cause anyone to forsake ambition, and go on the dole. He went out to find relaxation, his precious package being carefully placed in his inner breast pocket. Making his way to the Tivoli, he spent a couple of hours watching the films, after which he returned to the hotel, and, with his face set again in its discontented scowl, waited moodily for dinner. The stony silence, the stonier looks of the four or five fellow guests sitting there eventually got on his nerves; he gave up the unequal contest and retired to his room. At least he could sit there without finding cold, contemptuous eyes staring at him from every direction. For the first time in his life Carter realised what a terrible thing it is to be regarded with scorn by one's fellow creatures.

He had hardly entered his room, when his acute powers either of observation or instinct warned him that it had been searched. He stood by the door looking round him. The toilet articles on the dressing table, his shaving tackle on the washstand were neatly arranged, but he knew they were not in the positions in which he had left them. Feeling distinctly uneasy, he dragged his battered suitcase from under the bed and opened it. Here again articles were placed in orderly disposition, but were not as he had left them. A pad of cheap notepaper which he had brought with him, and used for the purpose of his reports to Sir Leonard, lay on top. He remembered distinctly putting it underneath the clothing. There was not a thing in the suitcase which could create suspicion. The shirts, collars and socks were old and worn – he had taken especial care that everything would suit the character he was playing. There was, he felt, no reason for alarm, still the feeling of uneasiness persisted. It was only natural, he argued, that Modjeska and Grote should wish to ascertain that they were not deceived in him – it was unlikely that anyone else would have been interested enough in him to have searched his belongings. The anarchists must have been reassured by their failure to find anything that might have caused them to have doubts about him. Even the revolver was in his hip pocket, though they would hardly have considered that an article of suspicion. Nevertheless, he could not altogether eradicate a vague feeling of alarm.

Suddenly he gave vent to a little cry of dismay. What a fool he had been! He had quite overlooked the fact that the blotting paper on the pad would bear telltale marks. Quickly he opened the tablet, and a sigh of relief escaped from him. The blotting paper had not been removed, it was still there. He carried it across to the looking glass; held it up in order that he could examine it closely. It had been used so much that it was almost black with ink, but here and there words were decipherable. He was greatly reassured to find that none of them were of any importance. If the blotting paper had been inspected it had told the intruder or intruders nothing. Nevertheless he felt a deep sense of chagrin that he had been so careless. Taking care to remove or destroy what might have been a damning piece of evidence against him was, after all, an elementary precaution. He counted the sheets of paper remaining in the pad and, making a swift calculation, decided that two or three had been removed, apart from those he had used. The realisation of that caused him to smile. He had employed an exceedingly soft-running fountain pen, and was, in addition, a very light writer. There could, therefore, be no pressure of words left on the sheets beneath. To make absolutely certain he wrote a few words; then subjected the next page to a close scrutiny. There was not a mark of any kind.

The dinner bell rang, and he descended, feeling easy in his mind once again, though he was still annoyed with himself for having overlooked the blotting paper. He underwent his usual experience in the dining room, but ate in stolid and sullen silence. The two foreigners eyed him from time to time, but took no more notice of him than the others. Afterwards he put on his overcoat and hat; went for a circuitous stroll, as he had done the preceding night, and entered the buffet at Waterloo a few minutes after nine. Hill was leaning on the counter engaged in conversation with the girl who had before served him. Carter remarked with a smile that they seemed to be getting on exceedingly well together. There were few other people present, and he and Hill had that part of the bar practically to themselves.

'A large John Haig, miss,' he ordered.

She turned away to supply his requirements.

'Don't attempt to hand me anything,' came in an almost inaudible whisper from Hill. 'I've a notion you're being watched. I saw a bloke wandering about the platform in your wake before you came in. He entered after you. Look in the mirror – first table – right-hand side of the door. Know him?'

A large mirror advertising Worthington hung almost directly in front of Carter. He raised his eyes casually, glanced at the table indicated. He had great difficulty in suppressing a start, as he recognised the man seated there. It was Julius Carberry. He was so surprised that he remained staring at the reflection of the fellow for several seconds. Luckily Carberry was not looking in his direction. The last man Carter would have suspected of being interested in his movements, it nevertheless appeared evident that he had been trailing him. Yet the Secret Service man had been extremely cautious; had felt certain when he entered the buffet that he had not been followed. This was certainly a big surprise, and most disconcerting. Where did Carberry enter into the scheme of things? It did not seem possible that he could have anything to do with Modjeska and Grote, yet what other reason could he have for following Carter? Of course he may not have been trailing him after all; there was nothing very unusual in his being there, but Hill seemed to think the effeminate-looking man had been following him. Hill would hardly make a mistake.

'Are you sleepy, or in love?' asked a feminine voice.

Carter found the barmaid regarding him with amusement. Placed in front of him was his whisky.

'Sorry,' he apologised, and fumbled for some money.

He had observed that Carberry was looking directly into the glass at his face, and had promptly resumed the expression which he kept for the guests of the Canute Hotel. The girl went away to get his change.

'The fellow is staying at the same hotel as I,' he whispered to Hill, his lips hardly moving. 'I don't think he has anything to do with our affair.'

'Well, he's watching you. I'm sure of it. Repeat the dose, dearest,' he said aloud as the barmaid came back, and pushed his glass towards her.

She tossed her head.

'I like your dearest,' she commented with pretended disdain.

'Do you, dearest? Then I'll repeat it, dearest.' She went off to replenish his glass. 'That's got rid of her for a moment,' whispered Hill. 'Stick your report inside my paper when that dago isn't looking this way – I'll gather it up. And watch him, Tommy; I don't like his looks.'

He negligently spread his evening paper on the counter, part of it touching Carter's arm. Almost at the same moment Carberry looked away, and the pseudo-Bolshevik performed a sleight-of-hand trick. Hill bent over the counter reading the news. When the girl returned with his drink he folded up the paper again, and placed it in the inner pocket of his coat. Wrapped up in it was Carter's report to his chief. The more he thought about the new situation that had arisen, the more puzzled Carter became. Who was Julius Carberry? Was his name an alias and his supposed profession of commercial traveller a blind? There was certainly a good deal of the foreigner about him. If he had in reality been trailing the Secret Service man that night, he had been remarkably clever about it; yet there he was, sitting quite openly at a table in the buffet, drinking the sickly-looking kind of mixture one would expect a fellow of his type to delight in. Probably he felt that Carter would not suspect him of being in any way interested in him, and consequently would think nothing of his appearance there. He was not to know that Hill had been watching for his colleague's arrival and had had his attention drawn to Carberry.

Carter toyed with the thought of challenging the effeminate-looking man, demanding to know why the latter was trailing him, but that would be manifestly absurd, at least until he had assured himself, beyond all doubt, that he was, in fact, being followed by Carberry. Suddenly he remembered that he had noticed in one of his communist papers the announcement of a meeting arranged for that evening in a hall at Lambeth. It was timed to commence at nine o'clock. Carter decided to go there; he would be late, but that would not matter. He wished to make certain of Carberry's interest in him. If the latter followed him, it might also tend to convince the man that he was actually what he seemed to be.

He finished his drink, bade the barmaid goodnight, and walked out of the buffet. He took not the slightest notice of Carberry, and left the station, walking down the slope to Westminster Bridge Road without once glancing round. Thereafter he strode rapidly to the hall where the meeting was being held. The place was crowded, but he managed to find a seat at the back. There he remained for an hour. Speaker followed speaker, each giving expression to the most virulent communistic utterances. Carter felt nauseated; longed to stand up and denounce them, but he clapped and cheered as loudly as anyone. He had not taken long to satisfy himself that Carberry had indeed followed him. The fellow had entered the hall, and was endeavouring to efface himself between two vicious-looking, pale-faced youths sitting near the end of the same row as the seat occupied by Carter. At half past ten the Secret Service agent decided that it was time he returned to the Canute Hotel. He also decided that he and Carberry would return together. He squeezed his way out of the building, noting from the corner of his eye that Julius had risen from his seat. Outside he positioned himself in such a manner that the man trailing him would not notice him until he was actually on him, and proceeded to light a cigarette. Suddenly someone cannoned into him with a good deal of force, the impact causing them both to stagger. It was Carberry, and he seemed in a great hurry.

'Why don't you look where you're going?' growled Carter. 'Hullo!' he added in tones of profound surprise. 'Fancy meeting you here. I didn't know you were one of us.'

In the rays of light cast by the lamp hanging over the hall door Carberry looked a distinctly sick individual at that moment. He licked his lips, while a finger tugged at his collar as though it were choking him.

'I – I – It isn't generally known,' he stuttered in a high-pitched voice.

'Why not?' demanded Carter. 'You're not ashamed of it are you?'

'No, no of course not, but – but my job. You see – I might lose it.'

'Bah!' grunted Carter. 'Why should you care? I lost my job because I told the boss exactly what my sentiments are. To hell with all capitalists who squeeze the lifeblood out of the people. Are you returning to the Canute?'

'Er – yes.'

'Then come along! We'll walk together.'

Carberry was obviously very reluctant, but he could not very well refuse. On the way Carter at first spoke enthusiastically of the 'cause', the coming downfall of monarchies and capitalism, with the fiery ardour of the fanatic, and as though glad of the opportunity of discoursing to a kindred spirit. Julius confined himself to monosyllabic replies. Before they had gone far, however, the Secret Service man gradually introduced a personal note into his remarks, proceeding very adroitly to pump his companion, but, despite the manner in which he wrapped up his questions, he learnt practically nothing. Carberry was obviously very much on his guard. His affected voice when he did speak, his effeminate mannerisms, sickened Carter. Long before they reached the Canute Hotel, Carter had given up attempting to get him to talk. In consequence he was left in a puzzled frame of mind. Of one thing he felt almost certain. It was that neither Modjeska nor Grote were likely to have employed Carberry. He was too inept, too invertebrate to give anyone confidence or encourage trust. In addition, he was not a Bolshevik or communist. The one thing Carter had succeeded in discovering about him was that his ideas on the doctrines which had emanated from Russia were so vague as to be negligible.

They parted at the hotel door, Carberry going on ahead up to his room with a muttered goodnight. Carter soon followed up to his, and undressed very thoughtfully. He had hardly climbed into bed when Modjeska silently entered the room, a smile on his flabby, sallow face. He had reached the bed, and was about to take a seat on it, when the door slowly opened again. Both the Pole and Carter gazed at it with startled eyes, each catching his breath in a gasp of apprehension. A man entered; stood looking at them. It was Julius Carberry.

CHAPTER TEN

Blackmail

A dead silence, lasting for quite half a minute, followed the entry into the room of the unexpected visitant. There was a sneering smile on the latter's face, while both Modjeska and Carter stared at him in dumbfounded astonishment. The Pole's expression was perfectly ludicrous. His strange, brown eyes were open to their widest extent, losing thereby a lot of their sinister quality, his lower jaw had fallen as though completely beyond control. Carter was the first to recover himself.

'What do you want?' he asked.

'I want to speak to you – and him,' replied Carberry in his affected tones.

'This is hardly the time or the place I should imagine for your purpose.'

'It is the right place and the right time, for my purpose is private and concerns you both.'

'Vell, shut the door,' hissed Modjeska recovering his faculties suddenly. 'Ve do not vant all the people in the hotel to know ve meet here.' Carberry obeyed, and advanced farther into the room. Carter noticed that the Pole quickly placed himself in such a position that he was now between the intruder and the door. 'Explain, please,' continued Modjeska, 'vhy you come here in manner so secret.'

Carberry's dark eyes were turned first on one, then on the other.

'Exactly how much,' he asked, 'are you prepared to pay to make it worth my while to keep my mouth closed?'

Although the question caused Carter as much surprise as it apparently did Modjeska, he was sensible of a feeling of relief. Carberry did not, after all, represent an unknown and possibly dangerous party, neither was he a spy employed by Modjeska. Apparently he had discovered something concerning the activities of the latter and, associating Carter with him, had decided upon a little blackmail. It was the kind of thing that would appeal to a fellow of his type, thought the Secret Service man contemptuously, but he could not know the danger in which he was placing himself. Modjeska and company would think as little of removing anyone from the world who threatened to become inconvenient as they would a speck of dust from their attire.

Modjeska at first was frankly startled. Carter noticed, however, that he showed neither perturbation nor embarrassment and, when the initial sense of shock wore off, even smiled. But it was a wicked smile. The mouth was twisted pitilessly, the eyes, from behind their pince-nez, gleamed with utter cruelty. Perhaps for the first time, Carter realised the brutality underlying the suave manner of Ivan Modjeska. Carberry undoubtedly became, at that moment, aware of the peril in which he had placed himself. His pale face turned bloodless, fear looked naked from his eyes. However, with a visible effort, he pulled himself together, fondly imagining perhaps that he held the trump cards.

'It seems to me, Mr Carberry,' observed Modjeska in tones that can only be described as a purr, 'that you are, for some reason vich ve do not know, trying to – vat is it you say in English?' he appealed to Carter.

'Blackmail us?'

'Ah! Yes, blackmail us. My friend, Mr Carter, vill not, I think, mind mooch if you sit in that chair and explain to us.'

He indicated a chair on the opposite side of the bed. Carter nodded, and Julius Carberry, after a slight show of hesitation, walked round and sat down.

'I know who you are, Ivan Modjeska,' he declared in his sickeningly effeminate voice, 'and I heard enough of your conversation with Mr Carter last night to assure me that you and he were about to join forces.'

Modjeska and Carter exchanged a quick and somewhat apprehensive glance.

'Our conversation?' repeated the former. 'My friend, I think you dream. Of vat conversation do you speak?'

'It is no use trying bluff,' declared Carberry. 'I refer to your conversation in this room after eleven. I saw you pass along the corridor. I was already very much interested in you, but your secretive manner increased my interest. You see my bedroom is number thirteen, which happens to be at the top of the stairs on the other side of the passage. I looked cautiously out and observed that you entered here. I knew this was Mr Carter's room, and he is well-known to possess doctrines which I privately knew to be similar to yours. I waited till all was quiet; then I crept along the corridor and listened with my ear to the keyhole. You little thought your very interesting talk was being overheard, did you?'

Modjeska's eyes became more wicked-looking than before.

'Ah! The eavesdropper!' he murmured, and shook his head with the air of an elder gently reproving a youngster for a minor transgression. 'It is very mooch bad form – that. Perhaps tonight comes another eavesdropper. Who knows?' He crossed quickly to the door, and, opening it softly, inspected the corridor. Presently he closed it again, and Carter did not fail to notice that this time he bolted it. 'I think it vill be vell if you start at the beginning,' he went on to the white-faced Carberry, 'and explain vhy you have the so-great interest in me.'

'I'll tell you all,' agreed Julius, 'and then you'll see that I have you – like this.' He closed his hands slowly, as though getting a tight grip on something.

'This is most entertaining, do you not think so?' Modjeska asked Carter.

'Very,' replied the Secret Service man dryly.

'You'll understand quite a lot,' continued Carberry, 'when I tell you that Luigi Casaroli, who died in Shirland Road, was my mother's brother!'

A little hiss escaped from between Modjeska's thin lips. Carter now understood the touch of the foreigner in Carberry.

'So you're half Italian,' he commented.

'I am,' acknowledged Julius, 'and I'm proud of it. My Italian blood gives me the artistic side of my nature which my employers appreciate so much.'

'Get on with your story,' urged the disgusted Carter.

'Luigi Casaroli,' proceeded Carberry, now with a little more confidence than he had hitherto shown, 'got into some unsavoury communistic trouble in Berlin, where he held a very good post. He fled to England to escape punishment, and my father, who used to be an important official of the Bootblack Brigade, persuaded him to become naturalised. He did, and my father found him a job. He and I became very friendly, and he grew very fond of me.' Julius drew his hand backwards over his sleek hair and lowered his eyes modestly, his lips pursed. Carter longed to punch his head. 'A short while before he died,' pursued Carberry, 'I called on him, and found him in a state of great terror. He confessed everything to me.'

'Vat do you mean by everything?' queried Modjeska.

'He told me that members of an anarchist society had followed him to England, and had forced him to act as their agent in this country on threat of divulging what had occurred in Berlin. He said that the object of the society was to assassinate royalty in every country that possessed a king. He had received news that King Peter, who had accepted an invitation to visit England, was to be murdered on arrival here. He had been instructed to arrange accommodation for the three anarchists who had been selected for the deed. There were some rooms vacant in the house in which he lived. He proposed to arrange for the three men to have those, but he was in deadly terror. He believed, he told me, that his own death would result from the venture. I asked him why he did not tell the police. He replied that he dared not, because if he did the affair in Berlin would come to light. It was the shooting of a police official, who had been investigating the activities of a secret society to which he belonged, and which was connected in some way with the anarchists. He made me swear not to betray him, but to do my best to think of means by which he could escape from the toils. I promised to do so. It was because he knew of the Canute Hotel through my staying there that he gave the name to you, Ivan Modjeska. He told me about you and Vladimir Dimitrinhov, and asked me to watch you when you came to London.

'I was away on my travels in the country when news of the raid on the house in Shirland Road reached me, and the death of my uncle and the three anarchists. None of the papers described exactly how the men were killed, though it was hinted in several that one of the anarchists had gone mad and shot down his associates before falling himself. I went to visit the ice cream man who lives in the basement when I returned to London. He had overheard the police speaking, and was able to tell me that my uncle, Luigi Casaroli, had threatened to betray the society to the English authorities, whereupon a man called Haeckel had snatched up a revolver, even though his wrists were handcuffed, and had shot him. Afterwards he killed the other two and himself. Now you know what I know, Ivan Modjeska, and you're going to pay me well not to speak.'

The Pole sat on the bed studying him through narrowed eyes. Suddenly he turned to Carter.

'You of course knew of that so-tragic Sheerland Road affair – no?'

'Yes,' admitted Carter, 'but I had no idea that—'

'That it was any of my concerns? But now you know, you also know vhy I vant go there. The friend I talk of to you vas the ice cream man. He tell me also the same he has told Mr Carberry. My society vas mooch anxious about vat the police know. I am happy that it is very leetle.' Abruptly he looked back at Julius, and his voice dropped to a purr again. 'But tonight,' he pronounced, 'I have find out something very mooch important I think. Ve all vonder how it is the police know to raid the house in Sheerland

Road. I have now the answer. Mr Carberry vas the man who told them.'

'That's a lie!' gasped Julius starting up from his chair. 'I did not go to the police at all.'

'You did not go – no; perhaps not. But you could write – yes?'

'I didn't write either. I kept my promise to my uncle. Even then I thought that it would mean more profit to myself to keep quiet.'

'It is not possible to believe that you did not tell them,' insisted Modjeska. 'Vat other person could do it? Nobody, my friend. Am I not right, Mr Carter?'

'It looks like it,' agreed Carter, though he knew the true facts. He turned a baleful look on Carberry, as Modjeska nodded approval. 'You fool,' growled the Secret Service man to Julius, who was again looking white-faced and shaken, 'what did you expect to gain by mixing yourself up in an affair like this?'

'I expect to gain quite a lot,' was the reply, though not too confidently spoken.

'Have you heard the English saying,' queried Modjeska softly, 'I like it very mooch – "Dead men tell not the tales"?'

Carberry laughed a trifle unsteadily.

'You – you can't frighten me like that,' he returned, though his looks belied his words. 'I have left a document with – with someone, which will be handed to the police if I – if anything happens to me.'

'All that sounds very terrible,' smiled Modjeska, 'but vat do I care for your blackmail, my friend? – nothing, nothing at all. If your so-wonderful document went to the police, they could not act on it. They would find Ivan Modjeska and Vladimir Dimitrinhov most innocent men, vith not one leetle bit of proof to catch them.'

'Bluff – all – all – bluff,' stammered Carberry. 'Whether there is proof to be found against you or – or not, my death would be – be significant, wouldn't it? And don't forget: the name of the society is in the document.'

For the first time Modjeska looked really perturbed.

'Perhaps also in that document,' he murmured, looking intently at Carberry, 'is the address of the place vere the headquarters of the society are?'

The other nodded triumphantly.

'I have not only given the address of the headquarters,' he replied, 'but also the address of the hiding place in Constantinople.'

The Pole removed his pince-nez, and polished them in his handkerchief, with hands that trembled a little. Now that the glasses were removed Carter, for the first time, obtained a real view of the man's uncanny eyes. Their vivid, hypnotic quality was revealed in all its naked iniquity. The Secret Service man became almost fascinated by them. He did not wonder at the gasp which escaped from Julius Carberry. Glancing at the latter, he saw him staring with fearful intensity at Modjeska, his hands clenched, his teeth biting deep into his lower lip. Carter decided that the Pole had removed his pince-nez for the very purpose of terrifying the blackmailer. He sat slowly rubbing the glasses, his eyes fixed unblinkingly on the other.

'Vere is it – this document?' he asked presently in a low vibrating voice.

'I won't tell you,' came the faltering reply.

'Oh, yes, you vill, my friend. Ivan Modjeska vills it that you tell him. Listen to me, very carefully. I say again you vill tell me vere the document is.'

'No – no! I won't!'

'You vill.' And the eyes continued gazing deep into those of the victim.

Carter realised, with a sense of horror, that the Pole was attempting to mesmerise Carberry. A vivid recollection of an occasion when an attempt of a similar nature had been made on him recurred to his mind. Somehow, even if it meant drawing the Pole's suspicion on himself, he must put a stop to the foul work. He knew very well that once Julius was forced to reveal the information which Modjeska was attempting to tear from him, his life would be forfeit.

'I won't tell you – I won't!' came now in great gasps from Carberry.

'You vill. Nothing can vithstand the vill of Ivan Modjeska. Speak! Vere is the document?'

The tortured man tried vainly to tear his gaze away from those terrible eyes, but could not. He was easy prey to such a man as Modjeska. Before long his resistance was palpably weakening. He began to sob his refusal; then whine in a manner that was so animal-like as to shock Carter.

The latter could stand it no longer.

'He is obstinate, isn't he?' he observed in matter-of-fact tones. 'Never mind, Mr Modjeska, we will—'

The Pole turned on him like a wild beast.

'You fool!' he snarled. 'You have spoilt it all vat I vas doing. Have you not the sense?'

A string of words in his own language sounding very much like profanity, burst in a torrent from his lips, but the tension was broken. Carberry was bending forward, his face hidden in his hands, his whole body trembling violently. Carter eyed Modjeska with well-simulated amazement.

'What have I done?' he demanded in a resentful voice.

'Could you not see? Could you not see?'

'See what? What was there to see? You were asking Carberry where his precious document is. I'm hanged if I can understand why.'

'You are a fool – a big fool.' Modjeska replaced his pince-nez. 'I do not think I have ever before know a fool so great.'

'Oh, you haven't have you!' snapped Carter. 'Then you can jolly well clear out of my room. Perhaps you will be able to find someone who is not a fool.'

Modjeska looked surprised, and a little concerned.

'Vat is this you say?' he demanded. 'Are you now refuse to be vone of us?'

'Do you think I'm going to allow you or anyone else to call me a fool?' grunted Carter, all the sullenness and resentment back in his face. 'You can take your plots back to your own country, with you. I don't want to have anything more to do with them. A fool am I?'

The Pole studied him for a moment, then smiled.

'It is a misunderstanding betven you and me – yes? I vill explain; after you vill know vhy I call you a big fool. Now I see you are not the fool – it is that you do not understand. Ven you know you vill be mooch angry vith yourself.'

'Well, explain then.'

'In a leetle time.' He turned to the still trembling Carberry. 'I think you have win, my friend,' he announced. 'You have us in your power – I admit it. For your silence ve must pay. Vat is it you ask?'

Such a complete change in his attitude was, to say the least of it, a little surprising. Carberry looked up at him and, although still pale and drawn, quickly now began to recover from his experience. The light of greed was in his eyes.

'I – I knew you would see you were in my power before long,' he muttered hoarsely.

Modjeska shrugged his shoulders.

'Ah, yes,' he confessed. 'It vas evident, but I hoped that I could bluff you.'

'It would take more than you to bluff me,' boasted Julius.

'Alas! I feel that you are right. Vell vat is the price vich you ask?'

Carter frowned thoughtfully. He knew very well that Modjeska had no intention of acceding to the blackmailer's demands, but was unable to understand his object in thus appearing to surrender. There was devilry of some sort behind it without a doubt. Although he had interrupted Modjeska's attempt at hypnotism, and for the time being had, he was quite certain, saved Carberry's life, the Secret Service man was well aware of the deadly peril which was overhanging the commercial traveller. He feared that he would not always be in a position to save him. Carberry had now forgotten his terror in the sense of triumph that had come to him. It was obvious he was quite convinced that Modjeska now fully realised that he held the whip-hand, and had decided that all he could do was to treat with him. He sat as though considering the question asked for a minute or two, one hand placed in an affected manner on his hip. The fellow was quite unable to forbear from posing. Carter caught a whiff of some pungent scent as he drew a handkerchief from his pocket and dabbed his lips. At length he gave Modjeska an arch look, his head on one side.

'I suppose,' he observed, 'you will think I am a very greedy man, if I ask for ten thousand pounds?'

'Very greedy, yes,' nodded the Pole, 'but man – never.'

'What do you mean?'

'Vat I have say. No vone vould take you for a man.'

'Oh, I say. What else could I be?'

'Ve vill not disguss the science of eugenics – no. You say you vant ten tousand pounds for to be silent. It is too mooch, my friend.'

Carberry, who seemed to have regained all his confidence, tossed his head in the style of a schoolgirl.

'I will not take a penny less,' he declared.

Modjeska sat for a while stroking his chin. Gone was all suggestion of fierceness from his manner, his expression was almost mild.

'Vere you tink ve get all that money?' he asked.

'You have a very big fund. You see, I know a great deal about your society.'

'Yes; I can see that,' admitted Modjeska. 'If you are paid this money, how are ve to know you vill then keep silence?'

'I will give you my word,' returned Carberry with a grand air.

The Pole grunted, but made no other comment. He again sat thoughtful for some moments, then he sighed.

'Tomorrow I vill give you my answer. You vill vait?'

Julius rose from his chair.

'If you come to my room before breakfast,' he agreed, 'I will wait till then with pleasure.'

'Ah! You do not give me too mooch time. Very vell. I vill come.'

The blackmailer sauntered round the bed to the door; withdrew the bolt. For a few seconds he stood elegantly poised, an object, to Carter, of profound contempt, though he felt a good deal of pity for the fellow. 'Please remember,' lisped Julius, 'that it is useless to try any tricks. It would be bad for you both if you forget that a friend of mine possesses a statement which, if published, would mean the end of the society you – er – adorn.'

'What have I to do with it?' growled Carter.

'I have also mentioned you in my little report, Mr Carter. It contains, you see, a summary of the conversation in this room last night. You will probably be interested to know that I searched your room this evening.'

'Oh, you did, did you?' Carter was greatly relieved now that the matter which had been troubling him was explained. 'What did you expect to find here?'

'Evidence against you,' replied Carberry with a smirk.

'You're nothing but a common blackmailer and a thief,' snarled the Secret Service man, 'and if you think I'm afraid of you, you dirty sneak, you—'

'Hush!' interposed Modjeska, but his lips were twitching in a cruel smile which Julius could not see. 'Remember, my friend, ve are in his power.'

'I am glad you are remembering it, Ivan Modjeska,' came from Carberry in approving tones. 'You are a wise man. As for you,' he looked again at Carter, 'you will be well advised to follow Modjeska's advice. I will take care that your excursion to that seditious meeting tonight is added to my statement – and at once. That in itself may not be criminal, but added to everything else it will tell against you.'

With that he went out, unbolting the door and closing it behind him, apparently quite unaware that he had made a fatal mistake. Carter had noticed it, and he quickly saw that Modjeska had also done so. The latter's eyes were gleaming as the Secret Service man turned to look at him.

'Ah! The so-wise Carberry,' chuckled the Pole softly. 'He has pretend the bluff. The so-precious document cannot be vith a friend, if he goes now to add vords to it.'

'Perhaps he means he will write another document,' hazarded Carter, his heart sinking as he realised the manner in which Carberry had so foolishly placed himself in Modjeska's power by a thoughtless remark.

'I do not tink that, my friend. Vere did you go tonight of vich he speak?' Carter told him. 'And the good Carberry follow you?'

'I suppose so. At any rate he was there. We came back together. Now I want to know what you meant by calling me a fool, and saying I had spoilt everything.'

Modjeska explained to him at great length, and with many expressions of self-praise, the faculty he possessed of being able to hypnotise others.

'I vas getting Carberry into my power,' he concluded. 'Soon he vould have told me vere that paper he had written vas, but you interrupt, I know because you did not understand vat I do, and it is all over – finished. The influence vas ruined.'

Carter stared at him like one amazed.

'Can you really do that?' he asked in a hushed voice. 'You are not fooling?'

Modjeska sat up with an air of great pride.

'There is no foolery. It is true. I, Ivan Modjeska, can mesmerise ven I vill. It is mooch useful gift.'

Carter took care that a look of great respect came into his face. The Pole noticed it, and was extremely gratified. For some moments he basked in the imagined adulation of his companion.

'I'm sorry I butted in,' apologised the Englishman humbly.

'It is no matter – you did not know. Another time you vill understand, yes? I, therefore, forgive.'

Carter looked duly grateful for the other's magnanimity.

'It is decent of you,' he murmured.

Modjeska leant forward; patted him on the arm.

'The more I see you, my friend,' he declared expansively, 'so mooch the more I like you. Ivan Modjeska vill alvays be your friend. You have my vord. Your leetle mistake matters not. Ve know now Mr Carberry, that clever vone, has not the document given avay. It is vith him. Oh, the poor Carberry!'

He laughed, and the utter cold-bloodedness of the laugh sent a shiver through the Englishman. He showed no sign of his feelings however.

'What do you intend to do?' he asked casually.

Modjeska shrugged his shoulders.

'Who knows vat may happen? In this vorld life is mooch uncertain. Vone day a man is in health so good, and the next day he is suddenly dead. It is sad, but ve cannot help it. The vorld goes on just the same.'

Carter did not press him to disclose his intentions for fear of raising suspicions in his mind, but he resolved to keep a watch on Carberry's room for the rest of the night. The Pole took a thick wallet from his pocket. From it he extracted a transcontinental rail and boat ticket which he handed to Carter. The latter examined it, and saw that it was dated two days hence. The destination was Vienna.

'On Sunday, my friend, you vill go to Vienna vith this. Ven you arrive I vill meet you at the station. Hermann Grote and I vill go tomorrow night by the boat train for Southampton. Ve have business in Havre, you see. Your train vill leave from Victoria at nine of the clock in the morning, and you vill go by vay of Dover, Ostend and Brussels. It is understood?'

'Perfectly.'

Modjeska gave him a roll of notes.

'There you have tventy pounds vich ve vill call expenses. You cannot say Ivan Modjeska is not generous.'

'I think you are very generous,' returned Carter in exultant tones. 'I haven't had as much money as this for a long time.'

'There is mooch more vere that come from. Ven you are of the society, you vill be mooch vell paid. Ve do not starve our comrades who serve the great cause. Now, my friend, I vill leave you. There vill be no more to be said until ve meet in Vienna.'

'Are you going to consult Mr Grote about Carberry?'

'I have not make up my mind. Perhaps. I vill tink vat is best to do. Goodnight.'

Carter waited some time after he had gone, to make sure that he was not still in the corridor. Then, after switching off the light, and slipping on his overcoat – he had no dressing gown with him – he quietly opened his door, placed a chair on the threshold and sat where he could see the door of Carberry's room without being seen himself. He was determined that somehow or other, even if it meant bringing himself under suspicion, he would save the blackmailer's life. If no attempt was made on him that night he would see that on the following day, at least until Modjeska and Grote had departed, he would be amply protected by the Secret Service. An hour, two hours went by, and Modjeska did not come back. Carter began to think that the Pole had no intention of doing anything that night. Perhaps, when he visited Carberry before breakfast, he would carry out the murderous designs he was undoubtedly nursing. It would be a very risky proceeding, and foolish in the extreme, but there was no knowing what might be in the evil mind of Modjeska. Suddenly the Secret Service man sat bolt upright. The door of room number thirteen had opened. In the dim light cast by the solitary electric lamp that had been left burning in the corridor he saw a man appear, close the door quietly behind him and go quietly down the stairs. There was no mistaking the somewhat corpulent form of Ivan Modjeska.

CHAPTER ELEVEN

Death by Misadventure

Carter rose to his feet; stood for several moments looking down the passage, a prey to several conflicting emotions. The one that predominated was a feeling of anger with himself. It had not occurred to him that Modjeska would go straight to Carberry's room after leaving him, as he must have done. He had been certain that the Pole would go to Grote, and tell the German-American what had happened. A dread that harm had already overtaken Carberry fought with the rather weak assurance that Modjeska would not dare to murder the blackmailer in the hotel. Carter tried to persuade himself that he would be certain to wait until an opportunity occurred for him to bring about Carberry's death in some manner that would give it the appearance of an accident. But he remained unconvinced. Deep in his heart the Secret Service agent felt that the man who had made such a foolish attempt at blackmail was already dead. He was puzzled, however, to know why Modjeska had spent over two hours in the other's room. He decided to investigate.

Drawing his coat round him, for the night was very cold, he tiptoed along the corridor, gently turned the handle of the door of number thirteen, and entered. It struck him then what an utterly unwise man Julius Carberry was. To have entered his room, after the interview he had had with Modjeska, and to have left the door unlocked and unbolted, as he must have done, was the very extreme of madness. Carter could not see anything, as the light had not been left burning, but no sound of breathing reached his ears. He stood listening intently for over a minute; then closed the door, gently sliding the bolt into place. His fingers felt for and found the switch. At once the electricity flared into life, and his eyes immediately sought the recumbent form in the bed. There did not, at first sight, appear to be anything wrong. Carberry lay on his side, as though in a deep sleep, the bedclothes drawn up to his chin. The room was not in disorder, as though a search had been conducted in it or violence had taken place. Everything, in fact, seemed perfectly normal. Carter stepped quietly up to the bed; bent low over the figure lying there. Then he knew; knew without a shadow of doubt. Julius Carberry was indeed dead.

He appeared to have died in his sleep. There were no marks of any kind on him, as far as the Secret Service man could tell from a cursory examination. He had certainly not been stabbed, there was no sign of strangulation, and Carter became extremely puzzled. What had caused death? He stood for some time looking down at the body, his brows knit in perplexed thought, then his eyes wandered to the bedside table, became immediately fixed on a small phial standing there. It was uncorked, and contained a few small tablets. He picked it up. One glance at the label was quite sufficient to tell him not only why Carberry had died, but how the crime had been accomplished. He was staring at the word Veronal. Almost as though he had been present, he visualised Modjeska hypnotising the unfortunate blackmailer; then, when the latter was entirely under his influence, forcing him to swallow, one by one, the deadly little lozenges, until he had taken more than enough to kill him. After that Modjeska had simply waited in the room until his victim had died. The body was still warm, and Carter calculated that death had occurred not more than half an hour before. At first he had thoughts of calling for assistance, sending for a doctor in the hope that a flicker of life might still remain, and Carberry be saved. But he knew too much about death; here, without the slightest doubt, lay one whom no power on earth could revive.

The utter fiendishness of the crime appalled him. It was terrible to reflect that any human being could have hypnotised a fellow creature into taking an overdose of an opiate; then remained waiting, waiting, waiting until death had claimed the victim of his diabolical villainy. And, to make the matter more dreadful, Carter would be compelled, at least for the time being, to stand aside, and allow the murderer to escape justice, even appear to countenance the crime. There could be no doubt that the inquest would result in a verdict of accidental death, perhaps suicide, though that was unlikely. No suspicion of foul play would be engendered in the minds of the authorities unless Carter spoke, and his lips were sealed. He stood there white with horror, with passionate loathing of the man who had done this vile thing. Mentally he vowed that he would not rest until Modjeska had in some way expiated his crime.

He wondered whether Carberry had been in the habit of taking veronal, or if Modjeska had had the small bottle of tablets in his pocket. He could not have gone to his room to obtain it. Carter would have seen him enter number thirteen in that case. The first seemed by far the more feasible explanation. Carberry was the type one could imagine taking a drug, while Modjeska would have had no object in carrying a bottle of such tablets in his pocket. He could not have foreseen what was going to happen. There appeared little doubt that, on entering Carberry's apartment with the idea of murdering him in some other way, the Pole had seen the veronal, and had conceived then and there the scheme by which he could remove the blackmailer without the slightest risk to himself.

Carter replaced the bottle on the table, first wiping it with his handkerchief to make certain there were no fingerprints on it. There was just a possibility that something might rouse the suspicions of the police. In that case it would be distinctly awkward if they examined the phial for impressions and afterwards discovered that his were on it. The thought gave rise to another reflection. What if they discovered the surprising fact that there were no fingerprints on it at all. That in itself would be a suspicious fact. Still holding his handkerchief in his right hand, Carter lifted up the little bottle by the neck; then, turning back the bedclothes, raised one of the dead man's hands and pressed the thumb and forefinger against it. That done he put down the phial, and gently lifted the sheet and blankets back into position.

There was nothing to detain him in the room. He crossed to the door, therefore, switched the light off, and let himself out, first assuring himself that there was nobody about. Back in his own room, he closed and bolted the door, took off his overcoat, and got into bed. There he lay thinking of the crime that had been committed and the man whose satanic cunning had devised it. Sleep refused to come to him for a long time. In a way he felt responsible for Carberry's death. If he had only anticipated that Modjeska would go direct to number thirteen, he might have prevented the murder. But it was no use worrying about what might have been. Julius Carberry was dead. No amount of vain regrets would bring him to life again.

The pale light of dawn was showing through the flimsy linen blind when, at last, Carter fell asleep. Thereafter he slept soundly; did not awake until a continuous knocking on his door roused him.

'Come in!' he called sleepily.

''Ow can I come in,' returned a muffled feminine voice, 'when you've bolted the door?' Carter remembered, sprang out of bed, unbolted it, and took his hot water and morning tea from the chambermaid standing outside. 'What's the matter with you?' she asked sourly; ''fraid of bein' kidnapped or something? You 'aven't bolted the door before.'

He did not reply, contented himself with frowning sullenly at her. His eyes were alert, however, to catch any sign of unwonted excitement in her face. There was nothing. Obviously she had not been to Carberry's room, or, if she had, had noticed nothing amiss. Carter shaved and dressed quickly; was seated in the lounge some time before breakfast. While there he heard the sound of mysterious comings and goings, voices speaking in stage whispers. The death of Carberry had been discovered, he concluded, and the proprietor was endeavouring to hush it up. The death of a guest in a hotel is not exactly a welcome advertisement. Mr Fellowes, however, might have spared himself the trouble. It may be possible to keep private a death in a big hotel containing hundreds of guests, but in a little place where the ten or a dozen residing there are perfectly well known to each other, and the arrival of a stranger immediately noted, it is out of the question. The coming of a police sergeant and a constable, followed a little later by an officer in plain clothes, whom Carter knew by sight, and a man carrying a bag, obviously a doctor, caused comment and a good deal of excitement among the people who had come down from their rooms. At breakfast the news was no longer secret. Everyone knew that Julius Carberry was dead.

The guests spoke in hushed, shocked voices, and, though nobody had had much to say to the dead man when he was alive, he suddenly became popular now that he had passed beyond the veil. Carter noticed, with a feeling of cynicism, how the people round him were applying to the late commercial traveller virtues which he certainly never had possessed, and of which, if he had, they would not have been aware. Grote and Modjeska entered the dining room looking placid and content with life. Watching them surreptitiously but intently, Carter saw no sign of disquiet either in their manner or expressions. Modjeska shot him a sharp, enquiring glance and, apparently satisfied, looked away. He and his companion bade a polite and cheerful good morning to the others.

'Have you heard the news – the terrible, tragic news, Mr Modjeska?' asked Miss Simpson, like all her kind anxious to be the first to impart it.

'Vat news, madame?' returned the Pole courteously. 'Ve have not yet read the newspapers.'

'It is not in the newspapers,' she hastened to tell him, 'but of course it will be. It has happened here – in this very hotel. It is so tragic.' She applied a handkerchief to her eyes. 'Poor, poor young man!'

'But vat is it, madame?' asked Modjeska, looking very much puzzled.

'Young Carberry is dead,' announced Curzon in a sepulchral voice; 'died in his sleep.'

Miss Simpson favoured him with a glance of suppressed fury. She had been baulked of the opportunity, so dear to her maiden heart, of causing a sensation. Modjeska and Grote gave a very fine impersonation of two men thoroughly dumbfounded. They did it most convincingly. Nobody would have suspected them of knowing already or of being concerned in any way with the event.

'But this is terrible!' ejaculated Modjeska. 'It is not possible.'

'It is possible,' put in Miss Simpson hurriedly, anxious to save to herself some, at least, of the triumph of announcement. 'It has happened. We have not heard much yet, but it is thought that he died of an overdose of some drug he took to make him sleep.'

'You astonish me,' declared Grote. 'I saw little of him, of course, but he struck me as a young man so full of health and virility. It is very sad.'

'Very mooch sad,' echoed Modjeska. 'I like him vell and now he is dead, you say, gone – pouff! Like that. I feel I do not vant the breakfast.'

'That's how we all feel,' agreed Mrs Curzon, a thin lady with a whining voice suitable to the occasion.

Carter noticed, however, that they all did ample justice to the viands placed before them. He was left severely alone. Even the death of Carberry and the consequent excitement did not incline anybody to speak to him. They talked among themselves, and their hypocritical sentiments sickened him. He was about to leave the dining room, when the detective entered.

'I regret to say,' he announced, 'that one of the guests, Mr Julius Carberry by name, has died during the night of, it is believed, an overdose of veronal. Do any of you ladies or gentlemen know anything about the dead man? There will be an inquest, of course, and any information you can supply will be needed.'

Nobody knew anything of use. The police officer looked from one to the other. He started slightly when he caught sight of Carter, but as he was standing with his back to the two foreigners at the time they noticed nothing. The Secret Service man's left eyelid – it happened to be hidden from Modjeska and Grote – fluttered very slightly. An answering wink assured him that the detective knew he was not to be recognised.

'Do you know anything likely to be of interest to the coroner, sir?' asked the man.

'Nothing whatever,' replied Carter.

The officer turned away, and the young man caught the fleeting expressions of relief and approval on the faces of the two foreigners before they, once again, became appropriately solemn. Carter went into the lounge. The detective looked in and found him there.

'Your presence here is in no way connected with Julius Carberry, sir, is it?'

'No,' returned Carter hastily; 'and for goodness' sake don't be seen talking to me.'

The other took the hint, and departed. A few minutes later Modjeska entered the room. He made sure there was nobody else in close proximity.

'This so-sudden death is useful,' he whispered. 'It saves us mooch trouble.'

'How did he die?' asked Carter eyeing him steadily.

'How do I know except that it is said a dose over of a drug that makes sleep.'

Carter allowed a slight smile to show on his face.

'You are a very clever man, Mr Modjeska,' he pronounced, 'but of course I have nothing to say. You got the document I hope?'

'It is destroyed, my friend. There is nothing for vorry. Tanks to Mr Carberry's so-great careless vith the drug, the society is safe. In Vienna ve meet – yes? Hush! Somevone comes.'

He took up a paper, and commenced to read. Carter lounged there in his usual moody manner for an hour; then strolled up the first flight of stairs. There was not a sign of a soul on the first corridor, though voices and footsteps could be heard above. He rapped softly on the door of number two. Almost immediately it opened.

'Come right in!' bade the voice of Oscar Miles. Carter entered, and the American closed and locked the door. 'I kinder expected you to blow in about now,' he stated. 'Say, Tommy, I've sure got to hand it to you.'

'That sounds complimentary,' murmured Carter, as he threw himself into the armchair at a gesture from the other.

'It's meant to be. Jerry Cousins and Hugh Shannon have nothing on you when it comes to slick work. I guess I feel like raising my hat every time I think of the British Secret Service. I went right along to see Sir Leonard Wallace – he arranged matters pronto when he heard Oscar J's well-known nightingale voice. Gee! The hearty welcome he gave me! It made me feel like a million dollars; then some. Well, I laid my cards plumb on the table, Tommy. He did ditto, and we got right together. He told me to tell you he was delighted with your work here.'

Carter's eyes glowed. Praise from the chief was worth a great deal to him.

'I am going out to ring him up presently,' he announced. 'Modjeska and Grote are leaving for Vienna tonight.'

'Are they? That's mighty interesting. It's more sudden than I expected, too. Jerry Cousins is going with them, so the sooner you give Sir Leonard the tip the better.'

'It won't really be necessary for Cousins to go, though perhaps it will be safer. Modjeska is meeting me in Vienna when I arrive.'

'Now isn't that kind of him? Well, I guess he'll be meeting Sir Leonard and me as well, though he won't know it. We'll be right along.'

'Quite a family party!' smiled Carter. 'It's a pity that both Modjeska and Grote know you by sight, though one knows you as Hawthorne and the other under your own name. You'll have to be careful in case you are recognised.'

'I guess we both will. It's quite likely these guys know Sir Leonard Wallace. But don't you worry any about us, we shan't be our own sweet selves. I never met anyone so slick at disguise as Sir Leonard, and I'm not so dusty.'

Carter glanced round the room. The bedclothes were thrown back in a heap, a breakfast tray, with the remains of the meal, stood on a side table. No attempt had apparently been made to tidy the apartment. Miles noticed the look.

'I'm sorry to receive you in a room like this,' he apologised. 'It ought to have been done while I was in my bath, but the girl hasn't happened along yet.'

'I was wondering if she would come while I am here,' Carter told him. 'It wouldn't do for her to see me.'

'She won't. I'll tell her she'll darn well have to wait, since she didn't come when she should.'

'I think I can guess why. Naturally Carberry's death has caused an upset.'

For a moment Miles stared at him in astonishment.

'Carberry's death!' he repeated wonderingly. 'Say, Tommy, you're not telling me that that Cissie guy has passed over.'

It was Carter's turn to look surprised.

'Didn't you know?' he demanded.

'No; I'm blamed if I did. Gee! That's mighty sudden. How did it happen?'

'An overdose of veronal.'

Miles grunted.

'Well, the manner of his death doesn't surprise me any. That certainly explains the delay in cleaning up this room. The girl said nothing to me when she brought the doings, though, come to think of it, she looked a bit queer. Guess she'd had orders to keep quiet. So the poor little guy took a couple of pills too many, did he? I can't say I want to burst into tears, but I reckon someone will be sorry.'

'I am perfectly certain,' declared Carter in quiet tones, 'that he was forced to kill himself.' Without hesitation, he plunged into an account of the manner in which Julius Carberry had trailed him on the preceding night, his sudden appearance in the Secret Service agent's bedroom soon after Modjeska's arrival and announcement of his purpose. He laid particular stress on the Pole's attempt to hypnotise the man and his own success in baulking it. Afterwards he told of the change in Modjeska's attitude, his suspicions of what was in the latter's mind; went on to tell of his two hours' vigil, the unexpected exit of the Pole from room number thirteen, and his own subsequent investigations. Miles listened to the end without interruption.

'By Heck!' he then ejaculated. 'What a fiend! Guess this Modjeska guy's more dangerous than I thought. Of course Carberry was a darn fool – he simply asked for it. To start with, he hadn't the nerve to make a successful blackmailer, and it looks like he hadn't any common sense either.'

When Carter rose to leave Miles' room, the American asked him if he could risk dining with him somewhere in the West End that evening. Carter was tempted to accept, especially as Modjeska and Grote would be gone by that time, but he knew Sir Leonard Wallace would require him to retain the character under which he was masquerading until the anarchists and their unholy society were destroyed. Wallace was ever thorough. He took no risks where they could be avoided. Carter, therefore, declined with many expressions of regret.

'I get you,' declared Miles, rising from his chair, and donning his spectacles, thus becoming an amiable, harmless-looking individual once again.

'Still it's a pity,' he added. 'I'm meeting Jerry Cousins and having a yarn with the old scout this afternoon. Afterwards Hugh and I had fixed to dine somewhere, and it would have been kinder nice if you could have come right along. Guess we'll have to postpone being ourselves together, Tommy, until this darned gang has been cleaned up good and proper.'

CHAPTER TWELVE

Carter Goes For a Walk

Carter placed some distance between himself and the Canute Hotel before entering a telephone booth. He was quickly put through to Sir Leonard's office when the clerk in charge of the telephone switchboard at Secret Service headquarters knew who was speaking. The chief listened to all he had to say, asking a question now and again, but not otherwise interrupting. At the conclusion of the recital he uttered a few words of approval which caused the young Secret Service man to feel a sense of deep pleasure. As Carter had anticipated, he was directed to continue living the character he had assumed, and to depart for Vienna without appearing at his home or headquarters or holding any communication whatever with friends or colleagues. Sir Leonard assured him that, unless something unforeseen happened, he would keep in constant touch with him from the moment he left London throughout his stay in Austria.

'You may not recognise me or those with me,' he concluded, 'but if accosted make certain that the man speaking to you has an artificial left arm. If, by some chance, I lose touch with you, call in the shop of Lalére and Company, in Vienna, and buy a bottle of scent. It might be as well to supply yourself with a woman friend in case that becomes necessary, Carter.'

The young man smiled to himself.

'I understand, sir,' he returned.

'You'd better use some of that money Modjeska gave you to buy an outfit. It would be the natural thing to do. Good luck!'

Carter went to a cheap shop in the Strand, and bought a ready-made suit, a few shirts and collars, and a somewhat striking felt hat of a dark shade of green. Loaded with his parcels he returned to the Canute Hotel. An Italian selling baked potatoes not far from the door showed a gleam of white teeth in a smile as he offered to sell him some. The Englishman declined. Grote was emerging as he entered, and favoured him with a nod which was obviously intended to be friendly.

'In Vienna,' he muttered, 'you will begin to live,' and passed on.

Taking his purchases up to his room, the Secret Service man packed them, with the exception of the hat, into his battered suitcase. That done he went down to see the proprietor. He found the latter sitting moodily in his office.

'I am leaving here early in the morning,' he announced. 'Can I have breakfast and the bill about eight?'

'What you, too!' quoth the landlord. 'I shouldn't have thought a death in the hotel would have bothered you.'

'It doesn't. I am leaving because I've a chance to get a job in the country.'

'Sez you!' sneered Mr Fellowes. He and his wife were inveterate film-goers. 'Mr Modjeska and Mr Grote go this evening, Mr and Mrs Curzon have already gone, and Mr Hawthorne goes this afternoon. I suppose they've all got a chance of jobs in the country. It's too bad a poor, hard-working hotel proprietor has to suffer, because a fellow who ought to have known better goes and kills himself.'

'You'll get others,' Carter consoled him, though his sullen countenance showed no sympathy. 'Anyhow, you can believe it or not, I'm going because I've got to get a job. What do you think I am – a bloodsucking capitalist?'

'Now then, none of that Bolshie talk, please. If you are after a job, take my advice, young man, and cut all that sort of talk right out. It won't ever do you any good.'

'Can I have breakfast at eight?' snapped Carter.

'Yes, you can.'

'Right – don't forget it.'

The pseudo-communist turned away, and came face-to-face with Miss Veronica Simpson. She wrinkled her nose as though a bad smell had suddenly troubled it; stepped as far from him as she could.

'Mr Fellowes,' he heard her say as he walked along the passage, 'has the body been removed? I feel nervous at going upstairs while—'

'Do you expect it to dance about rattling chains or something?' interrupted the irritable landlord. 'Well, it has been removed, so you can rest easy.'

'It's a pity that young man Carter wasn't taken instead of—'

The Secret Service agent heard no more as he turned into the lounge, but he smiled grimly to himself. Modjeska was the only other occupant, and was spread inelegantly in an armchair, sleeping gently, his hands clasped across his middle. How a man could be so utterly devoid of or deaf to conscience as to be able to slumber placidly when he had recently committed a diabolical crime was more than Carter could fathom. Suddenly he conceived a great distaste of remaining anywhere near the fellow. He left the hotel, and walked to the Strand, where he lunched in one of Slater's establishments. Afterwards he gave himself a half holiday; went to a football match. On returning, he arrived at the door of the Canute at the identical moment that Modjeska and Grote emerged carrying their bags. They nodded to him somewhat curtly as they passed by; he returned the salute as brusquely. He watched them walk towards Waterloo, and wondered why they chose to travel to the continent by way of Southampton and Havre instead of by one of the shorter and more obvious routes. What business could they have in Havre? However, there was no need for him to worry about that, Cousins would be travelling with them.

He lounged about the hotel for the rest of the evening, had dinner, then went out for his usual circuitous stroll. He did not consider such precautions necessary now, but his training had taught him never to take anything for granted. The incident of Julius Carberry was an example, in itself, of the manner in which unforeseen circumstances arise. It was possible, though not probable, that his movements were being watched by some other individual. Accordingly he never allowed himself to be off his guard for a moment as he sauntered along, giving the impression to anybody who might have taken the trouble to observe him that he was a young man simply killing time.

He entered Waterloo Station a few minutes before nine o'clock. On this occasion he had no report to send to Sir Leonard Wallace, but there might be a message for him. There was no sign of Hill or any other of his colleagues in the buffet, but he would wait. He ordered his usual whisky and soda from the girl who had served him the two previous occasions. She recognised him, and showed an inclination to enter into conversation, but he gave her no encouragement. Presently she retired to the background, stood talking with one of the other assistants. From the frequent unfriendly glances the two of them cast in his direction, Carter gathered that she was making disparaging remarks concerning him. Suddenly her face lit up; she hurried to the counter.

'Hullo, sweetheart,' came in Hill's cheery accents. 'How's business tonight?'

'Dull at present,' she returned. 'We've been very busy, but it's eased off. The usual?'

'Please.'

He put his hand in his pocket, drew out a paper and flicked it open. Part of it fell in front of Carter, who immediately glanced down at it. Pencilled in the margin was quite a long message. While pretending to sip his drink, he read it, and gradually surprise, not unmixed with dismay, took possession of him. It ran:

M. and G. did not travel by Havre boat train. C. saw no signs of men answering their descriptions, but travelled Southampton. Enquiries proved no one of their names crossing Havre tonight. Cousins returning London. Chief suspects misled you with object of keeping you under observation to make sure of you. Be on your guard. One of them will probably be watching when you read this. Chief wants you to write out a statement regarding death at hotel for Scotland Yard.

Carter turned away, his back to Hill, thus indicating that he had read the message. The latter twisted the paper over in order that the pencilled words could not be seen by any other person, but pretended to continue to read until the barmaid rallied him about preferring the paper to entering into conversation with her. Then he folded it up, putting it carefully away in an inside pocket of his coat. Shortly afterwards Carter left the buffet. Although not appearing to be taking any particular notice of anything or anybody, he was, nevertheless, very much on the alert. He resolved to satisfy himself that he actually was being watched. Striding along now as though he had some purpose in view, he went down the slope from the station, and made his way to Hungerford Bridge. Halfway across he stopped and, leaning over, stood as though studying the river, but he was searching the darkness for evidence that Modjeska or Grote or both were on his trail. Sure enough a few yards away, seen dimly between two lamps, was the form of a man also engaged apparently in contemplation of the Thames. As the night was bitterly cold, and it was very exposed at that point, it seemed unlikely, thought Carter, that any other man would be standing there leaning over the parapet, unless he were interested in him. The figure suggested Modjeska; it certainly was not that of Grote. Carter decided that he would cause the man to regret deeply, before he went to bed that night, that he had ever undertaken to trail the new recruit to the anarchist society.

Tommy Carter was an extremely hardy young man, and in perfect physical condition. He could bear the biting cold of that March night on the bleak and unsheltered bridge without a good deal of discomfort, but he did not imagine Modjeska could. The Pole was obviously unused to hardship, loved comfort, in fact took remarkably good care of himself. By the time Carter felt that even he had had enough Modjeska must have been in a woeful state. The Secret Service man then proceeded to take him for a fast and lengthy walk. He led the way across Trafalgar Square, up the Haymarket, along Regent Street; then Oxford Street to Selfridge's, where he turned up Orchard Street, continued along Baker Street and made a complete circuit of Regent's Park. Not satisfied with that, he went on through Camden Town until he reached Finsbury Park, stopping when he came to Holloway as though to inspect the grim prison for females, but in reality to give Modjeska time to catch up with him. He had long since ascertained that the man was, in fact, the Pole. He had turned round suddenly at Oxford Circus when waiting for the traffic to pass in order to cross the road. Modjeska had been only a few yards behind him then, and had immediately slunk back, but Carter had seen him, though naturally he gave no sign that he had done so. Going along Park Street towards Camden Town, the Secret Service agent had stolen another glance, to find that Modjeska was lagging badly.

Carter decided that Finsbury Park should be the furthermost point of his little stroll as he gleefully called it to himself. He retraced his steps, therefore, turning so abruptly that the Pole had barely time to slink into the shadows. The Englishman grinned as he noticed him crouching down in a gateway, not more than three yards from him, pretending to do up a bootlace. He walked back at a reduced speed, fearful that his shadower would be unable to keep in touch with him if he continued to hurry. It was his object to walk the Pole to the point when he could walk no longer. He returned to Camden Town; then turned down the Hampstead Road. By Carreras' striking factory he stood as though vastly interested in the black cats. A glance from the corner of his eye showed him Modjeska coming along, reeling from side to side like a drunken man. He was very near breaking point, but Carter felt no pity for him. A little suffering might act as some slight punishment for the fiendish crime the man had committed on the previous night. At the same time he felt a certain measure of respect for him. Scoundrel though he was, he had shown a good deal of grit. Carter led him along Tottenham Court Road, but lost him completely at Cambridge Circus. He waited some minutes in expectation of seeing him appear; then cautiously went back. He found him sitting on the edge of the pavement, surrounded by a crowd. A sympathetic policeman was bending over him. Carter stood on the verge of the gathering, highly amused at some of the remarks he heard.

''E do look ill, pore gentleman, an' 'e didn't want no 'elp neither. Seemed fair upset when the copper come up to 'im after 'e'd fallen over.'

'A furriner by the looks and sound of 'im. Says 'e lost his blinking way and come over queer like.'

'The bobby's gettin' 'im a taxi. They're good sorts on the whole, Chawley. Nasty blokes to run up agin when you've got summat on yer mind like wot is private, but puffect gentlemen when you're took ill.'

A hand plucked Carter's sleeve. He turned hastily and a trifle anxiously. The next moment he was smiling, broadly. Cartright, looking even more lugubrious than usual, was standing by his side.

'What the devil have you been playing at, Tommy?' groaned his colleague. 'I'm aching all over – I'll be stiff for weeks.'

'Do you mean to say—?' commenced Carter, but was unable to proceed further. A great outburst of laughter threatened to break from him, and he felt that, if he tried to say more, he would be unable to control it.

'I mean to say,' grumbled Cartright, 'that I was told by the chief to pick up that ugly bloke if I could. I got on to him at Waterloo, and have been following him ever since. As he has been following you, you know the answer. You've practically killed him, and I'm more shop-soiled than I've ever been in my life before. What was the game, anyway?'

'I've been punishing him for his sins,' spluttered Carter. 'I didn't know I was punishing you also. But, hang it all! You don't mind a little stroll, do you?'

'Stroll! Stroll!' Cartright's feelings were, for a moment, too deep for words. 'Lord! How I cursed you,' he muttered presently. 'I shall always loathe you for this, Tommy, you irresponsible idiot. You'd better hop it. Here's the taxi; I'm going to follow him in another – he's bound to give the constable a wrong address. Cheer ho, you darned torturer! I hope you lie awake all night with excruciating pain.'

'I shouldn't be surprised if Modjeska does,' returned Carter cheerfully. 'So long, James! Mind you tuck him in snug, and kiss him goodnight.'

Standing by the Dominion Theatre, he watched the policeman and another obliging citizen helping Modjeska into the cab. He seemed in a bad way. Carter walked on happily, every few minutes chuckling to himself at the thought that Cartright had, willy-nilly, been compelled to follow whither he had led Modjeska.

'Lord!' he remarked aloud, when nearing the Canute, 'It's the fruitiest joke of the year.'

At the hotel the young man wrote the necessary statement for Scotland Yard regarding his conviction that Julius Carberry had met his death by foul play, giving his reasons for that assumption, and laying particular stress on Ivan Modjeska's previous attempt to hypnotise the man. He also emphasised the fact that less than ten minutes had passed from the time Carberry had left his room until Modjeska had gone to him, and that the Pole was in the blackmailer's apartment for over two hours after that. The declaration finished, he signed it, placed it in an envelope, which he sealed and addressed to Major Brien. The latter would despatch it, with a confidential covering note, to the Commissioner of Police. The latter would take no criminal action until the Secret Service notified him that such would no longer interfere with the investigations of Sir Leonard Wallace and his agents. Carter undressed, put the document away in the pocket of his pyjama jacket, assured himself that the door of the room was locked and bolted, and went to bed. His long walk had not greatly fatigued him; he felt pleasantly tired, as well as delighted at having had the opportunity of scoring off Modjeska, and quickly fell into a dreamless sleep, which lasted until he was called in the morning.

He was in ample time for the boat train at Victoria. As he walked along the platform, clad in his new though somewhat ill-fitting suit, aggressive green felt hat, carrying his overcoat on one arm and battered suitcase in the other hand, he was keenly on the watch for Modjeska and Grote. He saw no signs of them, however, though he expected them to be on the train. Modjeska would be unable to meet him in Vienna otherwise, unless he went by air. On reflection Carter thought that that was probably what the Pole and Grote would do. There was a possibility, of course, and the idea caused the Englishman a good deal of quiet amusement, that Modjeska would not be in a fit condition to travel. In that case, he presumed, Grote would doubtless meet him on his arrival.

He selected a compartment in the first coach and, having deposited his bag in the rack and overcoat on a seat, descended to the platform. Presently a small man with a boyish figure came wandering along selling Sunday papers. He went from compartment to compartment, and appeared to be doing a great trade, for the train was packed. Something about him struck Carter as familiar; then, as he drew nearer, the former knew. It was his colleague, Cousins, one of the most brilliant of Sir Leonard's senior assistants. He played the part of news vendor as though born to it, as in fact, he enacted all the numerous roles he was from time to time called upon to assume. Cousins was an extraordinary fellow in more ways than one. A perfect mine of reliable information, some of it concerning the most abstruse subjects, he rarely found it necessary to consult a book of reference. He was a linguist par excellence. No one knew exactly how many languages he could speak, though Hugh Shannon had computed the number at fifteen. Major Brien on one occasion asked him. Cousins had scratched his head and looked puzzled. 'I can't speak Japanese or Chinese,' had been his reply. In addition he possessed a fluent knowledge of innumerable dialects. He was almost as good a shot with a revolver as Sir Leonard Wallace, could lasso like a cowboy, throw a knife better than most experts, and swim like a fish. There was hardly a spot on the globe with which he was not familiar, and his understanding of the mentality of people of foreign races, even that very intricate organism, the oriental mind, was something to wonder at. He had been a member of the Secret Service as long as Sir Leonard Wallace, graduating from Military Intelligence at about the same time. Cousins' passion was literature – both poetry and prose. He was always ready with a quotation on every conceivable occasion; never seemed at a loss. His age was difficult to calculate. He might have been thirty-five or he might have been sixty. His amazingly wrinkled face gave him the appearance of age, but he possessed the figure of a boy of fourteen and was no taller. His height, as a matter of fact, was exactly five feet. His eyes were a deep brown and exceedingly bright; his mouth seemed to have been fashioned for laughter, it was all humorous curves. When he smiled, which was frequently, his face became a mass of extraordinary little creases, each of which appeared to possess its own private little grin.

Gradually he drew nearer to Carter, and the latter studied him with admiration as well as amusement. The manner in which he expertly produced a newspaper called for, and counted out change; his voice, as he invoked custom, suggested that he had been employed in that manner for years. But in some subtle way he had become a different Cousins. His wrinkles had, by clever make-up, been almost eliminated. His mouth drooped; looked anything but humorous. It is certain that only those who knew him well would recognise him. Carter was assured that people on the train who might see him as himself afterwards would never know him for the same person as the small, youngish-looking man from whom they had bought papers. At last he was abreast of Carter.

'Paper, sir?' he called. '*Observer, Times, Chronicle, Dispatch, News of the World, People.*'

'*News of the World*, please,' decided the other.

Cousins slipped it from his bag with celerity.

'Here you are, sir.' He accepted a shilling and, as he counted out the change, added rapidly in a low voice. 'G and M are on the train in compartment at the rear with blinds down. Sir Leonard and Miles are close to them. I'm flying to Vienna – shall be somewhere about when you arrive. Have you the statement for Scotland Yard?'

'Posted it to Major Brien on my way here. How's Modjeska?'

'Looks a wreck. You put it across him all right. Sir L not too delighted – thinks you may have incurred M's enmity and thereby lose his support. Unreasonable of him, of course, but a man who has been walked almost to death is hardly likely to be reasonable. There you are, sir.'

Cousins passed on. Carter entered his compartment, threw his overcoat on to the rack, and sat down. He felt a trifle perturbed. It had not occurred to him that by making Modjeska follow him over half of London, he may have undone some of the good work he had accomplished. He realised it now, however. Although the Pole would think that Carter had not known he was being followed, his ire would undoubtedly be roused against a man who had caused him so much suffering. When he was fully recovered, he might no longer feel any resentment, but, on the other hand, it was possible he would allow it to linger and turn him against Carter. The latter began to regret his jest – it did not appear in such a humorous light now. Above all, he was chagrined at the fact that, having won the approbation of Sir Leonard Wallace, he had spoilt it by meriting his displeasure.

'Hang you for a fool, Tommy,' he muttered to himself. 'When are you going to learn to be a little less impetuous?'

The train started; was presently tearing on its way through the countryside of Kent – beautiful even at that time of the year – on its non-stop run to Dover. Carter attempted to read his paper, but reflection of the harm his thoughtless desire to score off Modjeska might have done continually obtruded. Before long he gave up attempting to peruse the news; concentrated on finding a way back to Modjeska's esteem, if indeed he had lost it. The laughter and chatter of the other people in the compartment – obviously a family party – were too distracting for deep thought, however, and he was unable to evolve any scheme of promise. His mind, by a natural process of thought, turned to wondering that Grote and Modjeska should have elected to travel by the same train as he. Having informed him that they were crossing to the continent on the previous day, what explanation would they make of their apparent change of plan, for they could hardly expect to escape his observation? Embarking on the boat at Dover, for instance, it would be well nigh impossible. He received his answer shortly after the train had thundered through Maidstone. The door communicating with the corridor was drawn back. Carter looked up, immediately experiencing a thrill of astonishment, which he made no attempt to hide. Standing there, looking down at him with a smile on his coarse features, was Hermann Grote.

'How do you do?' he greeted the Englishman. 'My friend and I are on the train. We shall be glad if you will join us.'

Without a word, Carter rose and followed him.

CHAPTER THIRTEEN

In Vienna

It was a long and not very easy walk along the narrow corridor of the careering, swaying train to the carriage where Modjeska awaited them. Carter glanced into every compartment he passed, but recognised neither Sir Leonard Wallace nor Oscar Miles. They must have disguised themselves exceedingly well, he thought, since he saw no one who even seemed to resemble either. At length, almost at the extreme end of the train, Grote stopped before the door of a first-class smoker the inside of which was hidden from view by drawn blinds. He slid open the door and bade the Englishman enter. Modjeska was lying at full length along one seat, the arms of which had been raised to give him room. He looked worn and more sallow than usual. There was nobody else in the compartment. Carter stood looking down at him for a moment, and was relieved to find that he apparently bore him no ill-will. He even smiled.

'Ah, my friend,' he remarked, 'you are surprised to see us vith you on this train – yes?'

'I am – very,' returned Carter. 'I don't understand.'

'Vell, you soon vill. Sit down, and Mr Grote vill talk. I am too fatigue.'

'Are you ill?' questioned the Englishman, as he sank into a corner seat opposite the Pole.

'I am so veary that I am ill. All my bones hurt me mooch – it is you who do it to me.'

'I! How?'

Carter had no need to pretend surprise – he was astonished at this candour. They were apparently intending to be frank with him. Grote assured himself that the door leading to the corridor was firmly closed; then sat by the Englishman's side.

'In an affair of this nature,' he observed, 'it is necessary to make certain that those we employ, or intend to employ, are beyond suspicion. Mr Modjeska and I were convinced, up to a point, that you were quite reliable, and the very man for the post we intend to recommend shall be offered to you. But we desired to be assured beyond shadow of doubt. You were, therefore, told that we were leaving England last night. Instead of that we went to Waterloo Station and, from there, took a taxicab to a hotel near Victoria. Ivan Modjeska then returned and watched the Canute Hotel. When you emerged he followed you, observing all your movements. Unfortunately for him, you seem to be a young man with an unlimited capacity for walking. He does not walk farther than he can help. You will gather that your long promenade knocked him out. He returned to our hotel last night more dead than alive.'

A mixture of astonishment and resentment was in Carter's face as he glared from one to the other.

'Do you mean to say,' he demanded of Modjeska, 'that you followed me when I went for that stroll last evening?'

'Stroll he call it!' groaned Modjeska. 'I always tink stroll is the English vord meaning little valk.'

'So it is.'

'And you say you vent for a little valk! I am mooch tankful you did not go for a big vone.'

'So you were following me all the time,' grunted Carter. 'You don't think I'll put up with that kind of thing, do you?'

'But surely you understand,' persisted Grote, 'that we were compelled, for the sake of the society, to take precautions? We are now perfectly sure of you.'

'Oh, are you? How am I to know that when we reach Vienna the same thing won't happen again?'

'Because, I tell you, we are now quite certain of you.'

The remark sounded a trifle significant, but Carter made no comment. It probably meant, he reflected, that if the other members of the committee of ten were not quite satisfied of his bona fides no risks would be taken with him. He would either return to England with the full confidence of all or never return at all.

'Oh, well,' he declared, 'I suppose you had your reasons, but I don't like being distrusted. After all, I didn't ask you to make me a member of the society, did I?'

'No, you did not. If you had, we should have had our suspicions aroused at once, for how could you know there was a society or that Ivan Modjeska belonged to it?'

'I mean, I didn't ask when he told me about the society. It was his idea.'

'Exactly, my friend,' nodded Modjeska, 'it vas my idea, and

why? Because I know you vill be of great use. If I did not tink you were to be trust, I vould not have told you anything. The vatching vas only a safeguard. Helas! I now regret mooch I make the so unnecessary observation of you.'

He rubbed his legs tenderly.

'I'm sorry,' apologised Carter, 'but it is your own fault for following me.'

'I admit it. I am mooch punished.'

'You can't be used to walking.'

'I am not. I hate it.'

Carter remained talking to them until the train was approaching Dover. He was gratified and vastly relieved to find that Modjeska bore him no ill-will. Sir Leonard's fears had fortunately not been realised, nevertheless Carter mentally resolved to weigh up all possibilities before taking action in the future. He boarded the cross-channel steamer alone. Being one of the first to reach her decks, he watched the other passengers come aboard. Modjeska walked painfully, leaning on his companion's sympathetic arm, and followed by a porter loaded with their baggage. They sought the warmth and comfort of the saloon. Carter again failed to recognise Sir Leonard Wallace or Miles in the throng, and after the boat had left Dover and was ploughing her way through the heavy sea running in the Straits, he sought shelter on a seat protected from the chilly wind. He had it to himself, most of the other passengers having elected to go below.

Presently a stout, bearded Frenchman, with bushy eyebrows and a large nose glowing red with the cold, appeared and sat by his side. He was muffled in a greatcoat, and wore a dark blue beret.

'Oh, la, la!' he exclaimed. 'It is a ver' bad time – this – to cross ze shannel. I do not lofe him. The feeling of mal-de-mer afflict my stomach. You also suffer, m'sieur?'

'No,' replied Carter. 'I am fortunate that way. It's a pretty beastly crossing though.'

'I've known worse,' came surprisingly in the well-known voice of Sir Leonard Wallace.

'Good Lord!' gasped Carter; turned to stare at his companion, who was holding out his left arm towards him, and withdrawing the glove which covered the hand. One glance was enough to satisfy Carter that it was artificial. 'It's a marvellous disguise, sir.'

'Merely temporary,' returned Sir Leonard. 'This stout Frenchman will leave you at Brussels. We are quite alone here, and Miles is keeping an eye on our friends. I saw you pass along the corridor with Grote, Carter. Has your little escapade of last night had any unfortunate results?'

'No, sir,' his assistant assured him eagerly. 'Grote and Modjeska were perfectly frank with me. They told me that they had pretended to be leaving last night in order to have an opportunity of watching me and thus making certain that I was in reality quite trustworthy.'

'What charming candour!' commented Wallace dryly. 'And Modjeska showed no resentment?'

'On the contrary, he has taken his experience rather well!'

'H'm! I expected him to feel aggrieved. However that's all to the good, but I shouldn't do anything in the future if I were you that is likely to hurt his feelings or those of his confederates, even though you may appear quite innocent.'

'I won't, sir,' murmured Carter humbly. 'You've done brilliantly so far. Don't spoil your work.'

A tall, well-dressed Indian, wearing a beautifully wound turban, walked by at that moment.

'Grote is coming on deck,' he observed, and disappeared.

Carter started slightly. It was hard to realise that he had seen Oscar Miles. Sir Leonard promptly rose to his feet.

'Ah!' he grumbled, 'zis sheep moves too much. I will be ver' glad when he stand still in Ostend.'

He followed in the wake of Miles, staggering with the movement of the boat, and muttering to himself in French. Two or three minutes passed by; then Grote came into view. He did not look very happy, and Carter quickly gathered that the pangs of mal-de-mer were troubling him. He nodded gloomily at the Englishman.

'Are you not feeling the motion?' he asked, standing for a moment in front of the other.

'I like it.'

'Perhaps you are used to it?'

'I've never been on a ship before,' declared Carter, hoping the lie would not be marked up against him in the Judgement Book.

'You're lucky. The sea never does agree with me.'

Hermann Grote vanished somewhat hastily, and the Secret Service agent chuckled softly to himself. He wondered if Modjeska was enjoying the passage any more than his companion. One of the last to leave the steamer at Ostend, he watched the stout Frenchman and the dignified Indian go ashore. They were not together. Grote and Modjeska followed soon afterwards, the former now appearing as shaky as the man he was assisting. A blue-smocked porter took possession of Carter's bag, pointing to his number and yelling a stream of French at him, which the Englishman understood perfectly well, but pretended was gibberish to him. His brand-new passport was duly stamped, and he passed through customs without much delay, finding himself eventually in a second-class compartment of the train, packed in with several men and women of outsized figures. From Brussels to Cologne, however, he was more fortunate; only two others sharing the compartment with him. At Cologne a family party of Germans bound for their home in Passau crowded in, and Carter spent an uncomfortable night attempting to snatch a little sleep squeezed in between a fat frau who snored loudly and a young man, undoubtedly her son, who took after his mother in almost every respect. When they left the train, the Englishman was relieved that only a solitary passenger entered. The Austrian customs officials, as ever, showed great courtesy. They troubled the passengers very little, apologising charmingly for the necessity of disturbing them at all.

Vienna at last! The train ran into the big station bustling with excitement and hurry, noisy with shouts and cries, and the panting of engines like most other large stations, but with an added impression of gaiety that was lacking in the majority. Carter took leave of his travelling companions, who seemed extremely sorry to bid him farewell, and shook hands with great cordiality. He descended to the platform and, refusing the polite offer of a porter to relieve him of his bag, stood waiting for the coming of Modjeska and Grote. A stoutish, happy-looking Tyrolese in his national costume, fair-haired, bronzed face glowing with the health of his beloved mountains, passed slowly by. It was not until he had gone that Carter realised he was Sir Leonard Wallace. A few minutes later a tall, lean man with a monocle, small moustache, and a complexion that suggested years spent under Indian suns came along. Obviously an Englishman, everything about him proclaimed the soldier. Carter had a very good view of him, and it almost gave him a shock when it dawned on him that he was Oscar Julius Miles, the Chief of the USA Secret Service. In some subtle way his features had been altered. It is quite certain that, if Carter had not known he was there, and had not been on the lookout for him, he would not have recognised him. His eyes sought vainly for Cousins, but he knew that somewhere in the vicinity the little man would be waiting and watching.

Modjeska came to him almost blithely. He seemed to have entirely recovered from the effects of his long walk. With him was a man of about his own size and build, dark-visaged, and fierce-moustached. He was introduced as Bresov; bowed elaborately to Carter, who guessed he was a native of Yugoslavia, and took an instant dislike to him.

'Mr Bresov,' announced Modjeska, 'vill look after you for today and tonight. He has very kindly offered to give you a room in the flat he has in Floridsdorf vhile you are in Vienna. He vill also show you mooch that vill delight you.'

'That is nice of him,' acknowledged Carter. 'Does he speak English?'

Bresov smiled, exhibiting two rows of large, ugly teeth.

'English,' he declared in that language, with hardly a trace of accent, 'is to me like my mother tongue. You should have no fears, therefore, that you and I will not understand each other.'

'That's a relief,' sighed the Englishman. 'I feel like a fish out of water over here with all these people – talking a lingo I know nothing about.'

Modjeska beamed.

'Vell your troubles are removed avay. Herr Bresov vill be your – vat you say? Ah! Mouthpiece – he vill be your mouthpiece. I go now with Herr Grote. Tomorrow morning at this time I will come for you.'

He walked away, leaving Carter with Bresov. The latter called a porter and instructed the man to carry Carter's bag to a taxicab. Then, taking the Englishman familiarly by the arm, he led him to the exit. The porter stood holding the door of a cab open and, at a word from his companion, Carter stepped in. A tremendous effort of self-control was required at that moment to prevent his displaying surprised emotion. He had not noticed the driver sitting quietly on the box – that driver was Gerald Cousins! Sir Leonard Wallace, as usual, had left nothing to chance. To a man like Carter, familiar with the ramifications of the Secret Service, it was not difficult to guess how matters had been arranged. The porter who had carried the bag to the taxicab was the same man who had politely solicited Carter's custom on arrival. No doubt he was in the employment of Beust, Sir Leonard's agent in Vienna, who had also arranged to obtain the taxicab for Cousins. The porter had remained in the vicinity in order that he was certain to be engaged by Bresov, had then carried the bag to the right vehicle. The Yugoslav entered after Carter, having given his address to the driver, and they were driven across the city to a great block of modern flats overlooking the Danube near the Floridsdorf Bridge.

Bresov's home consisted of three rooms very well lighted, and airy, and exceedingly clean. Carter was impressed. Bresov had retained the taxi and, after his guest had washed, shaved and generally tidied himself, they drove back to the Stephansplatz. There Cousins and his vehicle were dismissed, and rattled away with the ceaseless double toot on the same note that is so typical of the taxis of Vienna.

Carter was thoroughly tired when eventually they returned to the flat and, after thanking his host with forced enthusiasm for the manner in which he had looked after his entertainment, went off to bed. He took care to place his revolver under his pillow and, with his hand on it, fell fast asleep.

He awoke suddenly in the early hours of the morning; sat up with all his faculties about him and his revolver in his hand. He did not know what had disturbed him, but it seemed to him that there had been a hand under his pillow. He must have dreamt it, of course; there was not a sound in the room, and his ears were keenly attuned to anything out of the ordinary. If there had been anybody besides himself there, he would have heard breathing, however suppressed. No extraneous sounds disturbed the almost deadly silence. It was unfortunate that there was no electric light switch by the bed. There was one by the door, that was all. To reach it he would be compelled to cross the room, but there was no knowing what trap might await such a venture. After sitting perfectly quietly for some minutes, he decided to risk it. With a sudden bound he was out of bed, had darted across the room. His fingers found the switch, and the light blazed on. The little apartment was empty except for himself. He noticed, however, that the door was ajar; he felt quite certain he had closed it firmly before going to bed. Perhaps the latch did not catch very well. He tried it; found it to fasten perfectly. After that he no longer had any doubt. Someone had attempted to enter, and the opening of the door had awakened him. Without bothering to put on his coat or slippers he went out into the tiny hall bent on investigating. The door of Bresov's room was tightly closed, he could hear the sound of regular breathing coming from within. The remainder of the flat revealed no sign of any intruder and the entrance door was fast closed.

Considerably puzzled, Carter returned to his room, took care to shut himself in, and sat on the bed in deep cogitation. The would-be intruder must have been the Slav; it could have been no other. What could he have wanted? Were the anarchists still doubtful of him, and had instructed Bresov to search his belongings? Or had the fellow intended to search on his own account, bent, perhaps, on a little pilfering? Naturally enough Carter was unable to answer the questions he put to himself. He turned out the light, and got into bed, but not to sleep. He spent the rest of the night lying awake, his hand never far from his revolver. In the morning he resolved on complete frankness. Over their coffee with Schlagobers and delightfully hot rolls, he confided in his host. Bresov merely laughed.

'It is the latch of the door that disturbed you,' he returned. 'It does not fasten well. I have slept there, and have also been disturbed. It opens sometimes with the noise like a pistol shot.'

Carter was not convinced, however. He had ascertained that the latch did fasten well. He went out for an hour alone that morning, found his way on to the Floridsdorf Bridge. From that vantage point he had a wonderful view. The early morning sunshine touched the roofs of Vienna, over which towered the spire of St Stephen's Cathedral, with a glint of gold. The Danube itself, for once in a way, was earning the reputation conferred on it by Strauss's immortal waltz. As a rule it is a greyish green touched in places by a suspicion of ochre. That morning it was a genuine blue.

CHAPTER FOURTEEN

The Council of Ten

At noon precisely Ivan Modjeska arrived in a large saloon car into which he invited Carter to step. Bresov was not asked, but was apparently expected to accompany them. He entered the car after the Englishman, and sat himself on one side of him; Modjeska was on the other. Carter, for a moment, experienced the peculiar feeling that he was a prisoner, but smiled to himself at the absurdity of the idea. Modjeska chatted with great animation during the journey, though he volunteered no information regarding their destination. Carter knew Vienna very well, however, and was not at a loss. The car ran through the suburb of Dornbach, on the fringe of the Wiener Wald, and, turning through a wide gateway, the posts of which were surmounted by bronze lions, passed along a well-kept avenue until it reached a large mansion. It stopped before the ornate portico. Modjeska stepped to the ground, inviting Carter to follow. In response to the Pole's ring, the huge entrance door was opened by a wizened little man, who glanced keenly at the Englishman from beneath a pair of remarkably shaggy eyebrows. He muttered something to Modjeska which Carter did not catch, and stood aside to allow them to enter.

The Secret Service agent found himself in a magnificent baroque hall adorned with hundreds of the short, sharply curved horns of the chamois. Whatever it had become, the mansion had obviously once been owned by a great sportsman. Carter could not imagine an anarchist with the sporting instinct, skill in mountaineering and other attributes which mark chamois stalking as one of the most trying and difficult of sports. He was conducted to a small chamber, bare except for a table, two chairs and a rug.

'You vill please remain here,' remarked Modjeska. 'Soon you vill meet the Council of Ten. Refreshment vill be brought to you.'

'How long will it be before the committee interview me?' asked Carter.

For some reason which he could not define, he had begun to feel a trifle uneasy. The sight of Bresov's swarthy face looking at him over Modjeska's shoulder, his lips curled in a sneering smile, did nothing to reassure him.

'You vill not be keep long,' the Pole declared. 'Perhaps half an hour it vill be, not long more.'

He and Bresov departed, closing the door behind them. Carter glanced round the little room; discovered that on the outside of the closed window were strong-looking iron bars. There was nothing very strange in that, he decided. If the house were in reality the headquarters of the anarchist organisation it was only natural that precautions should have been taken to keep out possible intruders. But iron bars, he reflected grimly, were more often placed on windows to keep people in.

Over an hour went by before he received the summons he was expecting. Bresov came for him. He was conducted up a broad flight of polished, uncarpeted stairs leading from the hall to a gallery above adjoining a corridor that, as far as he was able to judge, ran the whole length of the building. This was punctuated at various intervals by numerous closed doors. A little way along they passed the foot of another staircase leading to the second and, as Carter guessed from the view he had obtained of the exterior of the house, the top floor. The guide stopped outside a door not far from this flight, threw it open, and invited the Englishman to enter. The latter promptly obeyed. He found himself in a large, panelled apartment lighted by two great windows that extended almost from floor to ceiling. In the centre was a long, beautifully carved oak table and, at this, were seated several men, their backs to the light. A solitary, high-backed chair was placed on his side of the table, and Carter gathered that it was there for him. He would be facing the light. Two or three other men – fierce-looking scoundrels he thought them – stood close to the door. All regarded him with great interest as he entered. A remarkably small individual, appearing like a child in the great chair in the centre, waved to him to be seated. Carter felt a chill as he looked at him. He was completely bald; there was not a vestige of hair on his head or face. The latter was of the colour, and seemed to be of the texture, of old parchment. His eyes were mere slits beneath drooping eyelids and were rendered more repulsive by the absence of eyebrows. His nose was thin, and resembled the beak of a hawk, his mouth was merely a slash in his face practically devoid of lips. Four men flanked this grotesque-looking creature on both sides, Modjeska sitting at one end of the table. They were a motley collection, appearing, from their physiognomy and colouring, to comprise several races. Carter took the chair indicated and glanced from one to another with a good deal of curiosity. Two or three were, he guessed, natives of Balkan countries, a couple looked like Russians, Modjeska he knew to be a Pole, Grote a German. It was impossible to conjecture the nationality of the man who appeared to be president of this flagitious committee. He might have been anything – he looked as though he had sprung from a grotesque world peopled by creatures the existence of which had been hitherto unsuspected on this globe. Somehow Carter felt glad to note that, as far as he was able to judge, none of the men in that room was of Austrian blood. They were a cruel, ruthless-looking lot, appearing, in fact, to be exactly what they were – assassins. The president commenced to speak.

'Your name is Carter?' he asked in a cracked, metallic kind of voice, but in excellent English.

'It is,' returned the Englishman.

'Can you speak German or French? Some of my colleagues are not acquainted with your tongue.'

'I am afraid I can't.' Something that might have been a sneer flitted momentarily across the otherwise expressionless face, and Carter was puzzled.

'Very well,' went on the hairless man, 'we will continue in English. It is your desire to become a member of our society, is it not so?'

'Yes.'

'Our friend Ivan Modjeska was impressed by the sentiments you expressed in his hearing. It was necessary that we have an agent in London. He thought that you were exactly the right type and, because of that, he cultivated you. Before an appointment of a nature so important could be made the approval of the Council of Ten was essential. You were therefore told that you must appear here. Well here you are, Herr Carter.' The monotonous, harsh voice ceased for a moment. Without knowing exactly why, the Englishman felt his uneasiness return. All eyes were on him, and in none of them was there any friendliness; on the contrary, most of them seemed to contain distinctly inimical expressions. 'Yes, you are here,' went on the spokesman, and now there was a threatening note underlying his utterance, '*and here you will remain.*'

There came some guttural sounds denoting approval from two or three of the others. Carter knew then that he was in a trap, and a feeling of apprehension and deep mortification filled him. How could he possibly have been found out? There did not seem any doubt that he was known to have been playing a part. His face showed nothing of his inner feelings. He looked very much surprised, that was all, having summoned the appropriate expression in the hope that he was mistaken in his supposition; that the president meant he was to be given a job in Vienna.

'What do you mean?' he demanded. 'I thought I was to be appointed agent in England. What can I do here? I do not know the language, and—'

'You can die here,' came the staccato reply. 'That is what you are about to do.'

Carter started to his feet with a well-simulated cry of fear and astonishment.

'Die!' he repeated. 'What do you mean? Why should I die?'

'Because you are a menace. Sit down, Herr Carter, and let us cast aside pretence. You are not a communist, we know it. You are an official of the secret police of Great Britain.'

So they knew everything! But Carter smiled ironically.

'You must be crazy,' he retorted. 'How on earth did you get such mad ideas into your head?' He turned, and looked at Modjeska.

'You know me, Mr Modjeska,' he went on; 'tell him that he is making a fool of himself.'

'Almost you make vone fool of me,' hissed the Pole, his eyes glaring weirdly from behind his pince-nez at the Englishman. 'In time I find out who you are, but bring you vith me and Herr Grote from England for purpose vich our leader, the great Ulyanov, vill tell you.'

'I will tell him very soon,' declared the president. 'First, I think, since he is trying to continue the pretence, we will explain how it was discovered who he really is. Ivan Modjeska,' he continued to Carter, 'is a very clever man in many ways, but he is impetuous – that, I think, is the correct word. He also has unbounded confidence in his ability to judge the characters of other men.' Modjeska grunted a little; shifted in his chair uneasily. 'You, no doubt, acted cleverly, Herr Carter, and you deceived Ivan so well that he even sent a telegraph message to us that he had discovered a most excellent substitute for the dead Luigi Casaroli, and would bring him to us for our approval. He impressed Herr Grote also, but Herr Grote was a little more cautious. He suggested that you should be watched.' He turned to the German who was sitting three places away on his right. 'Herr Grote,' he invited, 'perhaps you will continue the story in order that this young man may be convinced that it is useless for him to continue any longer the deception.'

Grote's little piglike eyes glittered, his loose mouth was twisted into an ugly smile.

'You desired to worm your way into our secrets,' he began, 'and, as we say in America, you nearly got away with it. You will be surprised to know that we first obtained our real suspicions of you from the statement Ivan Modjeska took from that fool Carberry.'

Carter started despite himself. 'Ah! I thought that would astonish you. Towards the end of it he wrote that that afternoon he had entered your room with the purpose of finding evidence against you. He had found nothing of importance, or so he said, except a writing pad. The blotting paper attached was examined with the help of a looking glass – he thought on it he might have found something which would give a clue to your revolutionary activities.' Grote laughed harshly, then went on: 'There was nothing legible, he wrote, except two lines at the very bottom of the blotting paper. They puzzled him, and he only noted them in his statement because he thought they contained a double meaning, and would be understood by the authorities, if his document ever reached their hands. He cut off the narrow strip of the blotting paper on which were the lines in question, with a pair of nail scissors, in order that you would not notice anything wrong. That strip was pinned to his statement. Would you like to know what it contained?'

Carter was feeling deeply chagrined and mortified. His carelessness over the blotting paper had, after all, proved a fatal oversight; the blunder had ruined Sir Leonard Wallace's great scheme. At that moment the young man felt bitterly ashamed – he thought he would have eagerly welcomed the death with which he had been threatened. He continued to control his features, however.

'Yes,' he replied carelessly to Grote's question; 'it would be interesting perhaps.'

'It was most interesting to Ivan Modjeska and me. There were eleven words without beginning or end. Some of the letters were not legible, as is usual on blotting paper, but there were not enough missing to confuse us. The words were: "comes of my conversation with Modjeska tonight, will telephone headquarters in—" You will understand that though they puzzled Julius Carberry they were more easily understood by us. We sat until the very early hours of the morning discussing the matter, and we at last decided to carry out our programme with the only alteration that Modjeska and I would remain to watch you instead of leaving that night for Havre. It occurred to us also, that, if indeed you were a spy, you would not be of the ordinary police, as it was clear to us then that your intention was to accompany us to Vienna in the hope of discovering the headquarters of our organisation. We knew of the existence of the British Secret Service controlled by a man who is world famous – I refer to Sir Leonard Wallace, of course – and we concluded you were of that service. It was when we had reached that inference that Ivan Modjeska had a clever idea. "How is it," he asked, "that Carter knew anything of me to come to this hotel? There can be only one solution: he was at the raid on the house in Shirland Road, and there my name and residence were mentioned, or he found something with them on." I pointed out that a colleague of yours might have obtained the information, and you have been instructed to act on it. Modjeska, in any case, decided to go to Shirland Road, find the ice cream vendor, who lives in the basement of the house, and persuade him to return with him to the Canute Hotel. There was a possibility you see, Herr Carter, that, if you had been present on the night of the raid, he might have seen you and would recognise you again. In that case we would be convinced of your identity.

'At breakfast that morning we were a trifle anxious when the officials arrived to investigate the death of Carberry, I must admit. You English have peculiar ideas about death and there was a possibility that, through perhaps a revulsion of feeling, you would make a statement which, though it could not have proved anything against Ivan Modjeska, might have had consequences which would have been – shall I say? – distinctly awkward. However, you said nothing. Your attitude, in fact, almost persuaded us that, after all, you were what you pretended to be, but the two blotted lines were too damning evidence against you. Modjeska had a word or two with you to find out how you reacted to that very convenient death of the fool Carberry, who chose to try blackmail on a man with the most dangerous gift in the world—'

Suddenly Carter swung round in his seat and pointed an accusing finger at the Pole.

'You murdered him in about the foulest manner possible, Ivan Modjeska,' he cried. 'Whether I am a communist or not, I'll take care you hang for it one day.'

'Ve vill see,' sneered the other. 'You forget that soon you vill be dead vith yourself. And first,' he added leaning forward and speaking with intense ferocity, 'it vill give me mooch great pleasure to make you suffer for that you make me valk all over London.'

'Enough!' snapped Ulyanov. 'We shall talk of that afterwards. It is satisfactory to find that Herr Carter is not altogether devoid of feeling. The little experiment we will presently try on him will thus be more likely to succeed. Continue, Herr Grote!'

'While Modjeska went to fetch the ice cream man from Shirland Road,' went on the German to Carter, 'I kept watch on you. I saw you go into room number two, although you were obviously intent on escaping observation. I found out that it was occupied by a person called Wilmer Peregrine Huckleberry Hawthorne. I had no recollection of having seen him about the hotel, but I resolved to discover what he was like. Fortunately for my purpose room number five directly opposite his was unoccupied. I entered, and waited there with my eye to the keyhole. I saw you leave number two. A little while afterwards he came out, and I recognised him to be Oscar Miles, the Chief of the United States Secret Service. I knew then that we were in grave danger. When Modjeska returned I told him, and we agreed that for the sake of the society, apart from all other considerations, we must get you and him as well, if possible, out of England and into our power. Ivan had brought back the ice cream vendor with him – in the wintertime he sells cooked potatoes. Did you not see an Italian selling potatoes from his little oven on wheels when you re-entered the hotel, Herr Carter?'

An almost imperceptible gasp escaped from the Secret Service man. He remembered now that he had noticed the Italian, when he had returned from telephoning Sir Leonard Wallace. Grote's ugly smile was again on his face. 'Ah! I see you did,' he commented, 'but you did not know why he was really there. You found Ivan Modjeska apparently asleep in the lounge and went out again. Modjeska had not been asleep. Directly you had gone he joined me – I was waiting outside – and we went to the Italian who told us he had seen you with the other officers on the night of the raid. Now you know why it is useless for you to keep up any longer the pretence of being a fiery communist. You are a member of the British Secret Service, Herr Carter.'

The young man shrugged his shoulders coolly. He realised only too well that it would be absurd, after what he had been told, to endeavour to carry on the masquerade. A feeling of intense bitterness pervaded his whole being. By a stupid little oversight he had destroyed all he had accomplished. Not only that, but he had been the innocent means of disclosing the real identity of the so-called Wilmer Hawthorne to the man he was after; had probably exposed the American and Sir Leonard Wallace to the gravest danger, as well as throwing the royal families of the world back into the fiendish, gaping jaws of the doom from which they were on the verge of escaping. He felt terribly downhearted. Not for one moment did he trouble about the peril in which he himself stood.

'You have heard,' came the rasping voice of Ulyanov, 'what Herr Grote has told you. Do you still wish to join the society as the London agent?'

'What do you intend to do?' asked Carter ignoring the mocking question.

'You were brought out here because we wish to know exactly how much information about us and our activities is possessed by the British authorities.'

'Oh!' commented the Englishman, 'and do you expect to obtain that information from me?'

The bald head was inclined slightly.

'We are wise enough to realise that our organisation is in a certain amount of peril, and our plans in danger of being frustrated. It was thought, when it became known who you are, that you had wormed your way into Ivan Modjeska's confidence for the purpose of discovering the headquarters of the society. That being so you would undoubtedly be followed by colleagues of yours, perhaps by the great Sir Leonard Wallace himself. If we could get this Wallace into our power, we felt that by exterminating him we should effectually remove the danger that at present hangs over our heads.'

'You're an optimist,' observed Carter. 'The British Secret Service never admits itself beaten even when everything is against it. The death of Sir Leonard Wallace would not remove your danger, rather it would enhance it, for not one man of the department would rest until your filthy society was destroyed completely and for ever.'

'But if the brain is wrecked, what is the use of the body? Listen, young man! I have a personal animus against Sir Leonard Wallace. I have never met him, but he has baulked the designs of my country on innumerable occasions. His death would be acclaimed in Russia alone as a great, a wonderful event. I would almost view the destruction of the society with equanimity, if I could see this Wallace lying dead.'

The volume of hatred which was concentrated into his harsh voice as he spoke then was appalling. Carter felt a chill run through him.

The man on Ulyanov's right, a big fellow, with a fair beard and shifty, restless eyes plucked him by the sleeve; whispered into his ear. Impatiently he snatched his arm away.

'You are a fool, Dimitrinhov,' he snapped in Russian. 'What does it matter what I tell him? He will die directly he has been made to speak.'

Carter eyed the bearded man with fresh interest. So that was Dimitrinhov, of whom he had heard quite a lot. He was reputed to be a very active member, with a genius for organisation. A man farther along the table observed that he thought there had been enough talk, that it was time for action. Ulyanov turned on him with all the deadly ferocity of a poisonous snake. The man, whose name appeared to be Kharkov and whom Carter guessed to be a Bulgarian, shrank back in his seat before the withering blast of vituperation that poured from the lipless mouth of his leader. There were no further interruptions. Ulyanov turned his veiled gaze again upon the Englishman.

'When you arrived in Vienna yesterday,' he grated, 'the station was full of our agents on the lookout for people who might be trailing you. A number of suspicious-looking individuals have been followed since and –' his voice fell to a horrible kind of purr '– one has proved to be the American, Miles. Herr Grote, who knows him well, has seen him and identified him, even though he is disguised, I am told, very cleverly. Another, who it is nearly certain must be a colleague of yours, is attired in Tyrolese costume. Tell me, Herr Carter, is he by a fortunate chance, your chief, Sir Leonard Wallace?'

Carter laughed at him.

'You must think I am a fool,' he returned. 'Do you think I would tell you if he were? And how do you expect me to recognise any man by a description which merely states that he is attired in Tyrolese costume?'

'You know who followed you,' snarled Ulyanov, 'and I will know also. Tell me,' he suddenly shouted, his metallic voice reverberating throughout the room; 'how many are there, and is one of them Wallace? Answer!'

Carter simply smiled. He coolly took a cigarette case from his pocket, selected a cigarette and put it into his mouth.

'Have you a match?' he asked.

There were gasps of astonishment from the others at such effrontery. Ulyanov uttered a sound that was beast-like and, throwing himself forward, flung out a talon-like hand in a fierce attempt to snatch the case from the Englishman. But he could not reach, and the latter returned it to his pocket.

'Ah!' he murmured lightly. 'I have a box. I thought I had left it in the little room below.'

He calmly lit his cigarette; puffed a cloud of smoke in Ulyanov's direction. Two or three of the other members of the Council of Ten had risen, the men who had been grouped by the door had advanced until they were close behind Carter. They only awaited a signal from their leader to precipitate themselves on the defiant Englishman, but the hairless atrocity in the presidential chair did not give it. Instead he waved his men back.

'So you dare to scorn my demand,' he said in much quieter tones. 'You are foolish, young man, utterly foolish. You will regret it greatly before very long.'

'I suppose you are going to tell me that if I divulge all you wish to know you will spare my life.'

'No, your life cannot be spared. You know too much – you must die. But there are different degrees of dying. There are some deaths that can be so prolonged and horrible, Herr Carter, that the victims weep and pray for death.'

'That is the kind you reserve for me, I presume?'

'Exactly. I will give you another chance. Tell me all that is known about the society of which I am president, and how information was obtained which enabled your people to raid the house in London in which Pestalozzi, Haeckel, Zanazaryk and Casaroli were killed. If you do that you will merely be shot. An easy death and a speedy one, you will agree. If you refuse –' his voice became strident again '– you will die by slow degrees, and every minute will be to you a year of exquisite agony.'

'The picture you draw is charming – delightfully artistic in fact,' commented Carter, showing not the least sign of agitation, though his blood felt as though it had frozen within him. 'Well here is my answer—'

'Just one moment. I do not ask you again to tell me who have followed you to Vienna. Soon they will be in my power as you are, for it is certain they have traced you here. There are between twenty and thirty men waiting for them, who have instructions to let them get well into the grounds before capturing them.' At that item of news Carter began to feel that all hope had gone; his heart seemed to become leaden. 'All I wish you to tell me is what the British Secret Service know of our activities, and what evidence is possessed against us.'

'Go to the devil!' snapped Carter, and this time blew a cloud of tobacco smoke direct into Ulyanov's face.

CHAPTER FIFTEEN

Three in a Cellar

The Englishman's action was the signal for another advance on him, while shouts of opprobrium were hurled at him from all sides. The vulturine creature in the great chair stilled the clamour however. With an almost imperceptible motion of one of his talon-like fingers he beckoned to Modjeska. The Pole rose from his seat and approached along Carter's side of the table until he was standing close to the latter.

'I think,' observed Ulyanov, 'that you will not have much difficulty in making him speak. Is it not so, Ivan Modjeska?'

The Pole's queer eyes glittered.

'Let me have entire silence,' he urged in German, 'otherwise it is not possible.'

He removed his pince-nez, and Carter knew that an attempt was about to be made to hypnotise him. He shivered involuntarily, not because of any fear he felt of the powers of Modjeska, but at the memory of another occasion, when he had almost succumbed to an attempt to hypnotise him into killing one of his own colleagues. He had nothing but disdain for the flabby-faced Pole; had no doubt whatever that he would be able to withstand the influence of the man's uncanny eyes.

'What are you going to do?' he asked in a conversational voice.

'You vill see very soon,' was the blunt reply.

'If you think you are going to hypnotise me, you can save yourself the trouble of trying. Did you ever hear of a joker called Prilukoff, my dear Ivan?'

Modjeska gave a violent start; Ulyanov leant forward until his chin was almost touching the table.

'What do you know of Dr Prilukoff?' he rasped.

Others awaited Carter's answer as though deeply interested. His mention of the name seemed to have caused a minor sensation.

'All I know about him is that he was reputed to be the finest hypnotist in the world, and was used by the Bolshies to further some of their infernal plots. He paid a visit to England – I don't know whether it was his first; it was certainly his last – during which he attempted to hypnotise me.'

'Did he not succeed?' snapped Ulyanov.

'Not quite. He died with a bullet in his heart.'

'And Sir Leonard Wallace shot him,' came with an oath in his own language from Dimitrinhov.

'Oh, so you know that, do you?'

'All Russia knows it. Dr Prilukoff had a great reputation in Russia. His death is one of the most important items in the heavy score the Soviet have against the name of Wallace.'

'We are waiting, Ivan Modjeska,' barked the metallic voice of Ulyanov.

'Yes; get on with your stuff,' added Carter, throwing down his cigarette end, and crushing it under his heel, 'but be careful, Modjeska, that history does not repeat itself. It would be strange if you also died – with a bullet through your heart.'

The Pole was looking worried. He realised that the calm young Englishman was not going to be an easy subject. He placed himself in front of Carter and commenced his fight to obtain possession of the latter's senses in order to make him give the information that was of such vital importance to him and his companions. His uncanny eyes began to bore piercingly into those of Carter and, with a shudder, the young man's mind went back to those terribly distorted eyes of Prilukoff's which had seemed to grow larger, more evil, every moment until the whole world to the Secret Service agent had appeared nothing but merciless, devouring, all-enveloping eyes. Modjeska could not gain an influence over him of that nature. From the start Carter knew he would be able to resist the mesmeric powers of the Polish anarchist. He exerted all the strength of his will, and a feeling of triumph surged through him as he saw beads of perspiration beginning to break out on the other's brow. He was defeating him, and defeating him badly. Grimly, despairingly now, Modjeska put all that was in him into the unholy effort to obtain control over his obstinate subject's mind. The other men in the room watched fascinated, hardly daring to breathe. Almost half an hour went by; then suddenly, with a great groan, the Pole collapsed against the table, his eyes closed. He was beaten. Carter gave a great laugh of triumph.

As though it were a signal, every man at the table rose, with the sole exception of Ulyanov. Bresov and the others behind the Englishman darted forward. Thinking that his last moment was at hand he sprang to his feet, determined to sell his life dearly. He adroitly eluded two who made a grab at him, and slipped quickly to an untenanted corner of the room, drawing his revolver as he did so. There, with his back to the wall, he faced them, with the light of battle in his eyes, a smile on his lips.

'The first man who moves a finger will die,' he cried in German. 'There are fourteen of you – I am one. Who will be the first to go west?'

There was a dead silence; everyone stood immobile glaring at him. Then Ulyanov's harsh cracked voice bit into the silence. He was in a convulsion of passion horrible to behold.

'Fool! Fool!' he screamed at Bresov in Russian. 'He stayed in your rooms last night. How is it you allowed him to retain a weapon?'

'I went to search him for one,' returned Bresov sullenly, 'when I thought him asleep, but he heard me, and I was forced to give up the attempt.'

'Coward! Pig! Dolt! Swine!' shouted Ulyanov foaming at the mouth. 'For your wretched weakness you will pay dearly. Are you all cowards?' he went on to the others. 'You are many; he is one. Why don't you take him?'

'Why don't you?' asked Carter coolly, speaking in the same language. 'Listen to me, Ulyanov, I will shoot down any of you who stir as I would a mad dog. There should be no mercy for assassins, and I will extend none. I wonder that I don't shoot you now and as many of those at the table with you. It would rid creation of the leaders of as foul an organisation as the world has ever seen.'

'Bah!' snarled Ulyanov striving to control himself. 'You crow like a proud cockerel for a little time, but how long can you stand there defying us? You would be better advised to submit quietly. The longer you hold out, the worse will be your fate. I swear it!'

'Swear away,' encouraged Carter cheerfully, 'at present I have the whip-hand, and I intend to keep it.'

Nevertheless, despite his defiance, he was wondering how long he would be able to hold them off. There were no doors or windows at that side of the room. In order to get out he would have to drive those barring his way before him at the point of his revolver. Then there would be the danger that he would be attacked from behind by the men at his end of the table. It would be well-nigh impossible to keep both those in front and on his right at bay at the same time. Modjeska had recovered himself by that time, and turned to glare at the Englishman, hatred, bestial, naked, looking from his eyes. Whether it was that his intense loathing of the man whom he had failed so signally to bring under the influence of his will made him blind to his danger, or that the string of epithets flung at him by the enraged Ulyanov drove him to desperation, it would be hard to tell. It certainly will never be known. Suddenly, with an animal-like scream of fury he launched himself at Carter. The latter sidestepped.

'Back!' he roared, 'Or I shoot.'

But Modjeska threw himself at him again. He fired. A little spurt of blood appeared from the Pole's right eye. He stopped dead as though he had plunged against a wall. For a perceptible fraction of a second he remained upright; then crashed to the floor. Carter looked down at him.

'History does repeat itself,' he murmured grimly. 'He won't hypnotise any more poor devils into killing themselves.'

Unfortunately for him, however, he had not noticed that, while he was engaged with Modjeska, Bresov had darted silently and swiftly along close to the wall; had thus succeeded in getting behind him. His first notification of the Yugoslav's presence came when he felt his revolver arm grappled. Desperately he fought to free himself, but, with yells of triumph, the other three threw themselves on him. Even then he continued fiercely to resist. He succeeded with a tremendous effort in forcing the revolver round and firing again. One of the men clapped his hands to his abdomen and, groaning with agony, staggered from the fight. Others now joined in, and Carter went down beneath the weight of numbers. His weapon was torn from his grasp; he was practically battered into unconsciousness. They treated him unmercifully, kicking and belabouring with brutal cruelty. At length they desisted, dragged him to the chair he had hitherto occupied, and pushed him into it. Ulyanov was very pleased with the turn affairs had taken, though he showed little of his delight in his expressionless, parchment-like face.

'You are sorry now that you were so foolish?' he questioned, his voice grating on Carter's throbbing brain.

The Englishman raised his bruised and battered face; eyed him defiantly.

'Not a bit,' he declared stubbornly. 'I have at least succeeded in ridding the world of one fiend, possibly two. Your turn and the turn of those with you will come, Ulyanov.'

'Take him below,' ordered the president. 'See that he is well guarded. Later we will see what we can do to loosen his tongue. I guarantee we will succeed where poor Modjeska failed.'

Cruel laughs from several of the others followed his words. Carter was dragged to his feet; hauled brutally across the room. His captors and he had almost reached the door when it was flung open. Into the apartment entered half a dozen men. In their midst, their arms tied behind their backs, their clothes torn, their faces bruised and covered with blood, were Sir Leonard Wallace and Oscar Miles. Both were still in the costumes and make-up, or as much as was left, that Carter had noticed at the railway station. Sir Leonard's eyes met those of his young assistant; he heard the groan which involuntarily broke from Carter as he observed that his beloved chief and Miles had been captured. Wallace actually smiled.

'I thought the game was up when we heard those shots, Carter,' he observed casually. 'Bad luck.'

'I guess this is some mess,' commented Miles.

The fresh captives were pushed towards the table, the nine remaining members of the Council of Ten making no attempt to disguise their feelings of triumph and delight. Ulyanov ordered Bresov to bring back Carter. He was placed in line with Sir Leonard and Miles. This was the last straw, he thought. He had hoped against hope that the two would have escaped capture. Now he was plunged into the very depths of despair and remorse. Hermann Grote was leaning forward, his coarse face alight with exultation, his little eyes fixed on Miles with gloating satisfaction.

'Miles!' he breathed. 'Mr Oscar Miles! This is indeed a very great pleasure.'

'I guess I'm glad you feel that way,' was the cool retort. 'I shall reciprocate the sentiment when I see your dead body. It will look a lot more wholesome than it does now.'

'So you are Herr Miles, the Chief of the United States Secret Service,' rasped Ulyanov in English. 'We are indeed fortunate to have this opportunity of entertaining a man so important and so famous.'

Miles stared at him.

'Gee!' he exclaimed. 'What kind of abortion are you? Barnum and Bailey would feel mighty sore if they had known they had missed you.' He turned to Wallace. 'Say, did you ever see a freak like it?' he asked.

Sir Leonard shook his head.

'I don't think I have,' he returned quietly. 'Perhaps it has dropped from Mars.'

'It sure wasn't Venus,' murmured Miles.

Ulyanov broke into another of his uncontrollable fits of rage, his metallic voice grating out a string of profane imprecations. Wallace listened to him with an air of disgust, Miles as though mildly interested. At length the flow ceased.

'My!' commented the American in tones of admiration. 'It goes well when it's wound up, but it runs down too quickly. I guess I know where it was manufactured – it's marked Czechoslovakia, isn't it, Tommy?'

'No,' returned Carter, grinning despite his aches and his depression. 'It's Russian, rejoices in the name of Ulyanov, and is the president of the Council of Ten – nine now, Modjeska's dead. I shot him.'

'Now, isn't that too bad? Poor Ivan! You've kinder spoilt his ideas, Tommy.'

'Be quiet!' snapped Ulyanov.

'What you say goes, I guess,' murmured the irrepressible American.

'Who are you?' demanded the monstrosity in the great chair, pointing one of his claw-like fingers at Sir Leonard.

'A friend I brought right along to say "how do",' put in Miles.

'Did I not tell you to be quiet? If you speak again I will have you gagged.'

'I will talk outer my turn. It's a bad habit I've got into.'

Ulyanov snarled an order to Bresov, who promptly clamped a handkerchief into Miles' mouth and tied it behind his head. The American winked at Carter. He actually seemed to be enjoying himself.

'I ask once more,' Ulyanov snarled at Wallace: 'Who are you?'

'Is my name of any importance?' drawled Sir Leonard.

'Yes; it is of great importance. You are an Englishman or an American – of that I am certain. But I must know your name and why you are here.'

The Englishman merely smiled at him, whereupon he ordered them all to be searched.

Rough hands at once commenced feeling among the clothing of the three prisoners, which became dishevelled and torn with unnecessary brutality. Everything in their pockets was abstracted and placed in three heaps on the table. Sir Leonard's picturesque coat was split down the back, the left sleeve ripped from the shoulder to the elbow. The shirt beneath was torn open, exposing the arm beneath. Then came a great cry from Dimitrinhov. He was on his feet, staring at Wallace, his finger pointing at the Englishman's arm.

'Look!' he shouted. 'It is artificial!'

'What of it?' demanded Ulyanov.

'Did you not know, comrade?' came from the other in a tone of great triumph. 'The Chief of the English Secret Service has a false arm. How often have we in Russia been told of that, when ordered to watch for him! This man is Wallace, I tell you – Sir Leonard Wallace!'

The rest were on their feet now, talking excitedly to each other, their eyes fixed exultantly, malignantly, on the Englishman. For the first time Ulyanov rose from his chair. Standing there he looked more repulsive than ever. He was a dwarf, not more than four feet six inches in height. His thin figure, like that of a boy, allied to the grotesque head that had the appearance of vast age, gave the onlookers a sense of deep horror.

'So,' he observed, speaking in German which apparently was a language all his colleagues understood, and in a low, gloating voice that was even more jarring to the senses than his previous sharp utterance, 'you are the man I have wished to meet for several years. You are Sir Leonard Wallace!'

'Do you think,' returned Sir Leonard calmly, in the same tongue, 'that there is only one man in this world with an artificial left arm?'

'Do you deny you are Wallace?'

The Englishman shrugged his shoulders.

'What if I am?' he asked.

'Only this, Sir Leonard Wallace, that to see you die will be the most enjoyable experience of my life. I am pledged to the extermination of royalty, but it will be far greater pleasure to exterminate you.'

'You do not seem to like me,' murmured Sir Leonard, casually.

'Like you!' came from the other with vehemence. 'There is hardly a man in Russia, or a woman either, who would not delight in your death. You have, time after time, interfered in her plans, upset her schemes, ruined designs that would have altered the map of the world. What you and these others know about the society of which I am president, I have yet to discover. I also will know how you found out anything about us. But now that you are on the verge of death, I will tell you this. This society is pledged to destroy completely and for ever all those who call themselves royal or have any pretence of royalty. Branches have been formed in many parts of the world, but the central committee – the Council of Ten – before which you now stand has, at present, its headquarters here—'

'And its funk-hole in Constantinople,' put in Sir Leonard calmly.

There came gasps of dismayed surprise from several of the anarchists standing behind the table. Ulyanov's eyelids were raised slightly, and Wallace caught a glimpse of a pair of colourless, merciless eyes that seemed entirely alien to a human being.

'You appear to possess more information than I conceived,' rasped Ulyanov. 'It will be a delight, later on, to draw it from you and from your friends item by item, bit by bit. At present I just satisfy myself by telling you that, in endeavouring to dig into the secrets of what you thought was just an anarchist organisation, you have fallen at last into the hands of a far greater power. When death is approaching and your agony is compelling you to weep and pray for it to come quickly, your torture will be increased by the bitter knowledge that that power at last encompassed your ruin. My pleasure in your dissolution will be infinitely sweetened by the reflection that mine are the honour and privilege to act as its agent, mine the honour and privilege to avenge all the indignities you have put upon my country.'

'I have met some pretty horrible specimens of humanity during my career,' observed Sir Leonard quietly, 'but I doubt if I have ever come across one who was quite such a monstrosity as well as a monster. Gentlemen,' he added, looking up and down the line of anarchists, 'I congratulate you on achieving the seemingly impossible. You must have gone to hell itself and dug from the very depths this freak you have elected as your leader.'

Ulyanov again burst into one of his appalling fits of rage, but it was suddenly ended by a harsh, cackling chuckle.

'I will be the last to laugh,' he snarled viciously. 'For the insult you will but suffer the more, Sir Leonard Wallace.' He turned over the articles on the table with his claw-like fingers. 'Nothing of interest here,' he muttered, 'but, of course, there would not be.'

He raised his eyes to Bresov. 'Take them all below to the cellar, and guard them as you would guard your own life, my Bresov. If they attempt to escape or do not conduct themselves in a submissive manner, you have my permission to teach them a lesson. Be careful, however, that in your enthusiasm for the cause you do not kill any of them.' He turned his gaze on Sir Leonard. 'Farewell for the present, Mr Interfering Englishman, who will interfere no more; it would be advisable if you and your friends spent your last few hours in making up your minds to supply the Council with the information it needs.'

'I don't think you will need much information where you will shortly be going,' returned Wallace. 'You will obtain your knowledge first hand – not from the press, so to speak. Your relative, Satan, will see to that.'

Three men took rough hold of him; hustled him after Miles, who was already being led away. Carter's hands were tightly tied behind his back, and Bresov, with the assistance of another man, was about to conduct him out of the room, when he nodded towards the wounded man who was writhing on the floor in agony, pitiful groans every now and then breaking between his lips from between his ashen lips.

'Aren't you going to do something for that poor fellow?' he asked the committee. 'Surely there is enough humanity in some of you to influence you to attend to one of your own men? Not a soul has taken the slightest notice of him since he was shot.'

'Oh, ho!' sneered Ulyanov. 'Comrade Carter tries to kill a man; then is sorry because he is in pain. Oh, what a tender heart!' His voice changed to its rasping, grating quality. 'You can leave us to attend to our own affairs, Herr Carter. We do not need your assistance or your advice. Go!'

Carter was pushed unceremoniously from the room. Wallace and Miles – the handkerchief had been removed from the latter's mouth – were awaiting him with their escort in the corridor outside. The three of them were marched down the stairs across the hall below and along another corridor. Presently they came to a great oak door which groaned ponderously when pulled open by Bresov. Beyond it was a flight of stone steps; then a short passage, terminating in another powerful door. This also was opened. Sir Leonard had barely time to glimpse dimly more stone steps when he was violently pushed from behind. Unable to save himself he fell headlong down, coming to rest at the bottom bruised and badly shaken. Miles and Carter received the same treatment, crashing down on top of him, and knocking all the breath out of his body. Brutal laughter reached their ears from above; then they heard the door slam, the key being turned in the lock, the sound of rusty bolts being driven into their sockets. The American and Carter rolled themselves weakly off the body of Sir Leonard. It was as black as pitch down there and, their hands being tied behind their back, they were unable to feel round them and thus obtain some idea of their surroundings.

'Gee! The brutes!' muttered Miles. 'When we get out of this, I'll teach them to manhandle white men.'

'When we get out!' echoed Carter. 'Our chances don't look over bright.'

'No; I guess you're right. We certainly seem to have struck a whole heap of trouble.' There was silence for some moments. 'Say,' added Miles suddenly, 'it kinder looks like Sir Leonard's been knocked unconscious.'

'I'm all right,' gasped the voice of Wallace, 'at least I soon will be. But you two hurtling down on top of me hardly conduced to further enjoyment of a fall down about a dozen stone steps.' They were very contrite, and he laughed. 'Anyone would imagine you did it on purpose, to hear you talk. I judge that we're in a lower cellar right underground, so our chances of getting out are not too rosy.'

Miles struggled to his feet and commenced to explore, walking cautiously in order to avoid obstacles and other pitfalls. Carter followed his example after a while; then Sir Leonard painfully rose and joined in. By keeping against the wall he was able to judge fairly well the extent of the place. He rubbed against bottle rack after bottle rack, but whether they were empty or full he was unable to tell; then he encountered several large casks, after which he collided with the bare wall, and was forced to make a turn at right angles. Some yards farther on he met Miles.

'I guess this is some cellar,' commented the latter. 'I imagine it extends right under the house.'

'Probably,' agreed Wallace. 'There's one comfort; we shall not suffocate. Though the air is heavy and unwholesome, there's plenty to last the three of us for many hours. Where are you, Carter?'

'Here, sir,' called a voice with a note of triumph in it. 'I've found a barrel with one of the hoops torn away, and there's a beautifully jagged edge to the broken end.'

'Attaboy!' cried Miles. 'That sounds like it ought to remove this darn cord from our wrists. We're coming right along. Sing your signature tune or something, so we won't lose the direction.'

CHAPTER SIXTEEN

'Wallace is Dead!'

Carter obliged by whistling and, treading cautiously, they reached him without trouble. Sitting on the ground, with his back to the barrel, he was engaged in industriously rubbing the cord binding his wrists up and down against the broken end of the hoop. The manoeuvre was not proving very successful, for the metal was loose and gave to the movement. However, when this was explained to Miles, he planted his foot on it, thus steadying it. Thereafter Carter progressed satisfactorily until he had cut through two or three strands. He had little difficulty then in removing the rest of the cord. After rubbing his wrists vigorously to restore the circulation, for they had been bound together very tightly, he set to work to release the hands of his companions. Before long they were all free. Miles massaged his own hands, while Carter performed a like service to Sir Leonard's one. They sat on the barrel and discussed the position.

'I always had a feeling,' pronounced Wallace, 'that Modjeska's conviction that you would be a useful man to have in the association, Carter, was a little bit suspicious. It happened too quickly. But I don't understand how he and Grote knew who you really were, and am not altogether clear as to the reason they brought you here.'

'Modjeska did accept me without hesitation, sir,' replied Carter frankly, though a feeling of hot shame surged through him. 'Grote was more cautious, but Modjeska had such amazing belief in his own infallible judgement that everything would have been all right, if I had not made an awful bloomer.'

'You!' exclaimed Sir Leonard. 'How?'

Carter then proceeded to tell how suspicion against him had been roused in the minds of Modjeska and Grote; their subsequent investigations and the result. He practically repeated word for word the story that Hermann Grote had told him so triumphantly in the presence of Ulyanov and the other members of the Council of Ten. Bitterness at the revelation of the consequences of his one little slip had burnt the words into his brain as though they had been composed of letters of fire. His companions listened quietly but with deep sympathy. They instinctively knew what he was feeling. At the conclusion Sir Leonard's hand sought for and found his shoulder to which he imparted a friendly, reassuring little squeeze.

'Bad luck, old chap,' he observed. 'You have done brilliantly all through and, if your one mistake has had undeserved consequences, it can't be helped. None of us is infallible you know. We have a sporting chance of winning through yet.'

'What do you mean, sir?' asked Carter eagerly.

'Although I thought your part in the affair might come unstuck, I must confess that I felt pretty certain Miles and I would get through unsuspected. Nevertheless, we took precautions. Cousins, as you know, is here. We followed the car in which you came; he followed us. After we had watched you turn into the avenue leading up to this house, we found a convenient shelter free from observation. I told him to watch and not venture into the grounds then. If we were not back in two hours he was to investigate. The two hours have long since gone by, and you can be certain he is on the job. Possibly he heard the shots, and will have been warned that something has gone wrong. If only one of us could get out or get hold of him and send him to the legation with your story we'd have a force along here. Miles had an interview with his minister and I saw Sir Richard Lindsay. They are aware of everything that has transpired up to the date of your arrival in Vienna. Directly they are in possession of the necessary evidence concerning the existence of the anarchist headquarters in Vienna they will go to the Minister of the Interior and put the facts before him.'

Carter began to feel renewed hope.

'God!' he muttered fervently. 'I hope Jerry escapes capture. I don't think they are likely to suspect that there are any more of us about, but they've got the wind up badly. Their anxiety concerns how much is known in England about them and their society.'

'Yes; I guess that raid on the house in Shirland Road,' put in Miles, 'and the death of every darn one of their men, was a nasty blow.'

'And they mean to torture our information out of us,' observed Sir Leonard grimly; 'if they can. They are fairly certain, I presume, that we are the only people who know where their headquarters are, and their future actions will depend upon what they can squeeze out of us.'

Carter told them of Modjeska's attempt to hypnotise him into divulging the required information, and the manner in which he had subsequently shot the Pole and, for a short period, obtained the upper hand. There was silence for a considerable time after that. Sir Leonard's brain was busy scheming, while the others were also doing their utmost to think of a way out of their predicament. They had long since ascertained that there was only one exit from the cellar; that was locked, bolted and, no doubt, guarded. All hope seemed to rest on Cousins, but how would he be able to discover where they were? Even if he succeeded, thought Carter, he would then have the impossible task of opening the way to freedom in the face of a guard of at least eight men.

'Everything depends on Cousins,' declared Wallace at last. 'If the opportunity comes to one or all of us, we must not attempt to escape. These fellows must be exterminated completely. There is probably in this house all the evidence we require, to wipe out every branch. If we escaped, they would simply disappear with all vital documents, and set up their headquarters elsewhere. If we could get word to Cousins we could make a shift to hold out till he came back with the police. The devil is to get in touch with him.'

'You can be pretty sure,' observed Miles, 'that he is doing his darndest to get in touch with us right now. How do you propose we should defend this cellar, Sir Leonard? Our hands are free, but we haven't any weapons.'

'Shall I search for something that might prove useful, sir?' asked Carter.

'No,' decided Wallace; 'we don't want to provide ourselves with weapons at all. We can't expect to defend this cellar; we should not have a dog's chance, nor could we have any hope of communicating with Cousins from here. When they come for us, we must go out meekly with our hands still apparently tied behind us. We shall walk with our guards until I find a likely spot; then I'll give the word, we'll turn on them, and take up our stand. Where, of course, depends upon circumstances. Not knowing the house makes it more difficult, but it can't be helped. Get hold of weapons from the men you bowl over if possible, but don't take any more risk than necessary.'

The scheme was discussed at length, and everything considered that might make for success. At the best it would be a desperate venture; nothing but a forlorn hope, but it held out a faint hazard, and to men of their gallant stock the smallest chance was quite sufficient to fill them with a quiet optimism.

Carter wound a cord round his chief's wrists, knotting it loosely. He performed the same service for Miles; then, winding his own in a loop and knotting the ends, held it behind his back, and pushed his hands through. He had hardly concluded when they heard the sound of bolts being withdrawn from their sockets.

'Ah!' came in a hiss from Sir Leonard. 'Get ready!'

The door above opened; the light of a torch suddenly lit up the great cellar.

'Where is the man Wallace?' called the voice of Bresov.

'Impudent swine!' growled Carter.

'I am here,' returned Sir Leonard. 'What do you want?'

'Come up! You are required. Only you – not the others.'

'Gee! That's torn up our scheme,' muttered Miles in dismay.

'They'll probably send me back,' whispered Wallace hastily. 'If not I'll have to act for myself and trust to luck. You two do the same; cheer ho!'

'Good luck, sir,' murmured Carter, a wish that was echoed by the American.

'Hurry!' shouted Bresov. 'If I have to come for you, you will be sorry.'

'I kinder think you'd be a darn sight sorrier,' growled Miles beneath his breath.

'I'm coming,' declared Sir Leonard.

He made his way to the steps, and ascended. As he reached the top, Bresov made a vicious grab at his arm, and pushed him among the waiting men, all of whom were armed with either revolvers or rifles. Bresov's cruel grip did not hurt the Englishman; in fact he did not feel it. The Slav had hold of the artificial arm! He quickly realised that fact himself apparently, for he let go with a muttered imprecation. Bending down he glanced at the cord round the prisoner's wrists. Wallace's lips came together in a grim line. Would the fellow notice that it was loose? A grunt of satisfaction reassured him. An order was given and he was marched away. The door was closed, again locked and bolted. Miles and Carter were left to their own reflections which, it must be admitted, were very much the reverse from pleasant.

Time passed slowly by, and they gave up talking. Each had been attempting to cheer the other, at the same time realising that he was vainly trying to deceive himself. In both their hearts was fear – not for themselves, but for the man they both admired and to whom Miles as well as Carter was devoted. Neither possessed a watch, it having been taken from him with his other possessions. The waiting, in consequence, was more agonising than it perhaps would have otherwise been. All the time their ears were keenly alert to catch any sound that might indicate that Sir Leonard was returning. Carter was miserably calculating that quite two hours must have gone by since the chief had been taken away, when, at last, came the noise of the bolts being withdrawn. Involuntary sighs of relief broke from both. In their hearts the dreadful feeling would persist that Sir Leonard had long since been murdered, but anything was better than the awful suspense which they had undergone. Like drowning men clinging to straws they clung to the faint hope that there was possibly some other explanation of his absence; that he was still in fact alive. The door opened, a ray of light was thrown into the cellar.

'Down you go!' ordered a voice in German, 'and do not try any tricks, my bold bandits.'

'Gosh!' cried Miles. 'It's Jerry, by heck!'

He darted to the foot of the steps, followed closely by the delighted Carter.

'"Then they for sudden joy did weep",' quoted Cousins. 'So you are here? Splendid! I guessed you were, when I saw this ruffianly-looking trio on guard above.' He was driving down the steps before him three men, the revolver he held in his right hand apparently being quite sufficient to cow them into subjection, though two of them carried rifles and one an automatic pistol. They could see little of him as there was no light behind him, but the torch he held in his left hand enabled him to see them. 'Your hands are tied, so you can't relieve these gentry of their arms. Never mind.'

'Can't we?' retorted Miles. He released his hands, and strode forward.

'Ah!' came from Cousins approvingly. '"Nor did you think it folly to keep your great pretences veil'd till when they needs must show themselves". It would be a good idea if you used the cord you have discarded to lash their wrists together.'

Miles and Carter quickly disarmed the three men, who submitted as though dazed by the turn events had taken. Their hands were then bound behind their backs, two handkerchiefs taken from them being used on the third for that purpose. Carter and Miles, mindful of the manner in which their own wrists had been pinioned, were not too considerate.

'Isn't Sir Leonard with you?' demanded Cousins.

'He was taken away about two hours ago,' Miles told him. 'I guess things look mighty bad, Jerry.'

There was a pregnant silence for two or three seconds, then:

'You mean—?' began the little Secret Service man slowly, and stopped.

'I reckon it looks that way.'

They heard the sharp, hissing sound as Cousins' breath was drawn in between clenched teeth.

'Come on,' he snapped. 'We'll find him. And if anything has happened to him, may God have mercy on the swine who did it – I shan't.'

'It can't be done,' remarked Carter. 'Whatever has taken place, Mr Miles and I must stay here, unless, of course you have a force with you and the place is surrounded.'

'No; I'm alone. But I don't understand.'

'Tommy is right,' put in Miles. 'Sir Leonard's explicit orders were that none of us were to escape even if the opportunity came. The Council of Ten which controls the organisation is right here. If we got away, they'd flit pronto with all the evidence. Sir Leonard planned to exterminate the lot and find out the addresses of every darn branch in the world, so that the whole society could be wiped out. That depended almost entirely upon whether we were able to get in touch with you. Get me?'

'Yes; but what about him? He might still be alive, and there might be a chance of saving him, while the longer we—'

'I know that, Jerry. Darn it, man! Don't you think I feel mighty bad about it too? But we can't allow personal feelings to influence us, even though it might mean—Hell! I just can't say it.'

'You're right of course,' came from Cousins, accompanied by a sound that was unmistakably a groan. 'What are the orders?'

'Do you think you'll have any difficulty in getting away?'

'It wasn't easy to get in. When I'd been on watch outside the gates for the period stipulated by the chief, and you and he had not returned, I commenced to investigate as ordered. The grounds are guarded, and the terraces round the house patrolled, and it was a devil of a job to get through. Still here I am. I came through the kitchens, and caught sight of these three beauties standing guard over a locked and bolted door. That made me feel pretty sure you were on the other side of it, for I guessed that you must have been taken, of course. Anyhow I couldn't have got by the three without being spotted, so I decided to capture them.' He spoke quite casually, as though what he had done was nothing out of the ordinary. 'They were far too surprised to resist. I made them open the door. A little persuasion was all that was necessary. Not finding you in the upper cellar I came here.'

'Well, Tommy will put you wise to the facts,' observed Miles, 'and I'll keep watch while he's doing it. Then, when you've got all the dope, Jerry, you'll have to go straight to the British Legation and hand the goods to Sir Richard Lindsay. He'll get in touch with the USA ambassador, and the two of them will go to the authorities. But for the Lord's sake urge on them the necessity of acting immediately.'

'Trust me for that. Come on, Tommy, let me have what Oscar calls the dope.'

While Carter gave him the information that it would be necessary for the two ambassadors to have to place before the

Austrian authorities, Miles went up the steps into the upper cellar and, standing behind the first door, listened for sounds that would indicate the approach of anyone. He had armed himself with one of the rifles taken from the prisoners. Nearly a quarter of an hour went by before Cousins joined him; Carter had been careful to tell his colleague everything, including the names he had heard of the members of the Council of Ten.

'If it's possible to get away, I'll do it,' said Cousins confidently, 'but don't be too cocksure, in case of accidents – the grounds are alive with men. All being well I ought to be back about eleven – it's eight now.'

'Gee! Is it as late as that? I guess Sir Leonard's been gone about three and a half to four hours. It don't look too good, does it? Good luck, Jerry!'

The two men gripped hands.

'Thanks, Oscar,' murmured Cousins adding fervently, 'I pray to God you find him – alive. But don't throw your own life away! Remember little Joan!'

'I guess I'm remembering her quite a lot,' returned Miles, a little huskily.

'I've left my torch with Carter, also cigarettes.' Cousins opened the door by inches, his revolver held ready in hand. Slowly he put his head through the aperture, remained in that attitude for several seconds, then looked back. 'OK, I think,' he whispered.

He slipped through, the door closed gently behind him. Miles returned to the lower cellar to find Carter sitting on the steps, a rifle across his knee, the automatic in his right hand, torch in his left. He was smoking a cigarette with evident enjoyment. Cowering before him, full in the rays of the lamp, were the three anarchists.

'Pity there's no electric light in this place,' commented Miles. 'Never mind, it can't be helped. Keep that torch and your gun focused on these guys, Tommy; I'm going to see what they have in their pockets.' He searched the men carefully, but found nothing on them of any significance, apart from long keen-edged knives in sheaths, and ammunition for the rifles, which he confiscated. All other articles were replaced in their pockets. He accepted the cigarette Carter lit and handed to him, but, after half a dozen grateful puffs, threw it down and stamped on it. 'I guess this is where we get busy,' he declared. 'You and I have got to search for Sir Leonard Wallace right now.'

At once Carter was on his feet.

'I was about to suggest that,' he observed. 'What about these fellows?'

'We'll leave them here.'

'Of course, but what if we're discovered?'

'Well, I guess we'll give the devils who attack us a whole lot to keep them occupied. So long as we're all known to be in the house, the precious Council is not likely to beat it.'

'They will, if these blighters tell them about another man.'

'I'll take darn good care they don't. You leave it to me.' He turned to the captives; added in German: 'We are going to leave you here. Nobody will hear you if you shout, so that sort of thing will only be a waste of breath. You had better make up your minds to answer all questions that are asked you later on frankly and without hesitation. Truthfulness is a virtue which you will find may possibly make things easier for you. Go on, Tommy!' he added in English. 'I'll follow. Keep the light on them.' Carter ascended the stairs backwards. He had reached the top when one of the men, with a snarl of mad rage, threw himself forward at the American.

The latter promptly swung his rifle by the barrel bringing the butt down with a sickening thud on the other's head. The man went to the ground like a log of wood. 'I guess it gave me a whole heap of pleasure to do that,' commented Miles. 'It was a sweet blow, and it sure has relieved my feelings some. Darn fool! What did he think he could do with his hands tied behind his back? Any more?' he asked in German of the other two. They crouched back, muttering to themselves. 'No offers. Well, I guess I'll beat it.'

He retreated up the steps and, with Carter, passed through to the upper cellar. The door was closed, barred and locked. Miles extracted the ponderous key; put it in his pocket. Hastening to the upper door, they opened it and looked carefully out. There was nobody about, the American gave the word and they stepped through. The same process was repeated, the door being bolted and locked, the American pocketing the key.

'It will puzzle them some to force that massive shebang,' he whispered, 'if the notion occurs to them, which isn't likely. Now which way do we turn?'

'Right, I think.'

'OK. Lead on, Tommy – wait a moment though; take one of these toothpicks. It may come in useful.'

He handed his companion one of the knives. The two of them then crept quietly out into a passage. There was not a soul in sight, not a sound. They might have been in a deserted building except that the lights indicated otherwise. With Carter still leading the way, they arrived presently in the great entrance hall. There they stood hidden behind a curtain for several minutes. In crossing the hall and ascending the stairs, they would be compelled to take a tremendous risk for, if anyone appeared, they would be seen at once, no cover being available and the whole being brilliantly illuminated. However, fortune seemed to be with them. When, having assured themselves that there was nobody about, they essayed the hazardous task, they succeeded in crossing the hall and ascending the stairs without incident. At the top they became, if possible, even more cautious. Miles stood looking up and down the corridor, while Carter moved stealthily along until he stood outside the door in which the Council of Ten had interviewed him and his companions. Bending down he listened with his ear to the keyhole, but heard nothing. After some minutes he returned to the American, and they stood discussing the situation in whispers. Carter then went back to the door and grasping the handle, gently turned it. A few seconds later he had insinuated his head into the room. It was lighted but was empty. A dark stain on the carpet at one end indicated where the man he had wounded had lain – he wondered if he had since died; hoped that he had not. Carter was averse to killing people, no matter how villainous they might be.

Having discovered that the only room they knew anything about was unoccupied, the two men went from door to door along the corridor listening at the keyholes for sounds that would indicate the presence of a person or persons within. They opened one or two with extreme caution, found the rooms comfortably, even elegantly, furnished, but all lacking traces of present occupation. They returned at length to the foot of the staircase leading to the upper storey of the house.

'I've a kinder notion,' whispered Miles, 'that we're more likely to find Sir Leonard up topsides than down here. Let's explore!'

The second staircase, a good deal narrower and less ornate than the first, took a sudden turn halfway up, which perhaps was a fortunate circumstance for them. Miles, who was ahead, was turning the corner, when he suddenly stopped, his hand sweeping out to stay Carter. At the top, standing in a listening attitude, he had seen a man – one of the members of the Council. They stood where they were, hardly daring to breathe until they heard footsteps receding in the distance. Then Miles cautiously looked round the corner, stood still a few moments, and beckoned Carter on. They reached the top, and found themselves on another corridor almost identical with the one below, but here several doors stood open. The murmur of voices could be heard, a faint crackling sound came from a room at the extreme end.

'What in heck's that?' muttered Miles.

'Wireless,' returned Carter pithily.

'Gee! So it is. Come on, Tommy, we'll go and find out whom they radio to. I've got an idea that, if we have to hold out anywhere, the radio room will be a darn sight better than most places. Maybe we'll be able to persuade the guy inside to tell us what's happened to Sir Leonard. Step softly now!'

Expecting every moment to hear a cry of alarm, Carter followed in the wake of the American. Fortunately in the direction they were taking only one door stood open. They passed it successfully, though a man stood inside the room, bending over a table on which was spread something that looked like a map. However, his back was partially turned to them, and they escaped notice. They had almost reached the wireless room, when there came the shout they had been more or less anticipating. Swinging round, they beheld Dimitrinhov. He was pulling frantically at his pocket, in an effort to draw forth a revolver which appeared to have caught momentarily in the lining. Without hesitation Miles raised his rifle and fired, as several other men appeared in the corridor. The door of the room from which the crackling sound had come was flung open. A thin, saturnine-looking Russian called Ilyich looked out. Before he could quite gather what was wrong, Carter had sprung on him, and with a perfectly delivered blow to the chin with the butt of his rifle, had sent him crashing back into the room. The Englishman followed him in, Miles being but a fraction of a second behind his companion. As the latter slammed the door and turned the key in the lock, several of the men in the corridor fired, their bullets being heard to strike the exterior. Miles chuckled, as he pushed two powerful-looking bolts into place.

'Steel-lined and padded,' he pronounced; drawing Carter's attention to the walls. 'We're as snug here as bugs in a rug and a darn sight safer. There aren't even any windows. Tommy, I guess this place was constructed for us.'

'I'm not so sure,' returned the Englishman. 'Cast your eyes aloft!'

The room was almost circular, the wall practically all the way round being padded, air being admitted through two ventilators high up. The floor was of polished stone. The only furniture consisted of a large table against and shaped to the wall, covered with the most up-to-date wireless apparatus, two chairs and a small square of carpet. In the ceiling overhead was a closed trapdoor, and flush with it, a ladder, which could be raised and lowered by means of a rope on a pulley. Miles looked up.

'It looks as though I spoke a little too soon,' he murmured. 'Guess I'd better go up and investigate.'

He undid the rope from its staple in the wall, and let down the ladder. A minute later he had climbed up, had unfastened the small bolt that secured the trapdoor and, lifting it, was looking out. In the meantime Carter had turned his attention to the man stretched out on the floor. The violent blow he had received had temporarily stunned him, but he groaned and opened his eyes as the Englishman looked down at him. Immediately his face became distorted into an expression of utter hatred.

'Where is Sir Leonard Wallace?' demanded Carter in the fellow's own language.

A malignant smile curved the lips of Ilyich, his eyes shone with evil triumph.

'The great, the distinguished, the famous Wallace,' he proclaimed, 'is dead.'

CHAPTER SEVENTEEN

A Desperate Defence

Carter stared at him for a moment, his brain dazed with horror. Then, giving a great cry, he bent down and, gripping Ilyich by the shoulders, hauled him to his feet. Thrusting the Russian against the wall, he grasped him by the throat and, despite the man's frantic struggles, began to squeeze with all the strength of his fingers, the while he swung his head to and fro. For the time being Carter was crazed by the horror with which Ilyich's statement had filled him. A firm touch on his shoulder brought him to himself when the Russian was very close to death. With a convulsive shudder he released the fellow, who collapsed unconscious to the floor. Carter turned to find Miles' deep-set, grey eyes fixed on him.

'Say, Tommy,' enquired the American, 'what's got you? You're as white as a sheet, and you look like you had seen a ghost.'

Carter, with a great effort, pulled himself together.

'If you hadn't interfered,' he shot out between his clenched teeth,

'I'd have killed the swine. He told me Sir Leonard is – is dead.'

'God!' ejaculated Miles, and his face became suddenly as white as the other's. He stood staring down at the prone man, in his eyes unutterable things. 'Maybe he lied to you,' he murmured presently.

Carter shook his head wearily.

'Why should he lie?' he asked.

'A guy of his rotten breed would be only too eager to hurt if he saw a chance.'

'But he was just gloating with evil triumph, I – I'm terribly, horribly, afraid he told me the truth.'

'If he has,' ground out the American, 'I shall regret to my dying day that I interfered when you had almost strangled him. When he recovers we'll get the truth out of him, if we have to cut it out. At the present moment we must look to the defence of this place. That trapdoor sure is a bit of a snag. It bolts and locks OK, but they could bash it through without much difficulty from above. The roof is flat and there are a couple of mighty tall wireless masts up there. The guy who selected this dump for the headquarters of the gang is sure crooked, but he has his dome screwed on the right way. The house is in a kinder dip surrounded by trees. Nobody outside the estate could possibly see those wireless masts.' He picked up his rifle. 'I'm going up to keep watch. I guess they'll attack that way. There's a moon, though, and, as we're right at the extreme end of the house, they can only come from one direction. Things look pretty good to me. If only—'

He did not conclude the sentence, but Carter knew of what he was thinking. Miles stood on the ladder, and arranged the trapdoor in such a manner as to give him just enough space to see along the roof and to move the barrel of his rifle freely.

'Now, if you'll switch off the light, Tommy,' he called down, 'it'll be fine.'

Carter promptly did as he was bidden. He then went down on his knees by the side of the unconscious Ilyich, and searched him. There was a revolver, a knife and a crowd of other articles, including what felt like several letters. He did not trouble to examine the latter then, though it would have been possible to have done so, as he had Cousins' flash lamp with him, but there were other more important matters to be considered at that moment. Ilyich must be trussed up in order that he could not interfere when he recovered consciousness, as he would be likely to do if Miles' and Carter's attention was engaged elsewhere. He wore a belt and with this Carter proceeded scientifically and securely to strap his legs. The Englishman then removed the long, flowing necktie he wore and, rolling him over on to his face, tied his wrists tightly together. To make assurance doubly sure he took the laces from his shoes and tied them over the necktie.

'I guess they're not in any hurry to attack,' Miles remarked in regretful tones after some time had passed.

'Perhaps there's no other way on to the roof,' returned Carter.

'Sure there must be. There's a room at the other end or what looks like a room. There is bound to be a way up to that anyhow. I'll start to feel lonesome, if they don't come soon. My left leg is beginning to—' He suddenly broke off and fired, the concussion sounding terrific in that confined space. 'Got him! Right in the bean, too, I think,' he cried exultantly. 'Gee! That was a near thing. He was crawling along in the shadows, and I didn't see him at first.'

'Any room for me up there?' asked Carter.

'House full notice is up, Tommy. There's not even standing room. You can relieve me when I've no ammunition left. Has that guy down there come to his senses yet?'

'No; but I've trussed him up.'

'Bully for you. Whoopee! Here are two of 'em!' Two shots in rapid succession rang out. 'One's bit the dust; the other's hopping back on one leg. By heck! This is the nearest I've come to sniping since the War. They're congregated up there somewhere. Can you hear them singing their national anthem?'

Faintly to Carter's ears came cries of rage and exacerbation. After that there was a lull, during which Miles kept up a kind of running commentary concerning the shadowy movements he could perceive at the other end of the roof, punctuated by contemptuous references to the anarchists' lack of courage. Suddenly the wireless started into life. Carter had not put on the earphones, which he had noticed on the table; nevertheless, he could hear the continuous tap, tap of a station somewhere calling in Morse. He now adjusted the instrument on his head; wondered if the repeated signal was intended for that house. There was a pencil among Ilyich's belongings, and he picked it up. He did not know, of course, whether there was any private symbol of acceptance but, taking a chance, he sought for and found the keyboard, and he tapped out the usual Morse indication that he was listening in. There was a slight pause; then came a rapid series of letters which he wrote down on a small pad he felt before him. It was awkward writing in the dark, and he was afraid he was mixing the letters up rather hopelessly. However, the message was not a long one. Suddenly it ceased. He indicated that he had received it. As he removed the earphones he heard Miles' interested voice.

'Who's on the air, Tommy? Not your sweetie, is it?'

'Haven't one,' returned Carter shortly.

He took Cousins' torch from his pocket and, shading the light in order to prevent it shining on Miles, strove to read the jumble of letters on the pad. At first he could not make head or tail of them. Then suddenly a word in Russian became plain to him. After that he quickly made out the whole message. It was not in code, as he had expected it to be, but was a very innocent-sounding communication in straightforward Russian without any indication of the name of the sender. He translated it to read:

Excellent suggestion.
Send him to Moscow by air.

For a few moments he stared at it; then a flood of light burst on him. He shouted out in delight.

'Oscar!' he cried – it was the first time he had accepted the American's invitation to call him by his Christian name – 'I believe Sir Leonard is alive after all. Listen to this!'

He repeated the message. His shout of joy was almost immediately echoed by the American.

'Gosh!' he exclaimed. 'I think you're right, Tommy. They've notified the Moscow lot that they have Sir Leonard here, and suggested sending him along to be dealt with there. Say! I sure feel like a million dollars again now. I can just confine myself to sheer enjoyment up here. Gee! That's the best news I've heard in years. He's alive, and that's all that darn well matters. He'll go to Moscow like hell. Guess they've another think coming.'

'Don't be too sure!' returned Carter somewhat dubiously. 'We may be wrong.'

'I don't think so. It fits in too pat. Sorry I'll have to break off the little chat, Tommy. There's something doing, and it looks like I'll be getting busy.'

A minute or two went by in silence; then he fired twice in rapid succession. Almost immediately came the staccato rat-tat-tat of a machine gun. He ducked his head below the opening. It was as well he did so, for Carter heard several dull thuds suggestive of bullets coming through, and hitting the wall high up. A hush followed which seemed somehow very deadly after that clatter. Carter felt that it presaged another perhaps even more murderous outbreak.

'Gosh!' exclaimed Miles. 'They're mighty well equipped. But that ought to bring the whole of Dornbach buzzing round wanting to be put wise to all this friendly chatter.'

'They must think they're fairly safe,' commented Carter, 'otherwise they would hardly risk using a machine gun. Dornbach is a good way away, and this estate is large.'

'Still the sound of a machine gun would carry a considerable distance on a night like this. Perhaps the good people of Dornbach and neighbourhood think it's a woodpecker on the job.'

Carter laughed at the conceit.

'I hope Cousins got through safely,' he observed.

Miles echoed that hope with great fervour.

'Maybe we helped,' he added. 'It is likely all the men have been withdrawn from the grounds to help in getting us. Say, Tommy, I guess I'd like to know where Sir Leonard is.'

'So should I,' returned the Englishman ruefully. 'If we could only find him and get him in here, I shouldn't have a worry in the world. I wonder—'

'You wonder what?' queried Miles suspiciously.

'I was wondering if I could get out of this room, without being spotted, and go on the prowl. There doesn't seem to be anyone outside the door as far as I can tell. They're probably all on the roof.'

At that moment came another terrific outburst of machine-gun fire. Miles slid to the bottom of the ladder.

'I guess I'll be more comfortable down here while that goes on,' he remarked. 'I don't kinder fancy being hit by a ricochet.'

The fusillade stopped. Miles promptly and quickly returned to his post. Almost at once he was firing regularly and methodically. The anarchists were making a determined attack. At his shout Carter squeezed up beside him. Quite a number of forms were silhouetted in the moonlight, some having approached very close. The Englishman, armed with the automatic, fired rapidly into them. Two or three fell; the rest hesitated; then broke, and dashed back into safety.

'That was warm while it lasted,' murmured Miles. 'They expected that we'd have been driven below by the machine-gun fire and that they would have been able to rush us before we got into position again, but they weren't quick enough.'

'You mean you were too quick for them.'

'Well, I guess it's all the same thing. Matters are getting serious though, Tommy. I've used nearly all my ammunition. How many rounds have you?'

'Twelve for the rifle – nothing extra for the automatic; there are about four rounds left in it now. Ilyich's revolver is fully loaded.'

'H'm! We can't hold out for ever on that.'

'All the more reason why I should go on the prowl. I might not only find Sir Leonard, but obtain an additional supply of ammunition as well.'

'You might also, and probably would, lose your life,' returned Miles dryly.

'I suppose there would be no chance of that if you went?' observed Carter sarcastically.

The American chuckled.

'OK,' he agreed. 'Go to it! But for the love of Mike don't take unnecessary risks. I kinder like you, Tommy, and I should hate like hell to be present at your funeral later on. Hand me that other rifle and the doings.'

Carter did as he was directed, giving him also the automatic.

'I'll retain the revolver,' he decided. 'What are they up to now? Can you see anything?'

'Nope. They seem to have gone to earth like a lot of bunnies. You'd better wait until they get busy again before you start exploring; they may be back in the corridor.'

A long period laden with anxiety went by, and the anarchists showed no signs of resuming hostilities.

Carter relieved Miles on the ladder after some time.

'By Jove!' he exclaimed in tones of admiration. 'You've certainly done some execution, my bloodthirsty comrade. Ten dead – at least I presume they've departed this life; they look extremely dead to me and, in addition, I suppose we can calculate that half a dozen have been wounded.'

'Did you say ten?' demanded Miles.

'Yes. I've just counted them.'

'Gosh! Let me have a peep!' He squeezed himself alongside Carter and glanced along the roof. 'Tommy,' he declared after a couple of seconds' silence, 'those aren't all casualties. I only counted six bodies. The other four are playing possum for some reason or other. Watch carefully! They're probably crawling towards us.'

They stood straining their eyes, but it was some time before they were able to distinguish between the dead bodies and the live men, so gradually did the latter move.

'It's a cute idea,' commented Carter when they had satisfied themselves. 'There are so many shadows, and it's so difficult to see with any degree of accuracy that we might have been deceived.'

'We should have been if you hadn't counted them. I'd already done my counting and wouldn't have noticed that the bag had been added to. I reckon it's time we notified them that we're wise to their little scheme. You take that one on the right, Tommy; I'll get the guy near the edge.'

They looked along the sights of their rifles.

'Ugh!' shuddered Carter. 'It's like deliberate murder, shooting a crawling man who's presenting his cranium as a target. Even a child couldn't miss.'

'It isn't nice!' agreed Miles. 'Still I guess, if we come all over kind-hearted and let them approach they'll kill us, and I'd sure hate to be dead.'

He fired as he finished speaking, Carter pulling his trigger immediately afterwards. They knew they had not, could not have missed, but there was nothing to indicate that they had done other than shoot two bodies already dead. Carter thought he noticed his man twitch, but could not be certain. The other two had not risen to their feet in terror or dismay at the fate of their companions and made a dash for safety. Probably they were hoping they had not been seen and were lying still.

'Oh! Lord!' grunted Carter. 'Shall we have to shoot them too? I thought that, as soon as their comrades had been spotted and killed, they would have sought safety.'

'Queer that you and I should feel like this about croaking these guys,' commented Miles. 'When you come to think that they are assassins bent on—Look out!' he shouted.

At the same time he pushed Carter so sharply that he fell down the ladder, landing rather forcibly on the floor at the bottom. Miles followed as there came a terrific concussion that literally shook the place. Directly afterwards there was another not quite so violent, but equally awesome. The American rose to his feet as soon as the effects of the second had worn off and darted back up the steps. The shock had shaken the trapdoor into place, but he forced it up and looked out. He saw the two men running towards the other end of the roof, but did not fire. It occurred to him that perhaps it would be as well to let the enemy think they had killed him and Carter for the present. A few yards in front of him was a gaping hole in the roof, another a little farther away. Debris and dust in a fine shower were still falling. The ladder shook and he felt Carter climbing to his side.

'What on earth happened?' demanded the latter.

'Bombs!' was the terse rejoinder. 'I saw one of the guys swinging his arm. Sorry I had to be so rough.'

Carter whistled softly. He surveyed the two cavities and whistled again.

'They seem determined to get us, even if they wreck the house,' he observed. 'I wonder why.'

'I guess they think we're highly dangerous customers to be at large.'

'Even so, why go to all this trouble? If they guarded the roof and the door they would know we couldn't get away. Throwing bombs seems to me to be a trifle unnecessary.'

'It's a darn good job those two hadn't the courage to stand up and throw their toys. Lying down cramped their style I guess, which was lucky for us. If one of those cute little balls had come down here, we'd be looking a bit of a mess now.'

'I wonder if they've forgotten Ilyich is here.'

'Maybe, or perhaps they reckon he's dead. They'll be right along presently to find out if we're in the same condition.'

His surmise proved correct. A few minutes passed by; then they made out the forms of three men approaching cautiously along the roof.

'There seem to be a lot of men,' mused Carter. 'Far more than I thought. What are we to do with these three? Shoot them?'

'I guess we'll let them get close; then hold them up. Maybe we'll be able to make terms with them for the return of Sir Leonard in exchange for Ilyich.'

'I can't see them agreeing to that.'

'Why not? They'll still think they have us in their power.'

'Supposing they have bombs!'

'That will be a darn shame – for them,' declared Miles grimly. 'Which reminds me: those two guys lying along there with bullets in their beans probably have bombs in their pockets. I sure would like to get hold of them. We might give our friends a little of their own medicine then.'

They watched the cautious approach of the three with a certain amount of amusement. They were taking advantage of every vestige of cover, lingering sometimes behind chimney pots as though most reluctant to advance. When they reached the last between themselves and the trapdoor, they paused for a very long time. The American was about to comment sarcastically upon their tardiness when suddenly a blinding light was focused full on him and his companion. They ducked quickly, but felt they had been seen, especially when they heard angry voices, though the sight of the devastation caused by the misdirected bombs may have been the cause of the outcry. However, Miles decided to parley. Taking care to keep his head below the level of the roof, he called out in German.

'Your comrade Ilyich is here alive and well,' he announced. 'He does not like the position at all, and wants to know why the heck you are playing the fool with bombs, or words to that effect.'

Apparently the others were surprised at the news that Ilyich was alive. Excited and dismayed conversation could be heard; then a voice responded to Miles.

'You should give yourselves up at once to prevent further bloodshed,' it declared in English. Considering that all the blood that had been shed was that of anarchists, the demand struck Carter and Miles as amusing. They laughed aloud.

'Who is that speaking?' asked the American.

'What matters who is speaking?' came the reply.

'I guess I want to know if you are anyone in authority.'

'Ah! It is terms you wish to make. Then I will tell you. I am Vladimir Dimitrinhov.'

Miles clicked his tongue.

'Now isn't that just too bad? I thought I shot you in the corridor. It isn't often I miss. You're a lucky man, Dimitrinhov.' It seemed to him that words of a distinctly profane nature rose from behind the chimney pot at that. 'Where is Comrade Ulyanov?' he asked.

'What business is that of yours?'

'I wish to speak to him.'

'I will do all the speaking that is necessary. What is it you wish to say?'

'You can have Ilyich back on condition that you hand over Sir Leonard Wallace to us.' Surprised exclamations rent the air. That somewhat puzzled Miles. He would have understood laughter and scorn, but surprise rather suggested that the Russians had no more idea where Sir Leonard Wallace was than he had himself. 'That sounds mighty strange,' he confided to Carter. 'Anyone would think that they believed Sir Leonard was with us. There's no mistaking the fact that they are wonderstruck at my request.'

'They're astonished at your nerve in offering to exchange Ilyich for Sir Leonard, I suppose.'

'It isn't that sort of astonishment, Tommy. Now where can Sir Leonard be?'

They heard Dimitrinhov's voice again.

'If you will let Comrade Ilyich come out, we will consider about your request for Sir Wallace.'

'Oh, yeah!' cried Miles with a depth of sarcasm that caused Carter to chuckle. 'Nothing doing, Vladimir Dimitrinhov. You will have Ilyich with you safe and sound only when Sir Leonard Wallace is with us safe and sound. And, see here! If you keep on throwing bombs about in the inconsequent way your men just illustrated, Ilyich will get it in the neck. Put that under your hat and keep it there. Now switch off that darn light and beat it. I'll count ten; then my friend and I will start shooting.'

'It will be better for you if you deliver up Comrade Ilyich, and yourselves come out.'

'One – two—' commenced Miles in a loud voice.

The lights went out. The two cautiously raised their heads, and saw the three men hurrying away from them. Miles grunted something about 'darn cowards' to himself. They were left in peace for some time after that; the fact that Ilyich was being held more or less as a hostage was apparently a problem which took a considerable amount of solving. When they had thought him dead, it had not mattered what they did. 'Once a body is dead,' as Miles put it, 'it cannot get any deader.' But now they had reason to believe that their colleague was alive, it behoved them to behave a little more circumspectly unless they cared to risk the chance of his being killed after all. There is no doubt they were distinctly surprised to hear that he was actually still in the land of the living. Being anarchists, with the mentalities of anarchists, they could think of no reason why their antagonists should burden themselves with a prisoner except as a hostage. That to their minds was a poor reason, because, rather than that Carter and Miles should escape, they would sacrifice their comrade Ilyich. Comrades often must be sacrificed for the good of the cause. Ilyich knew that, which is probably why he gave vent to groans every few minutes.

But if Dimitrinhov and his companions were puzzled, so also were Carter and Miles, but for a different reason. Miles particularly was convinced that the whereabouts of Sir Leonard Wallace was unknown to the anarchists. That being the case, the Chief of the British Secret Service must have escaped. The thought gave the two a tremendous amount of pleasure. They felt that it did not matter what risks they themselves ran so long as Sir Leonard was free from danger.

'But if he has escaped,' persisted Carter, who was not quite so convinced as the American, 'how is it they have not dispersed? They would realise that the first thing he would do would be to go to the Minister of the Interior.'

'For some reason they thought he was with us,' was the reply, 'but now they know he isn't, you can bet your last dollar they'll beat it. Anyhow, I guess there's no point in your going out to look for him now. It's twenty past ten. It begins to look as though we'll survive till Jerry and company arrive.'

Miles was wrong, as was very quickly proved, in his conjecture that the anarchists would vanish. Suddenly a determined attack was made on the door. From the clamour that deafened the ears of the defenders they judged that hatchets, hammers and other powerful instruments were being used.

'I don't think they'll succeed in breaking in,' shouted Miles encouragingly. 'Their idea of having it steel-lined will be their undoing.'

'They're attacking the part where the lock and bolts are,' yelled Carter. 'They might force them.'

The American shook his head, quite forgetful that his companion would not be able to see him in the dark. He stiffened somewhat convulsively a moment later, however, when Carter suggested that they might bomb the door.

'By heck!' he exclaimed. 'You and I had better not stop for that performance, Tommy. I sure have no wish to be top of the bill in a bombing act. Directly they drop the racket they're making now, we'd better beat it out on to the roof and trust to luck.'

'What about Ilyich?'

'Guess he can stay where he is. If they've no consideration for him, why should we?'

Carter, however, stepped from the ladder and, searching for the Russian's feet, unstrapped them. The fellow was trembling violently; seemed to be in a regular paroxysm of terror. The Englishman helped him to his feet, and stood by gripping him by the arm. The din went on for some considerable time until both Carter's and Miles' heads were throbbing painfully with the sound. The door shook violently; the wireless instruments rattled continuously with the vibration. At last the clatter ceased; was succeeded by a deadly silence.

'Come on!' cried Miles. 'I have a feeling we'll be a darn sight safer on the roof.' He pushed back the trapdoor. 'Make a beeline for the nearest chimney stack.'

'Go on! I'm coming with Ilyich,' returned Carter. 'If you do not want to be blown direct to hell,' he added tensely to the Russian in his own language, 'get out on to the roof. If you try to escape, I'll shoot you down.'

The fellow was eager enough to go. Carter pushed him up, for he had not unbound his arms. Miles had already gone. Ilyich was stepping out on to the roof when suddenly came the terrible rat-tat-tat of the machine gun. Carter, who was directly behind the Russian, heard a choking cry, saw him stagger, sway drunkenly for a moment, and topple over. All round him seemed to be a swarm of angry bees; he felt the air disturbed on both sides as bullets sped past his head; then he threw himself flat on his face, wriggling desperately towards cover. Something seemed to tear with red-hot fingers at his shoulder, a similar feeling came in his leg, as frantically he swung sideways in an effort to get out of the line of fire. Then came a tremendous crash, an extraordinary upheaval seemed to be taking place, the whole world was, he felt, collapsing round him. At first he seemed to be soaring upward; then falling down into a bottomless pit. His last conscious recollection was of a pair of hands gripping him until he wondered why he did not cry out with the pain. After that the universe went utterly, devastatingly, horribly black.

White and shaken, Miles sat behind the chimney stack, holding on to the unconscious form of Carter. He had reached safety before the machine gun had commenced to rattle out its deadly hail of bullets. He had seen Ilyich collapse; observed Carter dive to the roof and start desperately to wriggle towards him. Without hesitation he had commenced to crawl out to the help of the Englishman. Then had come the explosion. Carter had been literally tossed into the air; was being hurled past him. Somehow the American had caught hold of him; had clung on desperately and had saved him from being flung over the parapet. He could never remember afterwards how he had done it.

Dazed and quivering in every limb, he yet recollected that the anarchists would be coming to administer the *coup de grâce*. The cloud of debris had settled; he heard triumphant shouts, the patter of feet. Grimly he clutched one of the rifles he had brought with him in his shaking hands. Rolling Carter gently aside, he raised himself to his knees, lifted his weapon, and glanced round the brickwork. Yes; they were coming, several of them. He could not last long, of course, but he intended accounting for a few more before going under. He sighted the rifle and as he fired, whispered the name – 'Joan!' A grunt of satisfaction issued from his lips as he observed his object stagger and fall. The others stopped dead, as though taken completely by surprise. Then rose a cry of consternation, of utter dismay; abruptly they turned and fled, as though Satan himself were after them.

'What the—?' began Miles, but he, too, now saw the reason for the stampede. From his position he had a view of the grounds in the front of the house. The whole place was lit up, for coming up the avenue was car after car, from which men were jumping almost before they stopped. 'Good old Jerry!' chuckled Miles weakly. 'Bully for you, boy!'

He sank back against the chimney stack. Oscar J. Miles had fainted.

CHAPTER EIGHTEEN

Tortured

When Sir Leonard Wallace had been summoned from the cellar by Bresov, he had been conducted to a small room on the top floor. Here he found Ulyanov, Grote, Dimitrinhov and Ilyich awaiting him. The President of the International Anarchist Society was sitting at a desk, the others standing behind him. All except the leader were armed. The room was sparingly furnished containing nothing more than the desk, Ulyanov's chair and three others, a cupboard and a few articles on the desk and mantelpiece. There was not even a carpet on the floor though the boards were polished. A bright fire burnt in the old-fashioned grate, adding a note of friendliness that seemed very much out of place. Bresov remained standing behind Sir Leonard, the other man withdrawing at a peremptory signal from Ulyanov. The Russian leader appeared even more grotesque than when Wallace had first seen him.

He remained without movement for some minutes, apparently engaged in a gloating inspection of the man who was in his power. At last he spoke in German, his rasping voice cutting sharply into the silence.

'You fool,' he sneered, 'did you think to destroy the International Anarchist Society? You, a puny, insignificant simpleton to pit your wits against an organisation that is all-powerful, that has behind it the might of a membership comprising thousands!'

'It ill becomes one who is himself the puniest and most insignificant of creatures,' retorted Sir Leonard, 'to seek to attach such a label to others.'

A grating snarl of rage told him that his remark had struck home.

'Before you pass to your death, Englishman,' hissed the dwarf, 'you will make compensation to me that, for exquisite agony, will hardly have been equalled. I shall sit and watch you squirm, the expression of torture in your face will be to me as a beautiful picture that enraptures me, the screams and groans that break from your lips will be delightful music. But I will not kill you. No, my very clever Sir Leonard Wallace, your death will be arranged by those you have defied for so long, by those whose plans and enterprises you have so wantonly destroyed. It is my intention to hand you over to be dealt with in Moscow – when I have extracted my fill of entertainment from you.'

'Oh! And how do you propose to present me to Moscow?' asked Wallace quietly.

A cackling laugh came from the other, but no expression of amusement appeared on his face. It was as though the sound was being emitted from an ugly, inanimate gargoyle.

'There are many ways,' came the reply, 'but the easiest is to send you to Russia by air. In the grounds, very cleverly hidden, is a sunken runway for an aeroplane, and a hangar in which we keep a machine. Presently a wireless message will be despatched to Moscow to inform them there that you are in my power and suggesting that I send you to that great city for disposal. Yes, we have a wireless installation here. We are well-equipped, are we not? Can you not see the delight, hear the exclamations of triumph and pleasure that will follow the receipt of my message? Do you think for one moment, Herr Wallace, that they will refuse my gift?'

'If they have any common sense, they certainly will,' replied Sir Leonard. 'You fool, do you actually think you can do this sort of thing and escape without suffering drastic retribution?'

'I will offer to send you either by air or by rail,' went on Ulyanov, paying no attention whatever to the Englishman's remarks, 'but as there are likely to be more complications if you are packed in a box and sent by rail, it is certain that the aeroplane will be used for your conveyance. It will be a nice journey for you. I hope you will enjoy it.'

'If you have had me brought here just for the purpose of gloating over me, you can spare your poisonous breath, and send me back to the cellar. Your gibes leave me entirely unaffected.'

'Do they?' shouted the other. 'We shall see. You were not brought here for the purpose of gloating over you, as you describe it, my dear friend. There are some questions you will be required to answer. If you refuse, you will be punished until you do speak. If you still refuse, your comrades will speak for you. It will interest you to know that, at midnight tonight, I will hang them on one of the trees in this estate. I do not think Moscow will want to be troubled with them.'

'You fiend!' cried Wallace, roused at the thought of the fate that threatened his companions, when no threat of torture or death applied to himself had any power to move him from his icy calm. The glance from his steel-grey eyes which he shot at the dwarf must have warned the latter that if this man, by some chance, escaped from his clutches, he could expect no mercy from him.

He leant forward.

'Tell me,' he snapped, 'how did you find out that arrangements had been made to remove King Peter from this world? From where did your information come? Who betrayed the whereabouts of the lodgings of Pestalozzi, Haeckel and Zanazaryk? In short, Herr Wallace, I demand to know every item of information concerning this organisation which is in your possession or in that of your government, and the source from which you obtained it.'

Sir Leonard smiled.

'You are very worried about our knowledge, aren't you?' he commented. 'Do your demands also include the knowledge which the government of the United States possesses?'

'What is that?' shot out Hermann Grote in sudden consternation.

'Merely that you are, or were, the head of the branch in America,' drawled Wallace, a faint smile on his lips as he noted the anxious expression on the German's face; 'that you conveyed to Vienna a sum of three hundred thousand dollars in American notes – all of the numbers of which, I may as well add, are known – and further that—'

He was interrupted by the excited and dismayed exclamations of the anarchists. Grote's coarse face had turned a dirty white.

'The numbers are known!' he repeated wonderingly. 'How can that be?' Wallace shrugged his shoulders. 'It was all honest money,' persisted Grote; 'it was not stolen.'

'Can money collected from those in sympathy with anarchy, to further designs to assassinate innocent men and women, be accounted honest?' snapped Sir Leonard.

'Bah!' grated Ulyanov. 'You talk like the fool you are. That money was collected to go into our funds, and help us rid the world of the royal wasters who are a blot and a pest on it. Why were the numbers of the notes taken?'

'Presumably because it was known why the money was being collected. You will gather, Ulyanov, and you, Grote, that not one note of that money can go again into circulation without being traced. As far as you are concerned the three hundred thousand dollars are useless.'

An excited and perturbed discussion followed. Not one of the four apparently thought that Sir Leonard was merely bluffing them. Yet that is exactly what he was doing. The numbers of the notes had not, as far as he was aware, been taken – in fact he was certain they had not – but, if he failed in all else, he meant to ensure that at least the money brought from the United States would not be used to help anarchy reign in the world. Ulyanov at length turned back to him, his manner even more vehement than before.

'How is it these things about us are known?' he barked. 'Who is it or what is it that has supplied you with the information?' Sir Leonard did not reply. 'Answer me!' stormed the Russian. 'You will answer me, or I will tear out your tongue by the roots.'

'You could hardly expect to receive an answer then,' returned the Englishman.

'I am not jesting. Are you an imbecile so great that you do not think I mean what I say?'

'I realise that you are quite capable of carrying out your villainous threats, if that is any satisfaction to you.'

'Good! We then understand each other to that extent. You will, therefore, reply to my questions, and at once.'

'I shall not reply to questions concerning information in my possession or the possession of my department now or at any other time,' declared Sir Leonard firmly. 'You will save yourself a good deal of time and trouble therefore, if you realise that fact now.'

Ulyanov sprang to his feet with a cry that was more animal than human. For a moment he stood glaring at his prisoner from beneath those horrible, drooping eyelids of his; then he walked round the desk slowly, haltingly, as though he were not entirely master of his legs. He stopped barely a yard in front of Wallace, raised his head slowly, and looked up at him. The Englishman felt that nothing would have given him greater pleasure than to grip the creature by the throat and squeeze the life out of him. Temptation, in fact, was very strong. Little did Ulyanov realise the peril in which he stood at that moment. But Wallace felt that the time had not come to show that his hand was actually free. By a display of aggression at that juncture he might ruin all his plans. On the other hand, acquiescence even in brutality might still enable his hopes to be realised. There might remain a possibility of his companions in misfortune getting in touch with Cousins, even if he were unable to do so, and if he revealed that his hands were free it was quite possible that a strong force of men would be sent to make certain that Carter's and Miles' hands were not also free. Wallace was sure that they would themselves act on his suggestion, even if he did not return to them, once they were out of the cellar.

'You mean to defy me?' demanded Ulyanov, as though spitting at him.

'I shall certainly not answer your questions, if you consider that defying you.'

With a rapid movement the Russian reached up with his right hand and, digging the long, pointed nails of his fingers into Sir Leonard's face just below his left eye, tore the skin from cheekbone to chin. The Englishman felt the blood spurt out, cared nothing for the stinging pain, but that the loathsome little creature should lay his claws on him in such a manner was more than he was prepared to let pass unpunished. He did not free his arms; instead he kicked out with all the force of his powerful right leg. Ulyanov's shrunken body was lifted from the floor. He crashed over on to his back with a jar that shook the room. At once cries of alarm and opprobrium rent the air. Grote and Ilyich went to the assistance of their fallen leader; Dimitrinhov sprang on Wallace, crashed his closed fist into the Englishman's face. In return he received a kick on the shin that well-nigh broke the bone, and hopped back to the desk to stand on one leg, nursing the injured member in his hand, while he swore without restraint. Bresov grappled Sir Leonard, holding him, as he fondly imagined, quite powerless. But, though he knew he could have released himself had he so desired, Wallace made no attempt to do so.

Screaming maledictions, Ulyanov was raised from the floor.

'So!' snarled Ulyanov at length. 'You dared to attack me, you swine of an Englishman. For that your pains will be greater than ever. Call in your comrades!' he shouted to Bresov. 'Let there be no delay, unless they wish to be punished severely.'

The Slav hastened to obey, Ilyich and Grote raising their revolvers and pointing them at Wallace as a warning that they would shoot if he made any attempt to escape. He stood quietly, however, almost without movement.

Bresov quickly returned with half a dozen men who crowded

into the small room on his heels until there seemed hardly room
for anyone to move. At Ulyanov's orders Wallace was seized and
stretched full length on his back. He made no attempt at resistance,
still allowed his hands to remain loosely bound in the cord that he
could easily have shaken off. When he heard the dwarf give orders
for the poker to be thrust into the fire and heated, he clenched
his teeth, his body stiffened, but he otherwise gave no sign of the
horror that filled him. Was the little fiend about to put out his
eyes? The thought almost shook his resolution. It was unbearable
to think that never again would he look upon Molly or upon
his son Adrian; that after a career of success and achievement, of
devotion to his country and his king, it should end thus miserably,
that he should pass the remainder of his days in darkness, blinded
by the fiendish cruelty of this malignant devil of an anarchist, this
caricature of a man. Minutes passed slowly, agonisingly. Those who
were not engaged in holding him down were staring as though
fascinated at the poker in the fire.

At last Ulyanov decided that it was hot enough for his purpose.
He slipped off his chair, and limped to the fireplace. In his eagerness
he forgot that the heat would have travelled along to the handle
which was unprotected. He grasped it and immediately gave vent
to a scream of rage and pain. Sir Leonard could not see him, but
he could hear him and, guessing what had occurred, felt it some
slight compensation for his own sufferings. Ulyanov heaped curses
on those surrounding him as though they had been responsible for
his injudicious action. A guard of paper thickly folded was quickly
made for him, and again he took hold of the poker, this time
without mishap. He approached the recumbent form of his victim,
his men crushing back before him and his weapon. Sir Leonard
saw the glowing red-hot iron, and his nerves began to undergo a

tremendous strain. Barking orders to some of his followers to hold firmly to the Englishman, he commanded others to tear open the clothing covering his breast. Rough hands quickly laid bare his white, clear skin, but Wallace's sensation at that moment was one of profound relief. Ulyanov did not, after all, contemplate burning out his eyes.

'You know the questions I wish you to answer,' came in the harsh, grating voice. 'If you do not answer, I will brand you with the sign of the society. Answer!'

'No,' replied Sir Leonard at once, and in a tone of definite finality.

'I am not jesting, Englishman. The poker is getting closer and closer to that womanlike skin of yours. It would be a great pity to burn it, would it not?'

Sir Leonard could feel the heat now, but he did not flinch. 'I have given you my answer,' he pronounced.

The fiend gave a cry of anger. Immediately the glowing poker descended; there was a hissing sound, the odour of burning flesh. Sir Leonard turned deadly pale beneath the streaks of clotted blood, but not a sound left his white lips, his eyes closed involuntarily for a moment, but opened at once to glare scornfully, contemptuously at his torturer. Anticipating that his victim would writhe and scream out in agony, Ulyanov became infuriated by his calm fortitude. Again he pressed the fiery weapon into the shrinking flesh, but no sound could he draw from those bloodless lips pressed tightly together in agony. At last, with a cry of baffled fury he flung the poker from him, not caring whither it went. It struck a man on the head with tremendous force, causing him to collapse with a scream of pain. Ulyanov turned and glared at the fellow who, not rendered unconscious, grovelled on the floor, hands to his head. Not a word of sorrow or apology did the dwarf utter. He strode towards the man, touched him roughly with his foot.

'Get up and get out!' he snarled. Helped by his comrades, the injured fellow rose to his feet, and staggered from the room. 'Get out, all of you,' barked Ulyanov. 'You stay, Bresov.' Quickly the room was clear of all except those who had been originally there. Sir Leonard lay now, his eyes closed hardly seeming to breathe. 'Has he fainted?' asked Ulyanov, eagerly.

At once the Englishman's eyes opened.

'No; I have not,' he said, his voice just a trifle husky. 'I would not give you even that satisfaction, Ulyanov.'

'Damn you!' screamed the dwarf. 'Are you not human?'

He commenced kicking the prone man, but he had little strength in his legs, and did not cause him a great deal of pain. Probably he realised that himself, for he desisted and returned to his seat at the desk, where he sat for some time, his head between his hands, apparently in a fit of gloomy disappointment.

The intense pain he was suffering caused Sir Leonard to long to free his arms from the cord, if only to press the cool palm of the natural hand against the burns in an effort to soothe them. Nevertheless he made no movement. He preferred to endure his agony without attempting to ease or relieve it rather than that his captors should discover the secret he was nursing so carefully. Of them all only Grote displayed the least essence of feeling. He presently walked across to the Englishman and, bending down, arranged his torn clothing gently over the inflamed angry flesh.

'For that,' murmured Sir Leonard, 'I will have mercy on you, Grote, when my turn comes.'

'Don't be a fool!' snapped the other. 'You know you are doomed, but I cannot see the point of making you suffer unduly.'

'Thanks,' came quietly from the other.

At full realisation of the uncomplaining and heroic fortitude of the Englishman the German experienced a great revulsion of feeling. A sense of deep shame surged through him.

'Do you think you can stand?' he asked.

Wallace nodded, and Grote promptly helped him to his feet.

'What are you doing? Who told you to interfere?' came in the staccato accents of Ulyanov.

'Do you object to my assisting him to rise from the floor?' demanded Grote, eyeing his leader somewhat defiantly.

'I object to his being given any help at all. The more he suffers the greater will be my pleasure, and it should be yours also.'

'Well, it is not. It is one thing to die because he is a menace to the society. It is entirely unnecessary that he should be tortured in addition. Your action, Comrade Ulyanov, has disgusted me.'

'It seems that your veins contain water instead of blood, Hermann Grote,' sneered Dimitrinhov.

'Water!' rasped Ulyanov. 'Yes, water – dirty water – weak, sluggish, German water.'

'Be careful, Ulyanov,' cried Grote. 'You have been allowed to rule this society with a high hand, but there are limits beyond which even you cannot go. I am and always have been as loyal as any member of the society, but I will not allow you to ride roughshod over me.'

Shouting maledictions, Ulyanov rose to his feet, at the same time snatching a revolver from Ilyich who stood close by. He raised it slowly until it was pointing straight at a spot between Grote's eyes. The latter showed little perturbation.

'You dare not do it,' he declared deliberately. 'You, Ilyich and Dimitrinhov there, are the only Russians on the Council. The rest – Kharkov, Mossuth, Mikeroff, Papanasstou and Psarazelos already resent the manner in which the three of you force through measures without allowing them a proper say in decisions. Shoot me; then see what will happen. Put that revolver down, and do not be foolish, Comrade Ulyanov.'

Rather to Sir Leonard's surprise, the Russian obeyed. It was interesting to find that the fiery, demented dwarf recognised the unwisdom of his action. Apparently there had been dissensions in the Council of Ten.

'Take it,' snarled Ulyanov, pushing the revolver towards Ilyich. 'Comrade Grote and I will continue our little discussion at a more fitting time. You,' he added looking directly at Wallace, or rather appearing to look directly at him, for it was difficult to tell, when the lids were raised so slightly from the eyes, 'You perhaps think that the intervention of Herr Grote may save you further pain. But you are mistaken, Mr English Spy. I will make those obstinate lips of yours open yet. You can go!' he shot at Bresov. 'We will let him recover his strength before introducing him to Madame Knout. He shall have food and wine. See to it, Ilyich.'

The thin, saturnine Russian went out, reappearing some minutes later, followed by the wizened little man who had opened the door on Carter's arrival. The doorkeeper was carrying a tray on which was food and a flask of wine. Wallace could not touch the food, would not have done so if he could. Hermann Grote persuaded him to drink a couple of glasses of wine; found an opportunity to whisper:

'They shall not torture you, if I can prevent it. Perhaps later I may find means of helping you in other ways.'

What he exactly meant to convey by the latter remark Sir Leonard was unable to guess, but he bestowed on him a look of gratitude. He decided that Hermann Grote was not all evil, as his companions appeared to be. If ever he escaped from his present desperate situation, he would not be too hard on him. If ever he escaped! A wry little smile flickered momentarily round the pain-contracted lips of Sir Leonard Wallace. The chances appeared to be very slender.

CHAPTER NINETEEN

The Secret Chamber

When the doorkeeper had been dismissed with his tray, Wallace was conducted from the room by Dimitrinhov, Grote, and Ilyich, Ulyanov remaining behind and flinging a last jeering remark at him as he went out. Ilyich led the way along the corridor while Grote and Dimitrinhov walked close to the prisoner on either side. Occasionally they were forced to aid him, for the ordeal he had undergone had greatly weakened him, but whereas the Russian gripped him roughly, the German was extremely gentle, another point being marked up in his favour in Sir Leonard's mind. They reached a door at the extreme end of the corridor. Ilyich unlocked it and they entered, the door being closed again directly they were inside. Wallace thought he understood now why Bresov had been dismissed. It was evident, he reflected, that only members of the Council of Ten knew of the secret room, possibly only they were permitted to enter the wireless department.

Sir Leonard was surprised to find what a well-equipped apartment it was. It looked very much like the radio cabin on a large liner. Its circular conformation would have interested him if he had not been engaged in watching closely the movements of Ilyich. The Russian moved the small square of carpet to one side for no apparent reason that the Englishman could see. He then crawled under the table on which the wireless instruments rested. There came a sharp click, followed by a faint, buzzing sound, and before the interested eyes of Sir Leonard a slab about three feet square sank out of sight in the centre of the stone floor. He was pushed towards the hole and his feet guided to an iron ladder. Grote suggested freeing his arms, but Dimitrinhov and Ilyich dissented vehemently. It was awkward descending a perpendicular ladder without being able to use his arms, but the feat was accomplished, once again with the aid of Grote. Ilyich and Dimitrinhov would not have minded if he had fallen. At the bottom the German switched on a light – obviously an innovation installed since Ulyanov had occupied the house – and Wallace found himself in a square, box-like apartment of not more than six feet square. The walls were of plain brick, the floor of stone, unlike that above, unpolished. Documents, books, and large cash boxes were piled high at one side, there was nothing else in the room, if it could be called a room, at all.

'What need was there to put on the light?' Dimitrinhov called from above. 'It seems to me, Herr Grote, that you are behaving in a strangely mysterious manner. If you do not wish to be left down there with the man for whom your chicken heart feels so great a sympathy, I suggest you ascend.'

'I am sorry there is no room for you to lie down,' Grote observed to Sir Leonard, 'but, at least, it is possible for you to sit.'

He switched off the light, and ascended the ladder. A moment later came the dull, buzzing noise, sounding a trifle louder in the confined space. The square slab moved up into place, fitting perfectly. Sir Leonard felt as though he had been enclosed in a tomb. His first action, as soon as he was assured that his captors would not return, was to release his hands; his next to find the switch and put on the light. Then sitting down on a pile of books and papers, he drew aside the torn clothing covering his chest, and looked down at the terrible, inflamed burns disfiguring his skin. The pain was abominable, and he had no means of assuaging it. He sought comfort by dabbing the throbbing, fiery, blistered sores with the soft tatters of his undervest, afterwards lying back against the wall with his eyes closed in an attempt to regain the strength of which he had been robbed. At length the pain seemed to ease somewhat, or perhaps he had become more inured to it, and he felt better in himself. He stood up, and surveyed the collection of articles stored in that secret chamber. Here was work for him to do; there was no time to be wasted if he was to make himself thoroughly acquainted with the ramifications of the International Anarchist Society, and that was his intention.

Sir Leonard had not given up hope of escaping even then. Somehow he felt Miles and Carter would find him, unless luck was dead against them. Then there was Cousins – the great little man who would never give up searching for evidence and his chief while life remained to him. Unless he were captured, sooner or later he would find his way into the building, perhaps discover all the secrets it held. Even if Cousins failed, Beust possessed enough information to set him on the trail, though, not having been one of those to follow Carter, he would be faced with the difficult task of finding this headquarters of the anarchists. He had of necessity to be kept more or less in the background owing to his apparently innocent post of manager in Vienna of *Lalére et Cie*, the great Parisian perfumers – a post which cloaked his activities as agent of the British Secret Service. It was Beust who had originally, through the underground channels familiar to him, discovered that there were anarchical activities in Vienna and a plot to assassinate King Peter in London. Through those channels he might still be able to discover the whereabouts of the headquarters of the International Anarchist Society. He smiled grimly, a trifle painfully. The day of his death seemed at that moment very close. If he were taken to Moscow, he knew that no power on earth could save him.

Ulyanov must be very sure of himself to put him down in this treasure chest of evidence. Of course he had not known that the cord apparently binding Sir Leonard's wrists was loose. The Chief of the British Secret Service understood why Ilyich and Dimitrinhov had dissented with such vehemence when Grote had suggested freeing his hands. It would not be wise to allow even a man about to die to pry into the secrets of their terrible association, the object of which was to exterminate royalty completely and finally.

He commenced on his task, methodically exerting his great strength of will, and putting aside all pain and weakness as though they were non-existent. The position of each book, each document, was noted in order that it could be replaced exactly as he had found it. Time passed by, and he had become completely absorbed in his work, docketing in that wonderful mind of his facts that would cause the world to vibrate with horror and alarm. Everything he desired to know was revealed to him there. He found complete lists of agents and anarchists sworn to the service of the society and the destruction of royalty. There were no less than seventeen hundred names on the list from which assassins would be selected; ledgers were kept showing the sums paid out to them, others displayed rent paid for branches where the anarchists could meet. There were restaurants in Berlin, Paris, Rome, Madrid, Vienna, Copenhagen, New York, Cairo, Tokyo and a score of other great cities under the thrall of the society. There were members of police forces, armies, navies, government departments pledged to the dreadful, abominable assassination of those whose only crime was that they had been born with royal blood in their veins. It was a terrible, an awful, revelation, an unveiling of a murderous conception that shocked Sir Leonard to the very core of his being. He read elaborate plans callously put forth in the method of military orders for the murder of a king and queen here, a prince and princess there, of the assassination in cold blood of young children and old men and women.

It was anarchy at its very lowest, deepest, fiendish worst. It was almost beyond credence, diabolical beyond expression, monstrous.

When at last he had been carefully through all the books and documents and had replaced them as he had found them, he felt physically and mentally ill. His face was drawn and haggard, not now from the ordeal of suffering to which he had been subjected, but from a far worse ordeal that had disclosed to his horrified mind evil unparalleled, wholesale. How could he expect mercy from a creature whose distorted abominable brain had conceived schemes so monstrous? He no longer wondered that he, who had threatened destruction to all Ulyanov's cherished plans, was hated by the dwarf with such passionate virulence. He was unable to open the large cash boxes, as they were locked, and he had not with him that famous bunch of small steel instruments with which he was enabled to open even the most obstinate locks. It was as well, he reflected that he had left the bunch with Cousins. It would only have been confiscated with the other articles, which had been taken from his pockets.

He had been aware for some time of a faint, confused sort of sound above his head and, while concluding his perusal of the documents, had remained within easy reach of the electric light switch, ready to turn it off, if the secret trapdoor opened. The cord which had bound his wrists was arranged close by in order that he could again slip his hands into it if necessary. Having placed all the books and papers in position he sat down and listened. Long periods of intense silence were broken from time to time by what sounded like voices talking a long way away. Sometimes he thought he could hear the tap of feet; he even fancied that there was shooting going on. Eventually he rose and, climbing the ladder, stood with his ear pressed to a part of the roof where he calculated the trapdoor fitted into place. So cleverly had it been constructed, however, that it was impossible to find out exactly where the join was. He tried pushing at it with his fingers, but it did not give in the slightest degree. It was distinctly aggravating, he thought, that he could not hear more clearly. The little room was practically soundproof; the slight, confused noise he did hear reached him down the ventilating shaft. He managed to stretch across, placing his ear as close to it as possible. For a time silence reigned; then, in quick succession, came the faint but distinct sound of two rifle shots.

Vastly intrigued, Sir Leonard remained in his uncomfortable position for a long while, until he was forced to the conclusion that a fight of some sort was undoubtedly going on. Could it be, he debated, that Cousins had already obtained all the information necessary to persuade the Austrian authorities to act, and that the building was now being attacked by them? That seemed unlikely.

The alternative was that Carter and Miles had somehow broken out of the cellar, had obtained arms, and were now defending themselves in the vicinity. He wondered if they were actually in the radio room, but doubted it, for the place was, he had noticed, kept locked. Still there was a possibility that someone had been in there with the door unfastened, and that they had taken possession of it. If only he could get to them! He climbed down the ladder and started to search for the lever or button or whatever it happened to be that opened the trapdoor. It was inconceivable that it could only open from the outside; there must be a means of opening it from within. Yet, search as he did with methodical care, he found nothing at all, and was eventually compelled to admit himself baffled. He sat on one of the iron steps and considered the position. His keen eyes, as he rested there, explored every inch of the wall except of course that hidden by the books, boxes, and papers which he had already examined. He had inspected any peculiarity or irregularity about the brickwork he had come across, but he thought that perhaps, despite his vigilance, he had missed something. But nothing out of the ordinary rewarded his survey.

'It must be possible to manipulate that door from this side,' he muttered, 'but how is it done? I hate to be beaten by a little thing like that.'

Once again he went round the walls, climbed the ladder and examined the ceiling; still without result. He began to wonder whether he would be heard if he tried shouting up the ventilator shaft. It would not matter much if Carter and Miles were not in the wireless room; on the other hand, if by some chance they were, they might be able to discover how to open the trapdoor and let him out. He was about to stretch over towards the ventilator when a crashing sound reached his ears. It was much louder than all other noises had been; seemed as though people with hammers or hatchets were engaged in attempting to break in something solid. At once the solution burst on his mind. Miles and Carter were in the room above and the anarchists were endeavouring to force open the door. No use trying to make himself heard while that din was going on. It was loud enough down there; it would be a hundred times louder above, and calculated to drown his voice completely. He descended the steps again, and stood listening. The row went on for some time; then suddenly ceased. He thought he heard voices again, and was about to make another attempt to shout up the shaft, when his eye caught the top rung of the ladder. It is necessary to explain that the iron ladder was a fixture; that is to say that it fitted into the floor and ceiling. It occurred to Sir Leonard that the top step was unnecessary. It was not more than three inches below the ceiling, while the next one could be reached comfortably by anyone stepping down from above. Was it possible that it was actually not a rung at all but the lever for which he had been searching? No sooner had the idea come to him than he was up the steps trying it. He attempted to force it upwards, then downwards, but without result. After that he tried pushing it away from him. At once he gave vent to a low cry of exultation. He could feel it beginning to move. A buzzing sound delighted his ears, and the trapdoor started to open. It was at that moment there came a terrific explosion. The concussion flung him violently to the floor, where he lay half stunned, wondering vaguely what had happened, why the place seemed to be rocking.

The fulmination was followed by a dead silence for a few minutes; then came the exultant cries of men in a mixture of languages, the tread of many feet. He could hear quite plainly now, due no doubt to the fact that the trapdoor was slightly open. The jubilant shouts quickly changed to roars of rage and disappointment.

'They must have gone on the roof before the bomb was thrown,' Sir Leonard distinctly heard a voice cry in German. 'You cannot get up there since the ladder is destroyed – go the other way!'

Followed another rush of feet; then silence again. The Englishman smiled to himself. It was not difficult to gather what had happened. Carter and Miles had been defending the wireless room, whereupon the anarchists, after spending a long time attempting to overcome them, had bombed their way in, only to find that the two had escaped on to the roof. Sir Leonard grew very anxious. Now that they had been driven out of their stronghold, their chances of saving their lives appeared very slender. On the roof they would probably be exposed to attack on several sides at once. It appeared, however, that his own opportunity had come. Inclination urged him to go to the assistance of his friends, not that he would be a great deal of use, since he was weaponless; in fact he might prove a burden to them. But duty decreed that he must get out of the house if possible, find Cousins, if the latter had not been captured, and send him, as fast as he could go, to the ambassador. He wondered, as he climbed the steps and commenced to manipulate the false rung, what the little Secret Service man had been doing; had he heard the sound of shots? He certainly must have heard the explosion. To Sir Leonard's ears came again the sound of hurrying feet.

'Down below as quick as you can,' he heard the voice of Dimitrinhov shout excitedly. 'They'll be in the house in a few moments.'

With a muttered imprecation of keen disappointment Wallace slid down the ladder, switched off the light, and sat down. He picked up the looped cord and began to wriggle his right hand through it, after placing the artificial limb in it. The buzzing sound started which denoted that the trap was opening; there came a glow of light as somebody snatched the mat away. Sir Leonard heard the staccato voice of Ulyanov raised in frenzied anger, the soothing tones of another man endeavouring to calm him. Down the ladder came one man after another, until the little room was packed, the Englishman being crushed against the wall.

'Shut it! Shut it!' barked Ulyanov, apparently referring to the trapdoor.

'There may be still two or three who—' began Dimitrinhov.

'Shut it!' screamed the dwarf.

The humming recommenced, the light disappeared; then came a click and the little apartment was illuminated.

'Why,' cried the voice of Grote 'he is still here.'

Sir Leonard found himself the cynosure of all eyes. A shrill cry of triumph broke from the shrunken leader who was standing surrounded by six men.

'You seem surprised to see me,' commented Wallace. 'Considering you are responsible for my being here, perhaps you will not think it strange if I remark that I do not understand.'

'Your friends, damn them!' snarled Dimitrinhov, 'escaped by some means from the cellar in which they were confined. Not only did they escape, but they disarmed the guard and, we guess, locked them in the cellar. As they took the key away with them, and we have not had time or very much inclination to investigate, we do not know exactly what happened. At all events the two found their way to the wireless chamber above and resisted all attempts to destroy them. In the end we took the drastic course of bombing the door. The place was completely wrecked, but still they escaped.'

'You seem to have been very determined to catch or kill them,' observed Sir Leonard.

'Bah!' came from the dwarf in his ugly, grating voice. 'It was you we wanted. We thought they had found out where you were, and had come to rescue you. It is amusing, is it not, that they were above and you below, and they did not know you were here?' He cackled with that horrible, expressionless laughter of his; then suddenly gripped Wallace by his tattered coat. 'So!' he snarled, 'you are still in my power, and after all, you will be taken to Moscow. It is a great compensation for the destruction of my schemes. How did you arrange for this? Answer me! How did you arrange it?'

'Arrange what?' asked Sir Leonard coolly.

'That these police and soldiers should come. Are you a devil that you can do things like this even though you are in a prison from which you cannot escape?'

A great feeling of triumph surged through Wallace. He understood now why these men had entered the secret chamber, why they were looking anxious and, with the exception of Ulyanov, whose face, as usual, was expressionless, thoroughly frightened. They were seeking refuge from the Austrian authorities. Cousins had done his work perfectly. He laughed aloud in exultation.

'It is the end, Ulyanov,' he triumphed; 'the end of the International Anarchist Society.'

'It is the end of you,' screamed the Russian. 'You swine of an Englishman! You spy from hell! Do you think you will escape? Even now I will take you to Russia and watch you die. What triumph is it to you if you have, for the time, demolished the society? It will rise again like the phoenix, but you cannot rise.'

'You seem quite confident of reaching Moscow,' commented Sir Leonard. 'Personally I think your chances are nil.'

'Do you? Do you?' barked the other, threatening to be overcome by one of his extraordinary frenzies again. With a great effort he calmed himself, his hands fell from Sir Leonard's clothing. 'We will see,' he muttered harshly. 'I swear to take you to Moscow; then perhaps you will regret your temporary success over the society.'

'Nothing you can do to me will ever make me regret – my permanent and complete success,' retorted Wallace.

'It would be safer to kill him now,' growled Dimitrinhov. 'We are all armed with knives as well as revolvers. A well-directed stab and, whatever happens, we will know he can no longer do harm to the Soviet.'

'No! No! No!' barked Ulyanov. 'He will go to Moscow. Who will dare dispute with me?'

No one did. He seemed to wield a strange, horrible power over the men he ruled.

'Let him have his obsession, Dimitrinhov,' advised Wallace. 'Can't you see he's like a child with a new toy? Although I can't exactly commend your desire to stick a knife in me, I shall certainly not go to Moscow.'

Ulyanov and the bearded man were starting to reply violently at the same moment, when one of the others warned them to be silent. Dimitrinhov promptly clapped a great hand over Sir Leonard's mouth. Above, reaching their ears faintly, but nevertheless quite distinctly, they could hear the sound of many feet and many voices. The Englishman was tempted to fling the Russian's hand aside; shout out with all the power of his lungs. But what sense would there be in throwing his life away in the hour of triumph, especially when the chances were that he would not be heard. He could not see how Ulyanov and his companions could possibly escape. He refrained from attempting to give the alarm, therefore, standing quiescent to the brutal pressure of Dimitrinhov's hand. He noted, with a feeling of quiet amusement, how every man there seemed terror-stricken. Each was fingering the weapon in his hand nervously, as though apprehensive at the thought of having to use it, which would mean discovery. Little beads of perspiration, which were not caused by heat, trickled down Grote's coarse face. Once or twice he cast appealing glances in Sir Leonard's direction. Apart from him, Ulyanov and Dimitrinhov, there were present three men whom the Englishman knew to be members of the Council of Ten, but whose names were unknown to him, and another whom he had not seen before. Ilyich and Bresov were conspicuous by their absence.

At length the sounds of footsteps and voices in the room above died away. There were sighs expressive of deep relief, but almost at once a discussion arose concerning the possibility of escape. Dimitrinhov gave it as his opinion that the police and military would patrol the house and grounds for some days. Sooner or later, he thought, the hiding place would be discovered, and, even if it were not, eight men could not last long in a tiny room with only one ventilating shaft. Grote counselled making terms with the authorities. He thought that they would be able to bargain for their own lives and freedom as the price for allowing Sir Leonard Wallace to live. As was to be expected, his suggestion threw Ulyanov into a fiendish rage. He stormed and raved, frothing at the mouth, and hurling at the German a string of the most horrible epithets. But his power was beginning to wane. Wallace had an illustration that there was indeed dissension in the Council and that, after all, there were some who dared dispute with the dwarf. All the members of the committee present, with the exception of Dimitrinhov, appeared to side with Grote; the seventh man remained aloof, but it was not difficult to judge from the expression on his face where his sympathies were. In a sense Ulyanov stood alone, for while he had the support of his compatriot against making terms with the authorities, he was obstinately bent on conveying Wallace to Moscow, while Dimitrinhov continued to urge that the Englishman should be killed out of hand. The climax came when a tall, villainous-looking Greek, whose name turned out to be Papanasstou, declared that they would open the trap and parley with the Austrian commander without further hesitation unless Ulyanov could think of a better plan.

'Your idea of conveying this man to Russia, Comrade Ulyanov,' he proclaimed in very indifferent German, 'is mad now. It cannot be done. We must look out for ourselves. To recover him alive, they would agree to let us go free without a doubt.'

'Would you accept their promise?' sneered Dimitrinhov.

'What other chance have we? And the Englishman would see that the word was kept.'

'Let us open the trapdoor at once. We can send Vassallo to put our terms before the commandant.' The seventh man – apparently he was Vassallo – shrank back. Obviously the task did not appeal to him. 'If we wait here much longer,' persisted Papanasstou, 'they will find us. Where are Psarezelos and Nikeroff and Ilyich? They know of the existence of this secret compartment. Perhaps they are captured. If so how do you know that they will not tell?'

'Psarezelos and Nikeroff being Greeks,' sneered Dimitrinhov, 'might have done so, if they were alive. But as they were killed by those cursed spies when attacking the wireless room, they cannot. I do not know what happened to Ilyich – I fear he was either blown up or is a prisoner. But he will not speak – he is a Russian.'

His sarcastic comparison threatened to lead to trouble, but

Ulyanov broke in in his usual passionate manner. After roundly cursing the lot of them, he added:

'Do you think I am a fool? Would I have insisted on coming here to die like a rat in a trap? Imbeciles! Idiots! Buffoons! While I was here alone last summer I had constructed a way of escape ready for just such an emergency as this. But I kept it as my own secret. Now, Grote, and you, Mossuth, and you Kharkov, and you above all, Papanasstou, do you not admit that I am your master in all things?'

'Where is this way of escape, and why have we not used it before this?' demanded the man addressed as Mossuth.

'I waited, as I thought Comrade Ilyich might yet come,' returned Ulyanov, and, for once in a way, the harsh, metallic note was missing from his voice. 'It is useless to wait longer now; he is dead I fear. He was my son!'

CHAPTER TWENTY

Wallace at Bay

There seemed something revolting about the fact that a creature like Ulyanov should have a son. What manner of woman, wondered Sir Leonard, could the mother have been? The news seemed to astonish the other men in the room also, none of them appearing to have been aware of the relationship between Ilyich and Ulyanov. The dwarf observed their surprise and resented it.

'Is it so strange that I should possess a son?' he rasped. 'Dolts, all of you! Because I am small and ugly, you think no woman would look at me! Well, you are wrong, wrong, wrong! I choose where I will, and when I will. Do you hear? Nicolai Ilyich Ulyanov is more man than all of you together. Bah! I spurn you!'

He turned from them, and bending down, took hold of the last rung of the ladder and pulled. It worked apparently in the same manner as the top one had done. The interested onlookers heard a similar humming noise to that made by the trapdoor when opening, but it was not apparent at first what had happened. On Ulyanov commanding his followers to move the cash boxes, documents and books away from the wall, however, they disclosed a small opening about five feet high and three feet wide. Apparently a sliding door had moved aside, revealing the head of a narrow flight of stairs built into the wall itself. Despite Sir Leonard's careful examination he had failed to observe anything out of the ordinary. It must be confessed that he felt a trifle chagrined at the thought that, if he had only discovered the secret exit, he could have walked out. Greatly impressed by the dwarf's ingenuity, and once again completely under his sway, Kharkov, Mossuth, Papanasstou, and Vassallo each picked up, at his orders, a share of the articles that were of such great value to the members of the International Anarchist Society and would have been of such inestimable value as evidence against them. Thus loaded, they passed one by one down the narrow steps, and disappeared from view. Ulyanov, Dimitrinhov, Grote, and Sir Leonard were left alone; then the dwarf turned venomously on the German.

'You would defy me, would you?' he ground out harshly. 'You would attempt to befriend one whom I hate beyond all hatred; you would bargain with my enemies; you would seek to become leader, and turn members of the society against me? Well, Hermann Grote, you can remain here – your carcass can rot in this little chamber or be found and bear witness that Nicolai Ulyanov never forgives.'

Grote commenced to protest vehemently, but, with incredible rapidity, the dwarf sprang on him, at the same time drawing a long, thin-bladed knife. Sir Leonard darted forward to the rescue, but Dimitrinhov flung him back violently and he crashed to the floor. As he fell he saw Ulyanov plunge his dagger once, twice, thrice into the body of the German, who had had no time to draw a weapon or protect himself. A shrill cry that ended in a gurgle, and Hermann Grote pitched headlong to the floor; his body twitched once or twice, then lay still. Ulyanov stood looking down at him, a cackle of that horrible, expressionless laughter left his lips, and he turned to regard the Englishman.

'So!' he commented. 'You have lost your friend, Herr Wallace. It is a pity, you think, is it not so?'

'You callous cold-blooded fiend!' whispered Sir Leonard tensely. His grey eyes flashing his utter horror and repugnance. 'May your filthy, black soul burn in the very depths of hell for all eternity.'

'Get up!' snarled the dwarf.

Awkwardly Wallace rose to his feet, still keeping his hands behind him, though the cord had become detached as he had sprung to the assistance of Grote. He would have made his last desperate stand then, unarmed as he was, but he still hoped to prevent, somehow or other, Ulyanov and his companions from escaping with the precious documents that meant so much to them and to him. He kept his hands together behind him, therefore, trusting that the long, loose sleeves of his coat would hide from view the fact that they were unbound. Dimitrinhov pushed him roughly towards the opening in the wall.

'Go on!' he ordered.

Another cackle of laughter came from the misshapen monster standing watching him go.

'The first stage of your journey to Moscow, Mr Englishman,' he gabbled in a harsh, gloating, altogether evil voice.

Bending low, Sir Leonard passed through the low doorway. He found that he could descend the steps in an upright attitude, but so narrow were they that his arms brushed the wall on both sides. He reflected that big men like Papanasstou and Dimitrinhov must be experiencing considerable difficulty in descending. The humming sound recommenced behind him, and he concluded that the door had been closed. A beam of light shot out. Dimitrinhov or Ulyanov was provided with a torch. Down a considerable number of steps, set very nearly perpendicular, he went, coming at last to a passage, broader than the staircase and high enough to enable him to walk upright. He was surprised to find how long this underground gallery was; calculated that he must have walked over half a mile before at last he found himself ascending a slope. Waiting ahead of him were the other four, apparently unable to proceed farther. Ulyanov squeezed by him; went to the front. Again came a low, humming sound, another secret door had opened. Sir Leonard presently stepped into what appeared to be a large shed. A light flared up, and he discovered that it was an aeroplane hangar. Towering over him was a great Junkers machine of the all-metal type, and he felt he had to admit that the dwarf possessed considerable ingenuity. At the same time he began to feel that his chances of escaping were diminishing rapidly. The secret passage was closed, no door now being visible. The hangar was obviously built up against an elevation. The police and military were likely to concentrate on the house itself, and in consequence the chances of his being rescued before he had been forced into the aeroplane and carried out of reach were extremely small.

He was left to himself while his captors busied themselves round the great machine. Believing that his hands were tied and that he was unarmed, they did not trouble about him. They knew he could not escape. But Sir Leonard held different ideas. He not only intended to escape, if he could, but he was not going to allow them to get away if he could prevent them. He heard Ulyanov giving orders, saw Vassallo tinkering with the engine, and knew then why the latter had been included in the party. He was the pilot. The cash boxes, books, and documents were placed in the saloon; then apparently one of the four, who had left the secret room in the house before the murder, noticed the absence of Grote and enquired where he was. Ulyanov snarled a reply, and immediately a heated altercation took place. Sir Leonard was not near enough to hear all that was being said, but felt that a heaven-sent opportunity for him to act had arisen.

The four men were facing Ulyanov and Dimitrinhov by the doors of the hangar. If only he had possessed a weapon he would know exactly how to act. At that very moment his alert eyes alighted on a long crowbar lying on the ground a few feet behind Dimitrinhov. Promptly, but without any sign of haste, he moved towards it. The angry, excited men took little notice of his approach, probably thinking, if they thought about it at all, that he was merely walking towards them to listen to the quarrel. The distance between them and him gradually decreased. Ten yards remained. Eight! Six! Three! Ulyanov turned momentarily, but he was in one of his frenzies, the vitriolic words pouring from his lips with satanic vehemence, and he immediately looked back at the men he was endeavouring to blast with his scorching verbosity.

A moment to take in a complete picture of his surroundings, and Sir Leonard sprang forward, his right hand flashed from behind his back as he bent and grasped the crowbar. A shout of alarm and Dimitrinhov swung round. But he was far too late to attempt to defend himself. His arm half rose, but, with a flail-like sweep, the Englishman caught him on the temple. He went down as though he had been poleaxed. Then Sir Leonard was on the rest, hitting left and right with all the force of his powerful arm. Mossuth the Hungarian was beaten to the ground, Papanasstou was sent sprawling, both of them damaged but not rendered unconscious. Their raised arms had saved their heads. Kharkov stumbled over the body of Dimitrinhov in his haste to escape the deadly swing of the crowbar, thus luckily avoiding the fate that threatened him. Vassallo sprang back out of range, endeavouring to draw his revolver, but Sir Leonard was too quick for him. As he pulled the weapon from his pocket and started to raise it the Englishman darted forward, sweeping it out of his hand with a well-directed blow. A momentary feeling of regret that he could not pick up the pistol and retain the crowbar as well, and Wallace flung the latter at the screaming, cursing dwarf, who had hopped out of the way with remarkable celerity when the Englishman attacked. Ulyanov dodged, the crowbar striking the aeroplane with a sharp clang.

Papanasstou and Kharkov were by that time on their feet again; had drawn revolvers, but Sir Leonard now held the weapon dropped by Vassallo, who was leaning against the wall nursing his arm. The Englishman had them covered, and they saw quite clearly that a further movement on their parts would be exceedingly dangerous for them. There was death in those cold, grey eyes staring at them from out of the countenance still streaked with dried blood and bearing testimony to Ulyanov's brutality. The dwarf continued to shriek out maledictions, but Sir Leonard noticed that he was edging sideways with the view, no doubt, of making a sudden spring on his late captive from behind.

'If you move another step that way, Ulyanov,' snapped Wallace, 'I will shoot you down. Go and stand beside those two beauties there!' He indicated Papanasstou and Kharkov, but Ulyanov stood defiant, hurling curses at him. Sir Leonard stepped back a few paces in order that he would have a comprehensive view of them all. 'Do what you are told,' he ordered the dwarf, 'or you will die now.'

The position was distinctly perilous. Papanasstou and Kharkov stood together, but Vassallo was some yards from the Bulgarian to the right while Ulyanov was three or four yards away from Papanasstou on Sir Leonard's left. It was exceedingly difficult, in consequence, to keep a watch on them all. The dwarf continued defiant, and the Chief of the British Secret Service turned his revolver full on him.

'I will give you half a minute to obey orders,' he snapped.

Papanasstou misguidedly decided that his opportunity had come; threw up his weapon to fire but the Englishman swung quickly to face him, shooting him through the shoulder before he could pull the trigger. With a mingled cry of pain and anger the Greek dropped his pistol, but Ulyanov, howling like a wild beast threw himself at Wallace, his bloodstained knife glinting in his hand. He had not reckoned on the extraordinary swiftness of the Englishman, however. Perhaps if he had known of the latter's amazing skill with a revolver he might have hesitated at taking what seemed to him a great opportunity. He was in mid-air, the knife poised for the blow, when his wrist was shattered by a bullet, and he went down screaming horribly, rolling on the ground in agony. Sir Leonard could not face all ways at once, however. As he fired at Ulyanov, Vassallo launched himself on his back grappling him with desperate force. Quickly he bent forward, the unexpected manoeuvre took the pilot by surprise, and he shot over the Englishman's head to land in a heap on the grovelling dwarf. Immediately Kharkov took advantage of his chance, raised his revolver and fired. It was fortunate for Sir Leonard that the

Bulgarian was not a good shot or, at least, that he had taken aim hastily. At that range he should have had no difficulty in hitting Wallace in a vital spot. The bullet ploughed its way through the lower muscles of his arm rendering the hand nerveless and causing him to drop his revolver.

Kharkov yelled triumphantly and sprang forward, gripping the Englishman in a bear-like hug. Although his one arm was practically useless, Sir Leonard struggled desperately, and the Bulgarian by no means had matters all his own way. Twice Wallace almost got away from him, but then Vassallo, who had risen from the ground, joined in the fight. Mossuth staggered to his feet and added his efforts which, though weak, were effective. Hither and thither the combatants swayed, but, handicapped as he was, the odds were too great for Sir Leonard. Presently he was brought to the ground, the others crashing on top of him. One of them had him by the throat, another round the waist imprisoning his injured arm, the third gripped his legs and, although the Englishman continued to kick out desperately, hung on.

Observing how events were shaping, Ulyanov temporarily forgot his broken wrist. He sprang to his feet, yelling out encouragement to his henchmen, and dancing round like a demented hobgoblin, whenever he could get near enough he kicked at the man he hated with such utter intensity, once or twice even stamped on his face. At length Sir Leonard's powers of resistance were broken. The rough treatment he was undergoing, the pain in his arm, his tortured chest still aching abominably, proved too much for his spirit. He became quiescent, lay practically unconscious. Even then Kharkov continued to squeeze his throat, bent apparently on strangling him. Death felt very near, his lungs seemed on the point of bursting, a great thundering was in his ears. With the last remnants of his senses his thoughts were fastened on his wife, Molly, his blue lips strove to whisper her name. Then from afar he thought he heard a harsh, grating voice telling someone not to kill him, and he shrank into unconsciousness as Kharkov released him and rose reluctantly to his feet.

'Is he dead?' demanded Ulyanov, looking down at the object of his hatred, his whole demeanour denoting anxiety.

Mossuth pressed his ear against the unconscious man's heart, listened for a while, then shook his head.

'It is a pity,' growled Kharkov.

'It is well,' barked Ulyanov. 'If you had killed him I would have killed you.'

'Oh!' sneered the Bulgarian. 'How would you have done it?'

Ulyanov bent suddenly to pick up his knife with his left hand, but the other kicked it yards away. Immediately the Russian threatened to lapse into one of his frenzied outbursts, but Mossuth succeeded in soothing him.

'Do you not think, Comrade Ulyanov,' he remarked, 'that enough blood had been shed and enough damage done already? Perhaps if you had killed the three spies when they first fell into our hands the society would still be triumphant and secure. As it is, we are ruined. The sooner we depart for Russia the better for us all. Is it possible to start while it is still dark?' he asked Vassallo.

'Possible, but not easy, as we dare not use flares,' was the reply. 'The runway is good but not too long.'

'Will the noise of the engine be heard?' snapped Ulyanov.

'Yes, comrade, that is certain, but we shall be away before any can reach here and stop us; that is,' he added, 'if there are not already police and soldiers searching nearby.'

'Why should they be searching?' rasped the Russian. 'Get ready quickly, and we will depart. Let this cursed Englishman be bound from head to foot.'

The pain of his shattered wrist seemed to have taken a lot of the tigerish, overbearing tyranny out of the dwarf. He moved about uttering little moaning sounds horribly reminiscent of an animal in pain, but he snarled viciously when Kharkov offered to bind up his arm. A rope was procured from within the aeroplane and bound cruelly round Sir Leonard until his captors were assured that he could neither move hand nor foot. That done, they inspected injuries and did their best to clean and bandage them. With the exception of Kharkov they were all damaged in greater or lesser degree. Dimitrinhov still lay unconscious, it being fairly evident that his skull was fractured; Papanasstou had a bullet through his shoulder and his right arm was consequently useless; Mossuth's left arm, which he had raised to protect himself from the crowbar, was badly bruised and numbed, the blood still streamed from the glancing blow he had received on his head; Vassallo's right hand was temporarily out of action, due to the jolt administered to it when Sir Leonard had caused him to drop his revolver. They were an aching, vicious, woebegone crowd and the glances thrown at the unconscious form of the Englishman boded ill for him. If it had not been for Ulyanov's orders it is certain that they would have murdered him where he lay.

At length all was ready for the start of the flight. Dimitrinhov was lifted into the saloon of the machine, Sir Leonard was thrown in as though he had been a sack of potatoes, the shock bringing him to his senses. Then the doors of the hangar were rolled back, and Vassallo, Kharkov, Mossuth, and Papanasstou wheeled the aeroplane out into the open. It was darker now than it had been all night, the moon having set long since, while a great threatening bank of cloud had blown up. Vassallo glanced rather apprehensively at the sky, but, whatever his thoughts may have been, he did not voice them. No doubt he knew it would be useless, while he was as anxious to put a long distance between himself and Austria as were his companions.

There was some difficulty in starting the engine. It proved obstinate, probably on account of the cold, while the aching arms of all but Kharkov hardly conduced to great exertion. Ulyanov stood by watching their efforts, growing more vehemently impatient as the minutes passed. At last Vassallo succeeded. The powerful engine leapt into vibrating life with a roar. In haste now, lest their enemies might arrive before they could get away, they scrambled into the machine, Kharkov and Mossuth practically lifting in the dwarf. Vassallo took his place in the pilot's seat; the great aeroplane began to move forward. It was at that moment that a beam of light shot out from the trees on one side, became focused on the pilot. Two men, one tall, the other short, dashed out of cover.

'No time for ceremony,' muttered the latter to himself.

He fired and a bullet sped unerringly into the brain of Vassallo. He fell sideways, and the all-metal Junkers swung round, ran from the prepared ground, dashed headlong into the bushes and trees, coming to a sudden stop with a tearing, grinding sound.

CHAPTER TWENTY-ONE

Cousins Does His Job

On leaving Miles and Carter in the cellar, Cousins, the man on whom so much depended, crept cautiously through the domestic quarters of the house. His luck remained good, for they were unoccupied, as they had been when he had entered. Walking along a passage he reached the door by way of which he had broken in – it had been locked and bolted and he had been forced to use a couple of the finely-tempered steel instruments on the bunch left by Sir Leonard Wallace. Nobody had since locked it he was glad to observe, and opening it cautiously he peered out. He heard someone cough a little distance away on his right; from his left came the sound of low voices. The men on watch were still very much on the alert. Pity it was a moonlight night, thought Cousins. However, there was no time to lose; he could not wait until the guards had moved away. He stepped out, closing the door softly behind him. Fortunately there was a hedge a few yards away. Once he was in its shadow he would be comparatively safe from observation. The trouble was that in order to reach it he would be compelled to cross a bright patch of moonlight. He decided that he would be more likely to get away unsuspected if he made no attempt at concealment. While a man approaching the house would be subject to the sharpest surveillance, one leaving it would be hardly likely to have a great deal of notice taken of him, unless he showed a desire to hide himself or acted suspiciously in any other way.

Cousins strolled away quite openly from the door. He even whistled the Internationale. His sharp eyes noticed several shadowy figures on either side and at some distance from him. It was comforting to reflect that he was as shadowy to them as they were to him, but, if his heart were beating a little more rapidly than usual, he gave no sign of agitation or concern. He reached the hedge unchallenged, continued whistling for a little while, then stopped, stood still and listened intently. Having made certain that he was not being followed he slipped along the hedge, presently disappearing among the trees. For the next half hour he dodged from cover to cover with the stealth and expert tread of an Indian scout. Not a twig cracked under his feet, not a leaf rustled as he glided by. Two or three times he passed within a few feet of men patrolling the grounds; thought grimly that this Council of Ten guarded itself very thoroughly. He wondered if the house and estate were always as closely watched, or whether the present precautions were due to the events of the day.

He did not make for the main gates; they were too well picketed. He had found that out when entering the grounds;

he had been compelled to climb the wall at a remote end of the estate. He made for the same place now, but when he reached it found there were men in the vicinity. On he went, but every time he drew near to the wall his intentions of scaling it were frustrated by the presence of one or more of the vigilant anarchists. He began to despair of ever getting out when, making his way through a dense mass of untended shrubbery, he came to rising ground, wild, unkept and bosky. At least, he thought, he would be able to survey his surroundings from the top. He found it a difficult job getting through the thick, tangled brushwood, but eventually succeeded, to find, to his astonishment, that the slope came to a sudden termination. He was gazing down on the roof of a long building built flush against the hillside. Ahead as far as he was able to see, was a wide clearing.

Cousins was intrigued. He decided that although he was pressed for time a little investigation would not be out of place. He rolled rather than scrambled down the steep declivity, arriving at the bottom with his clothes rather the worse for the venture. He had not spent many minutes inspecting the building before he found, as he had expected, that it was an aeroplane hangar. Extending before the great doors for a couple of hundred yards – he calculated the distance by walking the length – was a well-laid-out runway. The knowledge he had gained, more or less by accident, might prove to be of great value later on he reflected. He was unable to spare the time to investigate further then; it was sufficient to be aware of the presence of an aeroplane. He walked on through the wooded slopes beyond the runway, coming at length to the wall again. There appeared to be no guard in that vicinity at all, but he made as certain as was possible before scaling it. It was not an easy feat, but Cousins made light of it.

Half an hour later he was in Dornbach, had reclaimed his motorcycle from the Keller where he had left it, and was speeding as fast as he could go towards the British Legation in the Reisnerstrasse. The American minister had dined with Sir Richard Lindsay, and they were sitting in the latter's study discussing the matter uppermost in their minds, when the arrival of Cousins was announced. Sir Richard gave orders for him to be admitted without delay. He immediately plunged into his story, the two ministers listening almost without daring to breathe lest they should lose something of the narrative, so great was their interest and concern. When they heard of the peril in which Sir Leonard Wallace, and, to a lesser extent, Miles and Carter stood, they became exceedingly apprehensive. Both were men of action and, having become possessed of facts and evidence necessary to prove to the Austrian government the existence of a great anarchist organisation with headquarters actually in a suburb of Vienna, they bestirred themselves promptly.

An appointment was made by telephone with the Minister of the Interior, the urgency of an immediate interview being impressed on him. He was also asked to invite the Minister of Justice to the conference. The two members of the government were vastly intrigued at the request, and received Sir Richard and his companion with every appearance of deep interest. They became two very astonished men when the whole story was related to them. At first they found it hard to credit. The house at Dornbach was supposed to belong to an eccentric but harmless Russian millionaire, who was thought to be an invalid, and kept himself in consequence severely secluded. But the significance of the circumstance that the ministers plenipotentiary of two such great nations as Great Britain and the United States had called in person to place the facts before them and urge immediate action, persuaded them that indeed their beloved capital had been used as the headquarters of a terrible organisation. The Minister of Justice sent at once for the Chief of Police; Colonel Wachter, the Minister of War, who lived within a short distance, was called in. Shortly after ten o'clock a strong force of police and military was under arms. Led by Colonel Wachter and the Chief of Police in person, and with Cousins riding ahead on his motorcycle, the men drove to Dornbach in thirty cars.

As the leading vehicles swept up the avenue there came a terrific explosion and a flash of flame showed for a moment at one end of the roof. A little later a single rifle shot rang out. The men tumbled out of the cars and under orders quickly surrounded the building and outhouses. It had been Colonel Wachter's original intention to summon the inmates to allow him and his men to enter; if they refused, to force an entry. The explosion and the rifle shot, however, decided him to dispense with the summons. The men were ordered to break in, others were sent to scour the grounds and take captive everyone they came across. Led by their officers, the policemen and soldiers smashed their way in with a hearty goodwill. Before long they were overrunning the house. Here and there they came across parties of anarchists who resisted desperately, and were shot down to a man. A few on the roof with a machine gun held out for some time, but were eventually exterminated. At length the building was in complete control of the authorities, only a few dejected-looking anarchists, now heavily manacled, remaining alive. Cousins went to the roof as soon as all resistance had ceased, the explosion and rifle shot having told him that his colleagues were up there. He found Carter and Miles by the chimney stack, the latter having just recovered from the faint which had been caused by a wound in his shoulder. He gratefully drank from the flask of brandy held out to him by the little Secret Service man. Carter was more seriously wounded – he had been hit four times, twice in the left leg, once in the left shoulder and once in his right side. He was quickly placed under the care of the doctor who had accompanied the force. Cousins and Miles heaved huge sighs of relief when told that he would recover.

The complete disappearance of Sir Leonard Wallace caused them immense alarm and anxiety. The suggestion that he had escaped was no longer considered, since he would have been certain to have got in touch with the authorities if he had. Cousins accompanied by Miles, who, as soon as his injury had been dressed, declared himself to be fit for anything, ransacked the building from cellar to roof, incidentally handing over the three men Carter and Miles had imprisoned down below. Their apprehension increased when Miles ascertained that Ulyanov, Dimitrinhov, Grote and three other members of the Council of Ten were also missing. It was then Cousins remembered the hangar, and decided to search it. Accompanied by an officer and ten men and of course Miles, who refused to be left behind, he led them unerringly to that wild, remote part of the estate which had been cleared as an aeroplane runway. Forcing their way through the tangled brushwood they heard the sudden roar of the engine. At once careless of torn clothing and lacerated hands, Miles and Cousins broke into a run, pulling forth their revolvers as they went. They emerged from cover just in time, as has already been related. The officer and his ten men were not very far behind them and, taking in the situation at a glance, for Cousins kept the powerful torch focused on the aeroplane, the officer ordered his men to surround the machine.

'Good Heavens!' gasped Cousins suddenly. 'What on earth is that?'

Looking out of the window of the saloon at them, his horrible, usually expressionless face now distorted with malevolent fury, was Ulyanov. On one side of him was Mossuth, on the other Kharkov; both were white, apparently with fear.

'I guess that's the cause of all the darn trouble,' declared Miles. 'That, Jerry, is Ulyanov the President of the Council of Ten.'

'"But thou are neither like thy sire nor dam",' murmured Cousins, "But like a foul misshapen stigmatic, Mark'd by the destinies to be avoided, as venom toads, or lizards' dreadful stings." What a caricature!' He stepped forward. 'Come out, all of you!' he shouted in German.

There appeared to be a fierce altercation going on inside. Ulyanov was bent on defying the men surrounding the machine, but Kharkov, Mossuth and Papanasstou had hopes of saving their lives perhaps, by surrendering. Suddenly the Greek threw open the door of the saloon; was about to step out, but with a shrill, gurgling cry he abruptly threw up his arms, swayed for a moment, then plunged out head first, to lie face downwards on the grass quivering out his life. Ulyanov had stabbed him in the back. At an order from the officer his men promptly fired, both

Mossuth and Kharkov being hit, but, as though anticipating the discharge, Ulyanov had ducked below the window. There came a cackle of horrible, mad laughter.

'Good God!' gasped Cousins. 'I believe he has Sir Leonard in there, and—'

He and Miles dashed forward together. The sight that met their eyes almost drove them to a frenzy. Bending over the cruelly bound form of Sir Leonard Wallace was the dwarf. Holding in his left hand the knife with which he had already committed two murders that night, he was engaged in stabbing Sir Leonard, not fatally, but deeply enough to cause the blood to flow profusely.

'Death by a thousand cuts!' he was cackling in a harsh, horrible, gloating voice.

With a cry of awful horror Cousins darted into the saloon, but Miles was even quicker. The American grasped Ulyanov by the collar of his coat and dragged him snarling, hissing venomously, out into the open. There he threw him to the ground, and was about to advise the soldiers to bind him with ropes when the abominable, repellent caricature of a man was on its feet again. With an unearthly cry it launched itself straight at the American, the long, thin knife gleaming malevolently in the light thrown on the scene by the soldiers' torches.

'Guess it won't be happy till it gets it,' muttered Miles, as he stepped back and fired.

Ulyanov was in mid-air when the bullet caught him. A long, wailing shriek struck a chill into the blood of everyone who heard it; the Russian pitched forward on to his head, rolled over into a crumpled heap, and lay still. Some of the men standing by crossed themselves. Miles, noticing the reverent gesture, nodded gravely.

'I reckon,' he murmured to himself, 'that if ever Satan inhabited a human body it was that guy's.'

He returned to the saloon of the aeroplane. Cousins, almost sobbing at sight of the terrible disfigurement to Sir Leonard's chest, and the officer were engaged in staunching the flow of blood and dressing the wounds as best they could until a doctor could attend to them properly. The rope had been cut away. Miles' eyes glittered with a cold fury.

'Did he do that to you, Sir Leonard?' he asked huskily.

Sir Leonard smiled a little weakly, and nodded.

'I will bear something always that will remind me that we wiped out the International Anarchist Society,' he remarked. 'It is entirely wiped out, isn't it?' he asked eagerly.

'Wiped out!' repeated Miles. 'I guess I never saw anything more wiped out.' He looked down at the bodies of Kharkov and Mossuth; then contemplated Dimitrinhov. 'Except for this guy,' he added, 'the members of the Council of Ten are all dead, while their followers have either been killed or captured. No; I forgot – there's Grote!'

'He's dead also,' Wallace told him. 'Ulyanov killed him. I am sorry, for Grote tried to be decent. Is Ulyanov dead?'

'As dead as mutton. I feel glad I put that bullet into his devil brain – I guess it kinder soothes my feelings for that.' He nodded at Sir Leonard's chest.

'All that stuff will enable us to give information that will clear the world entirely of the society,' remarked Wallace, indicating the documents. 'Somehow,' he added with a smile, 'Moscow will wriggle out of any responsibility, with their usual specious tales, but they will have to mind their p's and q's for a long time – for a very long time.'

'You've said a mouthful, Sir Leonard,' nodded Miles. 'My! They will hate the name of Wallace more than ever after this.'

'"*Oderint dum metuant!*"' murmured Cousins.

ALSO IN THE SERIES

To discover more great books and to
place an order visit our website at
allisonandbusby.com

Don't forget to sign up to our free newsletter at
allisonandbusby.com/newsletter
for latest releases, events and exclusive offers

Allison & Busby Books
@AllisonandBusby

You can also call us on
020 7580 1080
for orders, queries
and reading recommendations